THE SKY BLUE PARCEL

John Nightingale read English at Cambridge University. He now lives in London and Suffolk with his wife and two daughters. By day he is a civil servant specialising in fraud prevention.

THE SKY BLUE PARCEL

JOHN NIGHTINGALE

Copyright © John Nightingale 2006

The right of John Nightingale to be identified as
the author of this work has been asserted
in accordance with sections 77 and 78 of the
copyright Designs and Patents Act 1988.

All the characters in this book are fictitious,
and any resemblance to actual persons, living
or dead is purely coincidental.

All rights reserved. No part of this publication
may be reproduced, stored in a retrieval system,
or transmitted in any form or by any means,
electronic, mechanical, photocopying, recording,
or otherwise, without the permission of the author.

Typeset in Monotype Joanna.

Cover design by Grant Morrison.

First published in Great Britain in 2006 by
[M] The Minster Press, Wimborne, Dorset BH211JQ
Tel. 01202 882277 · www.printsolutions.co.uk

British Library Cataloging-In-Publication Data,
a catalogue record for this book is available from
the British Library

ISBN 1-899499-27-X

THE SKY BLUE PARCEL

For

Dennis Guerrier
&
Joan Richards

CHAPTER ONE

It was twelve days after the £250 million from the American bank disappeared that Jane Charles found the key to her apartment wouldn't turn. For a moment she imagined the lock had seized up like her car door, another mechanical casualty of the icy cold that had gripped London since the New Year. Then she heard a noise from inside, somebody moving. She took a step backwards in alarm but saw it was number 28, not 38, that she was trying to enter. It was the wrong door, distinguishable from all others in the block only by its number. She was in the right place but on the floor below her own.

Back in the lift the doors had barely closed before the central light flickered and died and the comforting whine of machinery in action abruptly stopped. Jane was left in the pitch black in a space that could only take three adults in comfort. She had to start to gulp down air to hold her fears back. It was just like the cupboard with the faulty lock in her uncle's house in Bath that had trapped her when she was seven and where she had first discovered her horror of confined spaces. She was aware of a rasping sound in the silence and it took her a moment or two to realise that she was listening to her own breathing. She braced herself against the side of the lift. Keep calm she told herself, breathe deeply, mind over matter, exercise free will, tomorrow use the stairs.

Her breathing slowed a little as she started counting the seconds. She had her telephone of course. She would, however, need to wait before she could justify calling anyone. I've been trapped in a lift for two minutes and in a moment I'm going to start screaming wasn't something she wanted to say. The lift had never stopped before. It was probably just a problem with the power supply caused by the freezing weather. She needed to be patient. She was searching in her bag for her mobile when the lights in the lift came on again and it cranked sluggishly back into life.

It was ten o'clock when she finally managed to push her own door open. The main room of the apartment stretched in front of her, a long oblong space leading to glass doors and a balcony overlooking the river. She threw her coat across the low leather sofa that had been left by the previous owner and let her briefcase drop on the floor. In the kitchen area that formed the landward end of the room she found a half empty bottle of wine gleaming greenish-yellow and lonely in the internal light of the fridge. She poured herself a glass and sat in the armchair.

There was a fax from the builders on her machine. The roof at Eastwood could be patched up using second-hand tiles for as little as £5,525 and guaranteed for twelve months. The work could be set in hand immediately on payment of a deposit of one-third of the total price and completed within four weeks. Mr Ken Smart looked forward to receiving her formal instructions.

Jane sighed. What Mr Smart was presenting as the most reasonable of prices was more than she had anticipated paying, or could afford. The house had inevitably deteriorated in the last couple of years with no one living in it and she was going to have to make a decision about its long-term future. The most rational decision would be to sell it. There was no logical reason not to. She had no sensible use for a decaying house in the country too far from London for commuting and too large for comfort. Six bedrooms might make a guesthouse but not a home, at least not a home for one. But they had both invested so much time in what it might become. Getting rid of Eastwood without giving the house a real chance would be a betrayal.

The answering machine was winking, providing a welcome distraction. "Jane? It's Sally. I just wanted to check you could make the dinner. We're expecting everyone about eight. And just to say that Robert is invited of course. Let me know if there is a problem. See you then. Bye."

Sally had stressed 'Robert is invited of course' in her matchmaking voice. Sally had decided that Robert Stuart was the answer to Jane's unuttered prayer. Robert was tall, handsome, amusing, single and rich. Sally had always maintained that a permutation of any four out of the five was more than Jane or any other woman could reasonably expect, let alone all five. But Jane didn't entirely share Sally's enthusiasm that he was destined to be the next man in her life. Robert, especially of late, had also seemed increasingly pre-occupied. Jane might have found that attractive if she had understood why, but Robert's emotions were something of a black hole. Robert seemed to collect energy from the admiring looks that young women in restaurants favoured him with, and Jane had contributed the odd positive pulse herself, but nothing much was travelling in the opposite direction. It would help for something to come back across Robert's emotion horizon, preferably something that made him more vulnerable and human.

She was hungry. Her desire to get her in-tray under control after the holiday had meant that she was home an hour later than she had planned, and the food shop on the corner had just closed. A sweep through the kitchen revealed the remains of a tub of violently pink taramasalata, some stuffed green olives, and an unopened packet of crackers. She remembered a banana in the fruit bowl that she had last seen in the bedroom. It was the beginnings of a meal. She poured the remains of the bottle of wine into her glass to fortify herself for the hunt.

Some hard searching produced not only the banana, but the remains of the bottom layer of a box of Belgian chocolates that her father-in-law, Edward Charles, had given her. She didn't remember bringing them back. She had eaten the top layer with Edward looking out over the ocean and the stars while he tried to convince her of the virtues of Mahler, bribing her with the last of the St Estephe that he said he had kept particularly for her. She had almost believed him, perhaps did about the wine, conscious only that he was capable of adapting a fact to his mood. She sighed. Christmas in Ireland, at Edward's house on the sheltered cove on the West Coast of Kerry, now seemed to belong to a quite different part of her existence, although she had only returned yesterday morning.

The flapping fronds of the palm trees in Edward's garden and the warm currents of the Gulf Stream had been replaced by an iced up London, the mild breeze from the ocean by freezing air from the Polar Regions, red wine by white wine, eternity by deadlines, music by missing money. Jane sat down with the chocolates.

Her plan in moving two years ago had been to force herself out of the rut she was in, not to find something equally deep. Tonight, after two days back in the office, she had managed to put together an alliance of northern nations to neutralise the Italian objections on the Community money laundering directive but had not been alert enough even to get out of the lift at the right floor. Jane sighed and finished the wine in a single gulp.

Her reflection in the bathroom mirror was more reassuring. The misty Irish air from her walks on the headland had magically cleared away London's grime. There was a surprising vitality in her face. She could almost detect a sparkle in her chocolate-brown eyes, and the jet-black hair she had inherited from her French grandmother looked glossy and alive. Sally had been right about having her hair cut shorter. It framed her high cheekbones better.

The telephone rang but Jane was reluctant to lose the face in the mirror. Her message on the answering machine announced that she was out but would get back to whoever was calling as soon as she could. She nodded conspiratorially to the person in the mirror who seemed to have the promise of a more exciting life than her own. Just for once whoever or whatever it was could wait until the morning.

It was only after the voice started speaking that she realised that perhaps it couldn't. The voice was male and one that Jane knew well. That didn't lessen the shock.

"Jane, it's Kenneth Ormond," the voice said, "I need your help. It's this Mandell business. Jack tells me that you're the Treasury's expert on financial regulation and corporate crime and the file is bound to have crossed your desk. The last thing the Government can cope with at the moment is another financial scandal. I need somebody to make sure that this gets sorted out fast. Mandell was a friend of mine. I'll see you get full co-operation. The missing money will be somewhere.

Look, I've got to go. Phone Jack Cook at the office, he can find a time when we can talk."

There was a click at the other end of the line as Jane was about to pick up the receiver. Ormond's call was surprising. Home Secretaries did not normally make calls to civil servants, even those who had worked with them closely before. They had Private Secretaries and Assistant Private Secretaries and Diary Secretaries to carry out these everyday functions.

Jane had headed Kenneth Ormond's office of civil servants when he had been a junior Minister. For two years Jane had shared his life in late nights in the Commons, in visits to the regions, and in keeping his in-tray and the Department's agenda of welfare reform under control. The relationship had started well and never wavered. Ormond had always been an idealistic, reforming politician who Jane found it easy to work for. The long hours in each other's company had bred a mutual sense of purpose and respect. They had remained in touch after Jane had left and Ormond had found time to call her the day after the accident had happened, although he had been in the middle of a political storm over violent offenders.

She got up and walked round the apartment. Ormond sounded as though he was under pressure and there might have been some reassurance that Jane could have given, if only that she had seen the papers, and that of course she would give what help she could. Her boss, Peter Green, had anyway already come fussing into her office to make sure that Mandell had reached the top of her priority list.

The interlocking Mandell firms had been controlled by David Mandell who had been a dominant Chief Executive and Chairman of the group he had founded. He also seemed to have made all key decisions himself. For thirty years David Mandell had built up a business empire by some fairly shrewd buying and selling of firms in the publishing and media sectors. There was a problem, however. David Mandell had borrowed £250 million from KM Investment Bank on Christmas Eve, ostensibly to finance some further takeover activity. Unfortunately these funds could no longer be found, nor any evidence that anything had been bought. Faced with a gaping hole in their finances, the Mandell companies now had insufficient assets to cover their liabilities. The situation needed to be sorted out quickly if they were going to stay in business.

The difficulty was that David Mandell wasn't available to answer any questions. It wasn't that he had left the country or was suffering from selective financial amnesia. His situation was perfectly clear. He was dead.

It was extremely puzzling. The money had disappeared but not the man who had taken it.

CHAPTER TWO

Jane telephoned Kenneth Ormond's office immediately she arrived at her desk the following morning. The branch Jane headed dealt with Her Majesty's Treasury's interest in combating large scale organized crime, which the analysts at the National Criminal Intelligence Service reckoned was costing Britain £40 billion a year, or £800, as Jane's Minister was fond of saying, for every man, woman and child in the country. Jane's remit covered everything from selling drugs on street corners to large-scale fraud, with people trafficking, VAT avoidance, money laundering, and a thousand other crimes or irregularities.

There were Turkish gangs in North London importing heroin from Eastern Europe; and Chinese snakehead gangs and Albanians fighting for a share of the Class A drugs market with British criminals moving out of the East End. The more established players in the game were able to call on lawyers and accountants as well as hit men to take care of rivals and debtors. And as the money and the asset base increased there was movement to more legitimate areas of investment. The gang bosses were emerging from the shadows into London's brighter lights, where in time they might aspire to rub shoulders with Russian oil oligarchs, American information billionaires, and the City's bankers and high rollers.

Both the modern business world and underworld were changing so fast that they required a far more flexible and integrated Government response to deal with them. New agencies and new methods were required and Jane was looking at a Home Office proposal for legislative changes in fraud cases that would permit a more flexible use of super grasses, and greater plea-bargaining. As far as she could see, however, it had the drawback of being drafted without any regard for human rights legislation. She had already raised her concerns with Peter Green who had been disinclined to intervene personally on something that was a priority bit of Government business

Jane put the telephone down. Ormond's Private Secretary, Jack Cook, had not yet arrived from Woking. There were problems with icing on the line but he was expected in an hour or so. Jane had said she would call again and avoided giving her name or any indication of the nature of her business. She had no idea how discreet Kenneth Ormond wished to be. She didn't expect David Mandell's financial affairs to be at the criminal end of the variety of activities she was engaged with. It was more likely to be a case of financial black holes in the company accounts that he had been trying to plug with fresh injections of cash.

She tapped her fingers and stared out of the window. She could see the modern concrete battlements of the top of the Home Office to the right and the Houses of Parliament and Westminster Abbey to the left. The main Treasury building was around the corner in Whitehall. Jane's unit of thirty-five had been decanted out before the refurbishment and never quite managed to get back. When Jane had taken them over a year ago the plan had still been to return, and as far as she knew that was still the long-term intention, but the summons had not yet arrived. There was a long-standing rumour, unsettling as far as Jane's people were concerned, that some or all of them might move to a new crime-fighting agency, located out of London. Jane made a note that she needed to check the position with Brian Harper, her meticulous, if somewhat fussy, second in command. She had asked him to use the contacts he had amassed over the last thirty years to try to find out precisely what was going on.

Something that Kenneth Ormond had said in his telephone call was also buzzing around in her brain. He had offered her full co-operation in anything she did. She needed to get a fix on precisely how far co-operation would actually go in practice. A Home Secretary, who was in the frame to be the next Prime Minister, had a lot of co-operation he could deliver.

Whatever the assistance on offer, Mandell Holdings had got to be the top of her priority list. She needed to put Ian Hart on the case straightaway. Ian was by far the brightest of her graduate trainees. Jane's job was his second posting in the Civil Service since he had graduated two years before with a mathematics degree from Cambridge. Jane was already thinking about the possibility of constructing a Grade 7 post in the branch and inviting him to apply. Grade 7 was the first significant middle management grade where the individual concerned would expect to be the complete master of a particular subject. Grades in the Civil Service got higher as numbers got lower. Anyone at Jane's level, Grade 5, or above was a member of the Senior Civil Service. At the top level, Permanent Secretaries, the heads of each of the Departments of State, were grade 1s, or in one exceptional case, Grade 0.

Ian had joined two years ago and it would be about as early a promotion as even a brilliant fast streamer could expect, She knew that Brian, who had laboured twenty years to get to that point and another ten to achieve Grade 6, would want to have at least half an hour's discussion on the advantages of experience against raw talent, before reluctantly agreeing with her. She groaned inwardly. She would need to speak to all her staff to ensure they were aware of her intentions before word leaked around on the grapevine. That would be time well spent but half an hour of her life to convince Brian and deal with the set objections he always advanced, wasn't appealing.

It might be better to get matters sewn up with Peter Green, and present it to Brian as a deal ordained from above. Whatever happened she needed to do everything she could to keep Ian on her team. He was the one person who worked for her she felt totally confident she could trust to deliver. He was also fun.

She spent twenty minutes composing a note on what she thought the most profitable line of investigation might be. Not that Ian would necessarily follow everything she suggested. He seemed to have a sixth sense in ferreting out the bottom line in the financial scandals that crossed his desk. He was normally right and Jane was happy to give him his head. She stapled an 'immediate' flag to the papers and gave them to her secretary, Suzanne, who had just arrived, with instructions

15

for their immediate delivery. Ian had an office on a far extremity of the next floor that entailed a five minute round trip.

When she telephoned again the Home Secretary's Principal Private Secretary had arrived. Kenneth Ormond, however, was not available. Jack Cook reassuringly seemed to know who she was but was adamant that the possibility of arranging a meeting, even an urgent one, over the next few days was remote. Jane got an assurance that he would take the matter up with Kenneth as soon as he was able to, and agreement that it was a matter of urgency, but that was all.

It had been an unsatisfactory conversation. Jane had assumed that Ormond's urgent tone of the night before would lead to an early meeting and more information. Now the Ormond end of the conversation seemed to have gone lukewarm. Not that Jack Cook's approach necessarily meant anything. Kenneth Ormond might not have put him fully in the picture and there might be any number of new crises more pressing than Mandell Holdings suddenly jostling for Ormond's attention.

Suzanne came in with a cup of coffee, a pile of papers, and a reminder that she had a series of meetings starting in fifteen minutes that would take most of the rest of the day. The papers were immaculately tabbed and strengthened Jane's resolve to follow her instincts and sort out a long-term job for Ian. Brian Harper had also maintained that Suzanne was too young and inexperienced for the job of Jane's chief aide. Twenty minutes into the conversation he had also ventured the view that Suzanne might be a distraction. Jane had concluded that the fact that Suzanne was nineteen, blonde, and had a perfect figure might be at the root of this objection, but had decided not to get drawn into a further debate. She had pronounced herself more than satisfied that Suzanne was clearly the best of the candidates on offer, and resisted the temptation of reminding Brian that being beautiful was not, in itself, a bar to employment.

She hadn't managed to make any significant progress on Mandell by seven that evening. In between her two morning meetings she had come to a more settled view of her failure to contact Ormond. It was clear that Ormond wanted the Mandell business sorted out, and he had at least two good reasons why. A financial scandal was certainly not good news for the Government, and he was clearly concerned about the good name of his dead friend. It wasn't surprising that he should turn to Jane.

At lunchtime she had put down her sandwich and detached the large photograph of David Mandell from the second folder of papers the Bank had sent and propped it against her computer screen. The black and white image was sharply defined, the head and shoulders of a strongly built man staring out confidently at the camera. The photo looked as though it had been taken for a company report to shareholders, a reassuring picture of the chairman at the helm.

In the course of the afternoon she found herself looking at it more than once. There was something about the certainty of the photograph that was completely at odds with the financial chaos that was descending on the Mandell companies .

Once she discovered Suzanne standing in front of her desk looking slightly perplexed, and she realized that she must have been staring at the picture. Normally Jane was able to surface from whatever problem she was engaged in immediately her secretary appeared, deal with whatever Suzanne wanted to talk to her about, and then dive back into the problem at the precise point she had left it. Today she was missing her normal total powers of concentration.

There had been a collection of press cuttings at the back of the file of papers. A week or so after Mandell's death had been reported the first notes of doubt had begun to appear in the financial pages. The initial analysis was that Mandell's driving personality and deft touch on a business deal had been the cornerstone of the success of the firm and he would be missed. As the days had gone by the uncertainties had become progressively more pronounced. At present the full extent of the financial crisis was still hidden from the public gaze, but crisply expressed in a memo at the top of the file. Mandell Holdings didn't have sufficient assets to cover missing cash of £250 million. The only cash that David Mandell had had ready to hand at the time of his death appeared to be a few thousand pounds in a personal account.

Jane put the papers back in the folder. A new scandal now could seriously threaten the passage of the regulation proposals in the Bill currently before Parliament. It was another reason to sort Mandell out quickly. Jane also needed a convincing line in the next twenty-four hours on why the Mandell situation was not a clear indication that what was proposed in legislation as a rigorous tightening of controls was not, in reality, still inadequate. Getting a proper sense of what could have happened to David Mandell and his companies would help her construct a more substantial defensive line. All she had at the moment was 'too early to comment on the case before we have some better knowledge of what the problem may be, if there is a problem at all'. She needed to speak to Ian Hart. Ian was always good at mounting a hypothesis to explain any situation.

When she got to Ian's office she found he had propped a drawing board in the only remaining free corner of what was already a cramped space. If Jane was not to sit on his chair she would need to stand in front of what seemed like a wiring diagram.

"What's the frantic interest in Mandell Holdings?" Ian asked as she came in. "Suzanne said you had spent most of the day looking at the papers the Bank sent over."

"Nothing in particular, if you ignore the sum involved and the political consequences. But now and again it is nice to get something sorted out quickly. Maybe this one has a simple explanation."

"Well, he hardly had time to spend it." Ian turned back to the drawing board.

Jane looked on as Ian added another box to the wiring diagram which, looking more closely, she saw showed the interlocking shareholding and cross ownership of a string of Kuopio companies.

"What's this?" Jane said. "I asked for something simple on Kuopio Industries. Is that the best you can do?"

"It is good isn't it?" Ian beamed, and ran his hand through his curly hair. I thought you would be pleased. I know you like a diagram. And you didn't ask for something simple. You asked for something on ownership that was both accurate and expressed in its simplest form."

"Fair enough," Jane said, looking at the weaving lines of control. "It's an illegal operation isn't it?"

"It sure is," Ian Hart said. "All the companies have virtually the same name so it's difficult to track what monies are going where. It's a simple ruse but an effective one, particularly if you have a few hundred of them. Remember the Barings scandal. But not difficult for the trained mind," he added, inking over a bold line that led to a company registered in the Cayman Islands. "The money is there. Kuopio 192."

"Good. Really good." Jane said. "But what about David Mandell and his companies? Do you know anything about them?"

Ian looked pained at her lack of appreciation.

"Ian, this is important. The analysis on Kuopio is great but it's small-time compared to Mandell."

"You are serious, aren't you?" Ian said. "Fair enough. I'll get on to it. I have had a quick look through the papers. As far as I can see the companies in the Mandell group are reasonably sound, not spectacularly profitable but not in any particular difficulty either. The problem seems to be this loan that has disappeared. If you want more detailed stuff I might be able to get something together by tomorrow afternoon."

"If you can't manage it before I suppose that will have to do. Get Fiona to help you. She's bright enough at numbers and she needs more of a challenge than she is getting at the moment." Jane paused. "At the moment I'm assuming there's nothing that points to a financial black hole in Mandell Industries."

"Not that I can see."

"Interesting," Jane said. "I'll get Suzanne to book you in for three o'clock. See if you can do a danger signs test by then as well."

"That shouldn't be a problem."

"Good," Jane smiled. "And don't work all night either. It's not good for you."

"Other things are worse. I suppose you are driving home again."

Jane nodded. Ian Hart pulled out a white plastic inhaler from his desk draw and waggled it under her nose. "Sooner or later the fumes are going to kill us all."

"I think you're over-training," Jane said. "If you suffer from asthma you shouldn't be finely tuning your body. I'd cut out cycling and all those visits to the gym if I were you. You won't have a joint that's working properly by the time you're fifty unless you do. Repetitive stress is what you need to worry about. Frankly I think it is just vanity. Besides, travelling by car eases my mental problems. Going by tube brings my claustrophobia to the fore. Sorting out this office would help as well. I can feel the furniture pressing in around me. It's quite horrible. Anyway I have an appointment tonight. I need the car."

"Leaving early then?" Ian said half-accusingly.

"Yes," Jane said firmly and looked at her watch. Seven-thirty. Robert Stuart had telephoned and suggested that they go out that evening and made it clear that he wouldn't take no for an answer. Jane had let her initial objections be set aside. It was time to go.

Ian had picked up something from the mound of papers on his desk that he was holding in front of her. It was a glossy magazine with a picture of two men. One she recognised as the film director, Nick Fyne. The other man also seemed familiar although she couldn't immediately place him.

"The man on the left you can't place is Mark Mandell," Ian said. He is backing Nick Fyne's picture. Some sort of period gangster movie set in the swinging Sixties. A British *Goodfellas* apparently. With a big budget."

"You should add a new category to your company danger signs," Jane said. "Backing British films sounds a good way of losing a lot of money."

"I might put it in between company jets and beautiful secretaries," Ian said. "By the way I don't think David Mandell had a jet but somebody said he had a beautiful secretary."

"I can't see one person costing him £250 million."

She picked up the magazine. She hadn't immediately noticed the obvious resemblance between father and son.

"Why don't you take it?" Ian Hart offered. "Familiarity will probably bring an end to your infatuation with the film business."

"I'm simply applying a little intuition, I would have thought the more we can understand the motives of David Mandell and his son, the closer we are likely to be to sorting this out."

"Perhaps, although you really just need to find out who has got control of the money at the moment. But rely on intuition if you must."

"See you tomorrow."

In her office Jane compared the photographs of father and son. Some of the dominant characteristics that were apparent in David Mandell had been reflected in his son's features except that, in the son, they had become softened, almost ironic.

At the back of the file she found credit card size pictures of David Mandell and his son that she cut out. Despite Ian's scepticism something told her that the more she could understand the Mandells the better chance they would have of finding the missing money.

She locked the file away and tried to tuck the photographs away in the wallet in her bag which was bulging under a rich diet of credit card slips and loose change which she had to spend a minute clearing out. As she consigned the slips to the waste paper basket in a mildly methodical manner she came across a third photograph. Robert Stuart smiled up at her.

She put Robert on the desk next to Mark Mandell. If she had been asked ten seconds before whether she possessed a photograph of Robert Stuart she would have been a hundred per cent sure that the answer was no. And yet here it was. She shivered slightly, only partly from the increasing cold as the room cooled for the night.

She searched back. For several seconds she flapped wildly around in her own past trying to locate the memory she knew must be there. Then her pulse slowed as she found it. It had been last summer, when she and Robert had first started seeing each other. Robert had insisted one evening that they should be photographed together in an automatic photograph booth in an underground station. Jane had agreed provided they did four different poses and that at least one photograph should be of Robert alone. With some fast changing of position they had managed it, and Robert's photograph had turned out surprisingly well. How could she have forgotten?

She gathered the three photographs up and inserted them into a credit card slot in the wallet she had cleared of plastic. She looked at her watch. It was more than time to go.

CHAPTER THREE

Robert, who was normally extremely punctual, was mercifully ten minutes later than they had arranged. Jane had a few extra moments to herself in her apartment. She still couldn't believe that she had managed to forget both that she had a photograph of Robert and the fun day they had had six months ago. Perhaps any rut she was in was primarily of her own making. The woman in the mirror looking back at her seemed, however, in total command of her senses and, for once, perfectly prepared for an evening engagement.

When he arrived Robert Stuart had tulips and roses in one hand and a small box in the other.

"Robert, how lovely," Jane said taking the flowers from him and moving to the kitchen area for a vase. "You really shouldn't have."

"Of course I should."

She put the flowers in the vase. He was holding out the small blue velvet box to her.

"Why don't you try these?"

Inside the box was a pair of diamond earrings. They sparkled up at her like an icy fire. They looked immensely valuable. The sort of thing Diana Vere would wear for her trips to Glyndebourne.

"They're a family heirloom but there is nobody in the family to wear them. I thought you might like to have use of them. There is no point in them staying hidden away in a cupboard."

Jane stretched out a hand to hide her eyes from the glitter. "That is terribly generous Robert, but really I can't. They might get stolen."

"They might get stolen wherever they are. They need to be put to use. I can't think of a better home for them. I thought you might like to wear them tonight."

"But I don't know where we are going."

"Just a restaurant I thought you would like. You said choose one and you would go along. I'm sorry it's taken me so long to arrange anything. I've been neglecting you, which is madness, particularly with someone as beautiful as you are. Look, just try them and see if you like them. If not, well, they'll have had an airing."

"It seems to be decided then. Thank you, Robert."

Jane gave him a light kiss on the cheek.

"But I am a little suspicious. What are you up to?"

"Nothing in particular. Well, that's not entirely accurate. I'll tell you in the restaurant."

Jane removed the earrings from the box in the palm of Robert's hand. The diamonds glowed cold and intense on their dark blue velvet bed. She picked them up and put them on with a flourish that she had seen Diana Vere perform a dozen times when they had shared a flat. In the small mirror on the wall the diamonds shimmered in the light.

"Perfect," Robert Stuart said.

She had another chance to check on his opinion as she encountered her reflection in the tinted glass door of the restaurant. The alternative Jane Charles she had encountered in her flat was glittering ever more intensely.

"So, Robert, are you going to tell me what this is all about?" she asked when the first course had been ordered. They were sitting at the back of the restaurant where two tables had been placed under a vaulted glass roof on which rime glistened.

"It was an impulse."

"I didn't think you acted on impulse."

"I don't normally. But I have been meaning to give them to you for some time. I just couldn't find the occasion."

"And what is the occasion today?"

Robert Stuart paused, gathering his thoughts.

"It's more of a prompt; I should have given them to you anyway. The thing is the bank has offered me a new job. Vice-President, Mergers and Acquisitions."

"Robert, that's tremendous. You must be thrilled."

"I am, I suppose. Yes, I am. There are some exciting opportunities. There's only one thing though. The job is in New York."

"I see that could be a problem," Jane said mischievously. "You would miss the Lord's Test."

"I might be able to get back for that."

"I can't see any obstacle then."

"There is one problem."

"Which is?"

"I'd like you to come with me."

Jane thought for a moment that she must have misheard.

"I'm sure you could get a good job out there if you wanted to," Robert continued. "I know you like your job here, but you said the other day you were thinking of a change. The bank has connections if you needed them, not that you would. Frankly with your background I can think of any number of companies that would be eager to employ you. We would be anxious to employ you ourselves – at twice, three times what you are getting here. Or you could get a secondment if you didn't want to leave the Civil Service. I just think it would be a great break for a couple of years, a sort of holiday. We could keep the flats here and Eastwood on. We could make regular trips back. We could have fun. What do you think?"

Jane didn't know.

"We could certainly have some fun," she said after a moment. "When is all this going to happen?"

"I'll have to move in the next couple of months. I'm going over to discuss arrangements early next week. But I wanted to talk to you first."

"Simon wanted to research a book in the States. A thriller he was writing – *Foreign Affairs*. He thought it would be his big break in the American market. We nearly went three years ago or so, just before the accident."

"I didn't know. Perhaps it's not such a good idea."

"No, no, Robert, the idea is fine. It's something I have always

25

wanted to do. Maybe now is the time."

There were other things she wanted to do of course. Renovating Eastwood would make no sense as a single person project. One day she needed to accept that or let go of the project altogether.

The arrival of the first course gave her time to think over Robert's proposition. The diamonds glittered in the glass in front of her. They seemed as unreal or as real as Robert's proposition. What precisely was she going to say?

"Look Jane," Robert was saying, "I'm serious. It's not a follow me option. I just think it would be a break from everything here. The fact that I've got a job there just makes it easier if we want to go. We could change everything tomorrow. Just say yes. What is there really to keep you here? I know the job is important but this seems an opportunity not to be missed."

"I think I would have said yes, yesterday," Jane said after a moment, and leaned forward confidentially, "but things are a little more difficult now. It's this Mandell business. You know that I used to work for Kenneth Ormond. He is involved and wants me to help. It's something I need to do. It could take time."

"I'm sure you're the best person to help, Jane, but are you sure you are being fair to yourself? Look, I can understand if you're not sure about us but wouldn't it be a good idea to get away from here and now, put all that's happened to you at a distance?"

"Robert, I,-"

But Jane was interrupted before she could answer.

"Jane - and Robert!" Sally Fry's bouncy voice announced her equally energetic presence, and close at hand. She had even managed to insert a dramatic pause between their two names. "What are you two doing here?"

Tonight she was looking more than her usual cheerful self and had an affectionate grip on her husband's arm. Sally and Martin had obviously booked the other table in the area below the glass roof. Jane supposed the area had been designed for couples to dine discreetly together. She wondered if Robert had deliberately chosen the table for that reason. Now he had managed to drop his fork on the floor and progressed to biting his lip. She had never seen him so irritated before.

Jane looked up at her old friend. Three children and six years of married life had produced, as far as Jane could judge, a period of unbroken happiness. Sally could be an advertisement for marriage and motherhood. But then Sally's life had always seemed more carefree from the day that she, Jane, and Diana as university students had agreed to share the flat in Kensington together. Jane could remember Diana Vere moodily looking out of the bay window of the flat's living room, a long curl of smoke rising from her cigarette, her aristocratic features composed into the stoical acceptance of melancholy that was an integral part of life. Jane would be bent over a book and Sally, work finished for the day, would be on the telephone in the kitchen talking to her latest boyfriend. Sally, Jane remembered, had always seemed to have had a boyfriend on the go. She had somehow managed to acquire the large bedroom with the double bed on the top floor and occupancy of the flat, particularly at weekends, was regularly increased to four. As Sally also managed to keep the fridge stocked and the flat cleaned neither Diana nor Jane had felt like complaining, particularly as Sally was adept at producing meals for three or four when Diana surfaced from her introspection and Jane from her studies. Diana had produced a theory that Sally managed to achieve so much because she lived entirely in the present. Jane envied her ability to balance her life so satisfactorily, but knew despite Sally's encouragement that she would never be able to manage her own life so well. Sally told Jane late one evening that as long as she had enough sex she was happy.

"We're celebrating," Sally continued as neither Jane nor Robert had said anything. "Martin's bonus."

"You must join us," Robert said in a controlled tone. "We can pull the tables together."

"What is going on?" Sally hissed when she had a moment alone with Jane. Jane could see the reflection of the diamonds glittering in Sally's eyes.

"Robert asked me out to dinner."

Sally adopted a resigned expression at this obvious evasion. "And?"

"We were discussing career options."

"And that's all you're saying?"

"Yes."

"Are you involved in this Mandell business Jane?" Martin Fry asked. "It's all over the business pages in the *Standard*. £300 million missing apparently."

"I'm not quite sure it's that much."

"It's hardly on the scale of Enron or anything like that," Robert Stuart said.

"No, but it's all in cash apparently, or it was." Sally Fry sounded positively excited. "And it's all disappeared. Just think what you could do with that amount of money. Absolute power."

"Hardly," Robert Stuart said. "It's not like being the President of the United States. You can't invade countries as you wish."

"As far as I can see money, or American commercial interests, is precisely what drives United States foreign policy," Martin said.

"I am sure there will be a solution to the Mandell problem without lives being put at risk," Jane said.

"I'm not sure about that," Sally said. "Wasn't there an article in the papers about how much it cost to get somebody eliminated in London? Was it £50,000? And no questions asked."

"This is all rather fanciful," said Jane. "Whatever has happened in the Mandell companies isn't likely to lead to murder. There may be some implications for the financial regulation stuff I'm involved in, but somebody has got to find out what happened first."

"Isn't that you?" Sally Fry sounded disappointed.

"Hardly. Anyway I'm sure there will be a perfectly ordinary explanation."

"I'm sure Jane's right," said Robert Stuart. "There was a rumour going round the bank that Mandell was after Neptune television. Maybe that was what he needed the money for, or maybe he *did* need the money to shore up his business."

"Precisely," Jane said ignoring Sally's wide-eyed glance.

"Anyway," Robert continued, "tell us more about this bonus Martin, and didn't Jane tell me the two of you were planning to move out of London? Where are you thinking of going?"

Robert's sudden deep interest in Fry affairs managed to distract Sally from digging too deeply into either Mandell or relationships.

It was two bottles of red wine later before Sally managed to corner Jane again.

"So what is going on with Robert?"

"I don't know," Jane said. "I really don't know."

She could see that Sally didn't believe her, but it was an entirely truthful answer.

At eleven, when she thought that Martin and Sally were bound to leave, Robert got a call on his mobile.

"Problems at the bank. I'll have to go. I'll get you a taxi."

"I'm sorry about Sally," Jane said at the door of the restaurant. Robert Stuart smiled.

"Don't be. I enjoyed it. We must have more evenings like this."

"One or two quieter ones as well."

"As many as we can get. Have you thought about New York?"

"A lot. Let's talk at the weekend."

"I am serious."

"I know."

Their embrace would have been longer and more lingering if Martin and Sally Fry hadn't appeared to find out what was happening.

CHAPTER FOUR

By the time she had drunk her second cup of office coffee the next morning Jane had decided that she might simply have said yes to Robert Stuart's proposition if Sally and Martin hadn't turned up. She was wondering what she should do about it when Suzanne appeared with a white envelope in her hand.

"Special delivery."

"We're not expecting anything are we? Who is it from?"

"Doesn't say. The people at the front door think it was a motorcycle messenger, but there was a lot of post coming in this morning and they're not sure. I did ask but they really don't know."

On the envelope was a handwritten address –

>   JANE QUINN
>   HM TREASURY
>   WHITEHALL

Someone else had crossed Whitehall out and put Jane's room number and building code on the envelope.

"Somebody who doesn't know we have moved," Jane said. "You'd better open it up."

It was the head and shoulders photograph of a man. Suzanne looked puzzled as she handed it across the desk.

"It's fine," Jane said. "I know who it is."

She would no longer have to rely on Ian Hart's magazine photograph to compare the character traits of father and son. Mark Mandell's eyes twinkled up at her from a photograph large enough to show the detail of the laughter lines around his eyes. On the back of the photograph was a message and a London telephone number in a firm hand and the initials 'MM'. The message read *It would be good to meet.* Underneath Mandell had added a PS *'Photo so you can recognise me if you need to..'* On the top right of the photograph itself was printed 'mark mandell' and below that 'mandell entertainment', both with a democratic disregard for capital letters.

"You managed to get hold of another photograph of him then?" Ian Hart said in a matter of fact voice from the doorway.

"This one was totally unsolicited."

"I believe you."

"It's the truth. Anyway what brings you here? I thought we were meant to be meeting this afternoon."

"Given that Mandell has got to the top of the pile I thought you might like to know how we were doing, but you may have new priorities."

"Top of the pile is about right for your office, but come and sit down and tell me more."

"All the major financial decisions affecting Mandell Holdings were always taken by David Mandell personally. I've checked with Perry at the Bank of England. They're also beavering away on this."

"Do they have any ideas about what happened?"

"Not exactly. The only thing they do seem sure of is there is nothing in the way Mandell has been behaving to suggest that he would contemplate a major fraud."

"Explain."

"They have been through all of the Mandell Holdings accounts and those of related companies for the last five years. David Mandell had all sorts of possibilities open to him for indulging in dubious business practices. He could have changed the accounting policy in the companies he acquired so that assets were depreciated over a longer period. That would have boosted his profits nicely. He didn't. He had companies with different financial year-ends trading with each other.

He could have arranged to sell stock he was finding it difficult to shift from one to the other. That would have increased his profits over the short term. He didn't do it. He could have re-valued the pension funds he acquired to give his companies a contributions holiday. He didn't. All the dealings they can find seem to be absolutely straight. There is absolutely nothing untoward except that there is £250 million plus missing and David Mandell had control of the money at the time that it finally went absent without leave. And yet in all his behaviour up till then there was not the slightest inkling that he was anything other than straightforward – at least in his accounting. According to Perry he would strike a hard bargain but be scrupulously fair. That doesn't fit with a man who is supposed to have stolen £250 million."

"So what legitimate reasons could he have had for wanting the money? A takeover bid?"

"That's a good thought; perhaps intuition is a good thing, after all."

"What about Mark Mandell and Mandell Entertainment? How do they fit into all this?"

"It's only a peripheral part of the group. I don't think it is of any particular importance in the scheme of things. Mark Mandell wasn't at the top table. Apparently he and his father weren't on the closest of terms."

"Somebody must know something more about the missing millions. Surely David Mandell had a Finance Director?"

"He did. A chap called Chorley. Mid-sixties, been with Mandell for years. Apparently very good at keeping the books in order, but doesn't seem to have been involved in making the key decisions."

"Which were all made by David Mandell?"

"Precisely."

"What about your danger signs?"

"No jets, speedboats, fast cars, or third and fourth homes. His accounting procedures seem whiter than white, as I said. He has stuck largely with KM Bank for finance for his deals in the last few years, although the £250 million was by far the biggest. He seems to have a good relationship with one of the KM main board members, an American called Karl di Rocca, who agreed the deal with him. He has never had any trouble with KM or any of his other bankers as far as

I can find out. The Mandell Holdings Board don't seem to have got too involved in decisions of the company which is a weakness but one which might be expected. There are also no flagpoles, fountains, marble, or undue extravagances in his office accommodation, rather the reverse."

"There must be something."

Ian Hart shrugged.

"There were only a couple of things."

"Which were?"

"The rumours about his beautiful secretary were right, although she is more of a personal aide. She is apparently something of a stunner. Perry says she comes from the East End and Mandell adopted her as his protégée. Reminded him of his roots or something."

"He would hardly need £250 million to impress a member of staff. What was the other factor?"

"There is a swimming pool in the basement of his house. He had it put in a few years ago. It's apparently modelled on Roman baths. It appears to have been his only indulgence. Ironic really."

"Why?"

"It didn't do him any good. It killed him. He was found drowned."

"Hardly a pleasant end."

"It's the third most common accidental cause of death," Ian Hart said.

Jane had a sudden, unpleasant, image of David Mandell fighting for life as the water engulfed him. She saw Mandell's face slipping below the water and a trail of bubbles come floating up from his mouth. She shook her head. The picture had been too real. She had obviously spent too long studying photographs the previous night.

"Look," Jane said, "follow up on this takeover angle. It's the most logical explanation that I can think of. Mandell had obviously accumulated the money for some purpose or other. If his companies were basically sound what other reason could there be? If he had been planning a takeover, somebody in Mandell Holdings must know something about it, even if they don't know the details. The Finance Director, Chorley or whatever his name is, can't be completely in the dark. He must have some sense of what David Mandell was up to."

"I'll see what I can do." Ian Hart got to his feet.

"Anything you can Ian, please. It is important to me."

Jane nodded encouragingly. She needed to speak to Peter Green about Kenneth Ormond's approach. Then she could be more forthcoming. She saw Ian whispering to Suzanne in the outer office. Perhaps he was complaining about her lack of frankness.

She telephoned Kenneth Ormond's office but the Home Secretary was away on a two day visit to Newcastle and contactable only on the most urgent business. He was not taking an overnight box of business papers so there was no opportunity for Jane to send him a message.

She took the photograph that Mark Mandell had sent her and propped it against her desk lamp. It took something of an ego to send a photograph of oneself to a perfect stranger. Mark Mandell did at least share his father's hypnotic eyes to drag you back firmly to the picture. Jane found herself smiling.

Suzanne buzzed through. Jane put the photograph in a drawer out of sight.

"Yes?"

"The meeting with the Economic Secretary," Suzanne said as though it were clearly evident that this was the topic uppermost in Jane's mind.

"I'm going," Jane said, picking up the sheaf of briefing papers that Suzanne had left on her desk.

The meeting lasted a couple of hours. Then she spent fifteen minutes compiling a list of all the follow-up actions that needed to be taken. She frowned. The extra figures on fraud that had been asked for would take her analytical team at least a week to produce. She needed to talk to Peter about resources again. She looked at her watch. It was time to check up on Ian Hart.

When she got to Ian's room she found he had covered a large white pad with a series of figures and doodles.

"I've heard a rumour," Jane said, "that David Mandell was planning to build a sizable stake in Neptune Television."

Ian Hart looked surprised. "Where did you hear that?"

"Somewhere around," Jane said vaguely. "Why, doesn't it make sense?"

Ian Hart nodded his head. "Perfect sense. But media was not an area where David Mandell operated a lot. Neptune are one of the smaller companies but with a good reputation for producing high quality television. The only trouble is that they are really too small in the current television world. They were bound to be taken over sooner or later. There are bid rumours for all the smaller television companies at the moment."

"And a takeover would attract a premium price?"

"Oh yes." Ian Hart was enthusiastic. "30 or 40 per cent, perhaps more. Prices are drifting up in the sector all the time but when it comes to the crunch the bid is always a bit over the top. I have never quite worked out how that macho factor should be weighted. It seems clear that the bid values the company by assuming that growth will continue as before. It's like buying a gold mine at a price which assumes that most of the gold has yet to be found."

"And somebody like David Mandell would understand that?"

"Sure. He had a history of bids where the companies turned out to be worth significantly more than he bid for them."

"So borrowing the money for a really big bid wouldn't be a problem for him?"

"£250 million isn't that big a bid in the media world. Neptune may not be massive in television terms but he wouldn't get control for that much."

"Could he have been building up a stake?"

"No reason why not. Mandell Holdings have some interests in regional newspapers but that is almost accidental. David Mandell normally bought complete companies, and broke them up."

"Perhaps he was taking advice from somebody."

"He could have been, I suppose. But he was reputed not to take advice from anyone."

"Let's just suppose it was his plan though. Suppose too he wanted to pick up shares gradually without alerting people to the fact that it was one individual that was building up a stake."

"It's possible," Ian Hart said. "But given the size of Neptune £250 million wouldn't have bought him much more than 20% of the company. He could just have bought that in one go."

"Suppose he decided to route the money he had borrowed through a number of accounts and companies to disguise the fact that it was a single individual who was building up a stake in Neptune. Nobody would know where the money had gone and nobody would be aware that these companies were acquiring shares on David Mandell's behalf in Neptune. The companies would of course be ultimately controlled by him or his nominees. Perhaps he was using Mandell Holdings as collateral for the loan but was basically involved in a simple share dealing transaction. Buy the shares and then sell them later, taking his profit. In the normal course of events the disguised nature of the transactions wouldn't be a problem. He wouldn't be buying enough of the shares to have to trigger a full bid. As long as the price went up everything would be fine. The only thing he hadn't reckoned on was his own death."

"So you mean it could be that the money is in accounts somewhere known only to David Mandell waiting for the buy instructions that are never going to come?"

"Exactly."

Ian Hart looked thoughtful. "It's ingenious enough but I don't buy it entirely."

"It's possible isn't it?" said Jane. "It fits the facts."

"Oh yes, it's possible. But there's something missing. It's too complicated just to disguise the source of a bid for shares. There would be no reason to go to those lengths. Money just doesn't disappear like that."

"So why does money disappear like that?"

"Because somebody wants it to."

"I don't get it. Why would David Mandell want that?"

"I'm not sure that he did."

"O.K. Ian," Jane said. "I've given you my working explanation. What's your answer?"

"I don't know," Ian Hart looked uncertain. "The bid idea seems sensible. Has anyone asked KM why they loaned Mandell the money?"

"Not as far as I am aware. Would they tell us?"

"There's probably not too much confidentiality with the dead, particularly if you're £250 million light but I'm not sure. Where did you get the Neptune takeover stuff from anyway?"

"It came up in a discussion about Mandell reports in the papers. I can't remember when," Jane said airily.

Ian Hart still looked as though he was troubled about something.

"Spill it, Ian. Tell me the takeover stuff is nonsense and there is another rational explanation."

"It's not that. I was thinking about something you said the other day. What was it? The intuition thing? I think we need to find out as much about David Mandell as we can. There's something strange about this whole set-up. Given David Mandell seemed to have been in charge of everything the explanation of whatever was going on is probably linked to him directly. The more we can find out about him and his way of working the better."

"If I said it I don't suppose it can do any harm. There's just the question of how precisely we do find out about David Mandell."

"I'm sure you'll think of something."

When Jane got back to her office she saw Suzanne beckoning to her to hurry.

"There's a call for you," Suzanne said.

"Who is it?"

"I'm afraid he wouldn't say. I did ask."

"That's all right," Jane said. "I'll got through and take it."

"Switching him through," Suzanne said.

"Hello," Jane said.

"Is that Jane Quinn?"

It was a man's voice.

"Yes, speaking."

"I apologise for calling you out of the blue," the voice said.

But Jane knew it wasn't quite out of the blue.

"It is just that I thought it might be helpful if we could meet. My name is.. "

Jane already knew. She mouthed the words silently as they were spoken at the other end of the line.

" .. Mark Mandell."

CHAPTER FIVE

"Yes," Jane said in as neutral a voice as she could muster, "a meeting would be a good idea." She could at least acquire the personal details that Ian Hart craved.

"I'm afraid I'm rather short of time. Could we meet today? Early this evening? Five-thirty?"

"That's no problem."

"There's a wine bar near your office. The Pompadour."

"I think I know it," Jane said.

He gave precise instructions and a minute later the telephone conversation was over. Jane wrote the name and address on a sheet of paper, folded it, and put it in her handbag. Then she took out Mark Mandell's photograph and looked at it. Mandell's voice had been warmer and lighter than she had been expecting, with a humorous tone.

Suzanne was in the doorway.

"Ian's back," she said.

"Wheel him in," Jane said. She put the photograph back in her desk drawer.

Ian was looking happier.

"I had a telephone call after you left. Looks like you were right – about some sort of bid anyway. I have a friend in Boulting Cox, David Mandell's brokers. She works for the Chairman. I telephoned yesterday and left a message. Apparently she spent a good part of

Christmas Eve waiting for a call from David Mandell. They had a team standing by for Mandell's final instructions. There was a bid he had been lining up."

"Neptune?"

"I mentioned Neptune but she wouldn't confirm it. She didn't deny it either. I don't think you'll get any more out of them without a court order."

"Did they do anything when Mandell didn't call?"

"They assumed he might have been having some trouble with his bankers. There had been some rumours that had suddenly started circulating about the quality of his profits. They thought that was causing the delay. They didn't get worried until they were seriously running out of time. David Mandell had a habit of cutting things very fine but eventually they realized nothing was going to happen. They tried to get in touch with him but they couldn't raise him at either his office or home number. They gave up at five. It was far too late to do anything by then but he was an important client and they wanted to be sure."

"And they didn't get him at all, no contact of any kind that day?"

"Nothing. It surprised them. When David Mandell had got something lined up he invariably went through with it.

"So you don't think there is any possibility that he was using Boulting Cox as a smokescreen while he mounted the bid from a more concealed source?"

"I don't see the point of paying out fees for nothing. Boulting Cox don't come cheap."

"What if he was just planning to walk off with the money?"

"That's more plausible. He could have been using them to disguise his real intentions. Boulting Cox normally acted for David Mandell. The fact they were lined up for something would probably have got back to his bankers. It would have been extra insurance for KM if they needed it."

"So you think David Mandell could have been planning to run off with the money?"

"It makes as much sense as anything else."

Jane nodded thoughtfully.

"I'll see if I can find anybody else who has heard any rumours."

"Before you go, there are a couple of things," Jane said. "Neptune's share price. What's happened to it in the last week?"

"Gone up," Ian said.

"How much?"

"5% or so. A little over £12 million profit if you had invested the odd £250 million you had, if that's what you're thinking."

"I probably was," said Jane.

"And?"

"And what?"

"What was the other thing?"

"Oh yes, I almost forgot. This intuitive stuff about what David Mandell was like. What precisely had you in mind?"

"Oh, boy's stuff, hobbies, favourite team, that sort of thing."

"Football team?"

"Football probably, you could also try cricket."

"And you're not going to tell me why, I imagine."

"Just a hunch, probably turn out to be nothing."

As Ian's hunches were normally profitable Jane would have pressed him more if Suzanne had not appeared in the doorway.

"Richard is at the front door."

"Richard?"

"Your brother. Shall I go and get him?"

"No need thanks." Jane got to her feet. "I'll go. I'd forgotten it was today. He is dropping off some papers for my mother."

Richard Quinn had promised to deliver the last papers her mother had to sign to finalise her father's estate. One or two irritating loose ends had already taken far too many years to resolve. The only beneficiaries of the delay had been the lawyers and Jane had been determined the whole matter should now be concluded as quickly as possible. She had volunteered to get her mother to sign the papers on her next visit to Silverlawns and her brother had agreed to collect them from the solicitors and drop them off at her office.

Suzanne was buzzing.

"I've got Sally Fry on the line."

"Did you say I was here?"

"No."

"Tell her I'm not back."

Jane looked at her watch. She had no time to talk to Sally now. There were one or two loose ends from the meeting with the Economic Secretary that needed tidying up and the conversation with Ian Hart had eaten up a few more minutes. The arrangement with Mark Mandell meant she was even shorter of time than usual. She really hadn't got the time to talk to Sally. She looked at the list of uncompleted tasks on her pad and sighed.

Richard Quinn was standing in the middle of the entrance hallway looking up at her. Her younger, and only, brother was clad in a long black leather coat. A pair of goggles had been pushed up over his thick curly hair and he was holding a crash helmet in his hand. Despite the weather conditions he was obviously still travelling on the Motoguzzi. Jane uttered another sigh. Why her brother should think the freezing conditions outside, with traffic sliding all over the road, were suitable for a motorbike that must weigh at least a quarter of a ton was beyond her.

"How is it going?" he said as she approached.

"Not bad," Jane said. "Fairly frantic, but just bearable."

"No change then. Anyway, you look well on it. I bumped into Sally Fry. She said things were going well with Robert. For my money he's a shade dull but worth thinking about."

"Richard, you're being ridiculous."

"I'm not sure that I am. Not that I am saying," continued Richard quickly, "that you couldn't do better. But you must give him high marks for persistence. I'm sure he will ask you some day. I should think it over seriously. Sally mentioned some diamonds he's given you. Looks promising. If you are working all the time there isn't exactly a great deal of opportunity to meet the ideal mate."

"I'm not in the remotest bit interested in Robert as a husband," Jane said. "Robert is extremely charming but that is as far as it goes."

"Something *must* have happened," Richard said. "You don't normally bother to deny it."

"I suppose Robert has been a little more attentive than usual."

"You'll be telling me next that you're just good friends."

"Richard, do stop being irritating. Have you got those documents?"

"That's why I'm here. But I did hear something about Robert that might interest you."

"What?"

"It's confidential, I'll need to whisper."

"Aren't you ever going to grow up?"

"Seriously Jane," Richard rolled his eyes in mock warning toward the security guard behind the main desk.

"So what is this news?" Jane half whispered.

"I've heard he's a spook, that he works for MI5."

"That's ridiculous," Jane hissed. "How on earth would you know anyway?"

"I was running a course last week at Sunningdale, re-orientating your organization to meet today's challenges or something like that. Half of GCHQ were there. Robert's name came up in conversation at the bar. It was rather late but naturally I was interested on your behalf and loyally stayed on until it thinned out a bit. Some of the people were quite talkative. Maybe it's guilt about knowing all those secrets. It must be a dreadful strain, particularly if you're drunk. Anyway I rather gathered Robert was on the payroll. Sort of a sleeper."

"I don't believe a word of it."

"Fair enough," Richard said in his responsible voice. "I wouldn't dream of compromising him – or you. I won't mention it again."

"Good," Jane said picking up a brown envelope that Richard had produced from within his leather coat. "Is this everything?"

"Elizabeth just has to sign and date each form and that should be it - at last."

Richard had recently taking to referring to their mother by her Christian name. It was a development that made Jane uneasy, but more about her own relationship with her mother than his.

"How about offering me a cup of coffee?" Richard continued. "It would also give me an opportunity of seeing the lovely Suzanne again."

"Sorry," Jane said. "No can do. I've got a pile of work to do and I have to be out of here just after five."

"Your life does seem to be changing," Richard said. "I thought you would have at least another three or four hours work before you could leave. None of this nine to five stuff. I must tell you that as a taxpayer

I feel rather affronted. Why do you have to be out of here?"

"I'm meeting someone at a wine bar."

Richard's eyebrows shot up.

"Not a spy?"

"Richard, I'm warning you. It isn't Robert. He isn't a spy. This is business."

"Oh yes," Richard said unbelievingly. "Make sure you have a good time."

CHAPTER SIX

The entrance to the Pompadour Wine Bar was marked by a canopy so gleaming with frost that it was difficult to distinguish the name. The stairs leading downwards were in deep shadow. Jane stepped through the half open doors and descended into the depths.

There was a murmur of noise coming from below and the air became warmer as she walked down the steps. She went through another door that creaked ominously and then she found herself in the first of a series of large interconnecting cellars with a brightly lit long bar serving wine and food. Tables and chairs were scattered amid supporting stone pillars and dark wooden panelling. The place was nearly deserted. It was the dead hour before the evening office trade started.

Jane looked round. Mark Mandell was sitting at a table in a secluded corner. A candle in a glass globe threw ever-changing images of his head and upper body onto the walls so that he seemed at one moment large and dominating, and the next faint and insubstantial. As Jane approached she saw that he was bent over a crossword in which he had filled in five or six clues. Behind her she felt a cold draught that was probably the current of air that she had brought with her from outside.

Before she could get to the table he looked up. It seemed to take him a second or two to focus on her. Something had obviously been preoccupying him.

"Jane Quinn?"

Jane nodded.

Mandell was on his feet. He lent forward and kissed her once on each cheek. It was an easy, familiar, gesture; the sort of thing that Robert Stuart had worked round to after three months. She might have been a relative in a close-knit French village.

He was taller than she expected, a couple of inches over six foot, and rugged, with broad shoulders. Close to, the humour and vitality that had seemed possible from the photograph were confirmed as real.

"I was expecting somebody older."

"I'm sorry to disappoint you."

"You don't. Rather the reverse. I was also anticipating more of a civil service type."

"I'm not sure that I know what a civil service type is."

"Oh, you know..." Mandell stopped. "Neither do I, anymore. Look, how about a drink? Something red? To keep the cold out."

"Fine."

Mandell went away to the bar. Jane found herself irritatingly breathless. Being underground always quickened her pulse and made her feel faint.

Mark Mandell had returned, bottle in hand.

"Are you alright? You look pale."

"I'm just a little claustrophobic," Jane found herself confessing. "It's nothing. Normally it is just tunnels that have this effect. I will be fine in a moment."

"Are you sure?" Mandell waved the bottle in his hand dismissively. "We can easily go somewhere else."

"No, no really, I'm fine now." Jane felt embarrassment come to her aid and insert some colour into her cheeks. She did not usually confide in strangers at a moment's notice. "If you pour me a drink I am sure that would complete the recovery."

Mandell nodded.

"Do you like crosswords?" Jane indicated the newspaper on the table. She was keen to change the subject. If they started talking about claustrophobia she had an awful feeling that she would find herself compelled to tell Mandell of the time she had been trapped underground as a child. She started wriggling her toes. Her father had always said that was what he had had to do to stop fainting.

"Not really," Mandell said looking ruefully at the clues in front of him. "My father used to do the crossword every day. I was thinking about him before you came in. He was a fanatic for all sorts of puzzles, mathematical ones particularly. I never understood quite what the fascination was entirely. I used to think it was fun when I was a child. I remember he wrote 'Happy Birthday' on the hard-boiled egg I had for breakfast when I was seven. You make ink out of alum and vinegar and write on the shell. The shell is porous and the message is left on the egg. He wouldn't tell me how he did it; I had to find that out for myself."

Jane felt her faintness retreat to a reassuring distance as she started forming a picture of the relationship of father and son in the Mandell household.

"Did you do other things together?"

"He would take me to football matches, a bit of county cricket in the holidays. That was about it. Most of the time he was busy working."

"What teams did you support?"

"The local teams, Nottingham Forest at football and Nottinghamshire at cricket. When I was young we lived a few miles away. Neither of them are quite what they were but the allegiance remains the same. It's the one thing that my father and I kept in common over the years. What about you?"

"Teams?"

"Yes. You seem interested in them."

"I'm not really the supporting kind. Not football, cricket anyway, not that sort of thing."

"Netball perhaps?" Mandell ventured. "I think the women's team is still in the top four in the world. They even get some television coverage, although somewhat early in the morning."

"Not really my thing."

"That's probably wise, although it seems to me that it is rather a more skilful game than basketball and probably under-rated."

"Actually," Jane said indulging a sudden compulsion to tell the truth, "I think it is really only the teams you support that I find interesting."

"Really?"

"To be frank I am just trying to get a better sense of precisely what happened. Knowing what your father was like could be a valuable lead."

"I'm a little hurt. But I thought you wanted to know the teams I supported?"

"Like father, like son."

Mandell considered the proposition for a moment.

"I very much hope not," he said.

It seemed to be a considered judgement.

"Look," Jane continued filling in what was becoming a slightly awkward silence, "I should have said before. I was sorry to hear about your father's death."

"That's kind of you, but we weren't entirely close, and we haven't been for years, so I can't say I'm heartbroken. It was an odd feeling though; something ending that you never thought would." Mandell pushed a glass of burgundy in her direction. "But one thing I know about him is that he wouldn't have wanted us to be mournful. I think a toast would be more appropriate. He would have approved of you. He liked beautiful women, particularly intelligent ones."

Jane raised her glass. "May he rest in peace."

"*Eventually* rest in peace. The police are not releasing his body."

"Why ever not?"

"They haven't said exactly. They don't seem to be able to work out quite how he died. But do drink. My father was never one for solemn mourning whatever else might have been wrong with him. We could also get some sandwiches if you're hungry. They're good here."

Mandell was already signalling to a waiter at the bar. The sandwiches were ordered in seconds with Mandell suggesting the best mixture. There was something about his energy that was disarming.

"So," Jane said, when the sandwiches had arrived. "Why the telephone call? How can I help?"

"I'm not sure I know exactly. Kenneth Ormond telephoned me and said he thought we should meet up. He's anxious to get this whole business sorted out. He thought if anyone in Whitehall knew what was going on it was likely to be you. He said you had worked together before."

"Not for a few years."

"Well, anyway, he seemed to have the highest regard for your ability to sort this if anyone could. He thought I might be able to help you and said I should get in touch. So I did, and here we are."

"Yes, indeed we are," Jane said looking round. The cellars were still mostly empty, their nearest companions a man and a woman at a table twenty feet away who seemed to be involved in personal rather than business negotiations. The couple had their hands locked tightly together in what seemed to Jane to be, given the early hour, an unduly public display of affection.

"So," Mandell said, "what else do you want to know?"

Jane saw that Mark Mandell was looking at her intently, his dark brown eyes moving impatiently over each of the features of her face.

"I don't quite understand the connection with Kenneth. How do you know him?"

"I don't exactly. Yesterday was the first time I had spoken to him in ten years. He's actually my godfather, but that hasn't exactly been an active role over the last thirty years. He came to my mother's funeral, he exchanges cards at Christmas with my father, and I gather from what he said yesterday that they used to meet from time to time. But that's really it. He seemed to be upset about my father's death and was worried about his good name and another financial scandal hitting the Government. So, I said I would help. Actually," Mandell smiled, "I would like to get whatever is going on sorted out myself. This sort of financial uncertainty isn't good for me either."

"You own Mandell Entertainment don't you? It's independent of the rest of the group isn't it?"

"You have been doing your homework." Mandell's smile broadened, but some of the humour had gone. "Yes, I do own Mandell Entertainment and yes, it's completely independent of the rest of the group."

"Confusing."

"Hardly, everyone knows that my father and I run separate organizations. I only got to use the name because my mother insisted."

"And there are no formal links between Mandell Entertainment and the Mandell Group as a whole?"

"None."

"Would people know that?"

"People who know me would. I can't speak for those who had dealings with my father. I think they would but my father never volunteered any information about his business dealings unless he had to. He is – he was – extremely secretive by temperament – he reckoned it gave him a business edge."

"Did you father confide in you about his business dealings?"

"No. We have never been close. It's probably because we are too like each other, too independently minded."

"So why would he need £250 million?"

"My father's speciality was buying and selling companies. I imagine he had something like that in mind. I should know more about it but I don't. The three people you could talk to are the Finance Director, Geoffrey Chorley, or my father's secretary, or his personal assistant. They were much closer to him that I was."

Jane got a pen and notepad from her bag.

"Tell me about them."

"Chorley has been with him ever since I can remember. Sorts the details out rather than makes the decisions. My father took on Paula Black, his personal aide, a few months ago. She is bright enough, very good looking, somebody he enjoyed taking round with him."

"And his secretary?"

"Eve Jackson. She has been with him for twenty years. She takes care of all his day-to-day appointments, Christmas shopping, road tax, getting a cleaner for his house, anything and everything."

Jane scribbled in her notebook.

"Is that it?"

"So can you help me?"

Jane didn't reply for a moment. There was a sudden chatter of conversation from somewhere close at hand, one of the voices rather hysterical and noisy in the general quiet. It was odd and distracting.

"So can you help me?" Mandell said again.

"Your father had alerted his brokers that he was planning to build up a sizable stake in a public company. The rumour is that it was Neptune."

"Sounds plausible, but it would be a big deal for him to swallow. If he had been planning to do it I would have been impressed. Where

THE SKY BLUE PARCEL

did you get that from?"

"I can't say I'm afraid."

"You could trust me."

"I don't know anything about you."

"First impressions count for a lot don't they? I mean people never really deviate from how they are the first or second time you meet them."

Mandell paused as if reflecting on what he had just said and then added "I'm sorry about the photograph. It was an ill-timed bit of publicity. I have a few thousand left, and finances being somewhat strained it's a reasonable substitute for office notepaper."

There was a new current of air and the candle on the table between them flickered wildly and threw distorted shadows onto the walls. Jane saw herself represented by a tall angular figure, the outline of the evil queen in a Disney cartoon. Then there were more voices, other people entering the Pompadour.

"Look," Jane said trying to concentrate. "There are some things we should try to work out. Something unusual happened on Christmas Eve. Your father deposited the £250 million he had received from KM in a number of accounts, making the money almost impossible to trace. A lot of the actions taken seem explicable only if that was the aim. One of the things to do is to try to find out what else that was odd was happening at the same time."

"I'm not sure I get it."

"I'm just looking for actions that were out of the ordinary, any actions. Anything extraordinary about anybody, anything singular, Sherlock Holmes stuff."

Not, of course, that it was the great detective's methods exactly, more Ian Hart's.

"Well," Mark Mandell said, "I know nothing odd about the KM deal. Although there was one thing that was unusual. But it is nothing really, nothing that could have any relevance."

"So what was it?"

"My father used to like swimming. He has a house in Wandsworth overlooking the common. It is where my mother wanted to live but where they hadn't quite managed to get to when she died. There was a swimming pool in the basement of the house that he eventually bought which he enlarged. He used to swim there everyday. It was his

51

chief luxury. On Christmas Day I went out to the house to see him. I got to the house but there was no reply, so I let myself in. The house was cold, which was unusual because my father liked to keep warm. There seemed to be nobody about and I nearly left. Then it occurred to me that he might be swimming in the basement. It was perfectly possible that he might not have heard me from there. So I went down. You probably know the rest. He was in the pool. They think he may have had a heart attack or something. There he was."

"It must have been a terrible shock finding him."

"Yes it was." Mandell hesitated. "My father used to swim every day as I said. He found it relaxing. He used to come down, take his clothes off, and dive in the pool. When I found him he had a pair of blue swimming trunks on. Normally he never used to wear trunks. He would just plunge in and come out twenty minutes later. There was normally no one about and he preferred swimming naked. I found him with his trunks on."

"Is that significant?"

"I don't know. It is certainly odd, anomalous, or whatever you were getting at. I told the Police Inspector who came round about it. A chap called Norman, very fat. Not the sort you would employ to chase a fugitive."

The candle flickered violently again. Somewhere in the building a door was pushed shut with a bang.

"The interview was all rather strange.."

Mandell was speaking, but Jane was hardly listening. There was something hypnotic about Mandell's eyes.

There was another factor too that needed a moment's consideration. That David Mandell had been found in his swimming trunks when this was not his normal practice pointed to one obvious conclusion. David Mandell had committed suicide. People who committed suicide did not normally wish to be found naked.

That fact though presented another problem. What motive could David Mandell have? He had command of funds of £250 million when he died. He had a deal lined up on Neptune, or so it was rumoured, that would have made him a healthy profit. Why commit suicide?

CHAPTER SEVEN

Jane stood motionless in the shadow of the trees around Silverlawns, her mother's retirement home. It was the first time that day that she had had the opportunity to think and the car journey down through Clapham and Streatham hadn't quite given her enough time to marshal her thoughts. Her conversation with Mark Mandell at the Pompadour seemed to have taken place weeks ago, not just twenty-four hours. Despite the Economic Secretary's panic that had controlled most of the events of the day she had managed to find time to contact KM and arrange an appointment with a Christopher Bellmore, who had been responsible for the mechanics of the transfer of the £250 million from the bank to Mandell Holdings. She had also asked Ian Hart to keep on digging away and see if he could come up with anything more on the overall financial structure of the Mandell Group.

Bellmore had taken a measure of persuading that he did really need to see her. Jane had had to convince him that it was both urgent and essential, particularly if there was going to be any short term prospect of recovering the missing money which, she had added, must be in KM's interest. Bellmore, very reluctantly, had finally agreed in principle, but had had to be pushed again before fixing a meeting for Tuesday, absolutely the earliest date he could do. It had been such hard going that Jane had sworn when she finished the call. She supposed the last thing a banker wanted was to be reminded of a deal that had gone spectacularly sour.

After she had left Mark Mandell the night before events had conspired to ensure that she had had little time to think. When she had pushed open the apartment door the telephone had rung and she had found Sally Fry in her most talkative mood.

On the expanse of grass in front of her the frozen ground was glistening in the lights of cars swinging round the bend at the top of the hill. It was nearly nine. She had parked the Peugeot in her usual spot at the end of the drive that ran down the side of Silverlawns. Normally she would have hurried back to the front entrance, but tonight she had taken a few steps the other way, so that she found herself buried among the close packed trunks of the silver birches that screened the garden.

She shivered, but not from the cold. In her dreams the previous night she had seen David Mandell floating away down a pipe that had been revealed when hidden doors in the side of the swimming pool opened. There had been a current in the water pulling her after him. After she had awoken and tried to dismiss the image she had only succeeded in summoning up unpleasant pictures of green hedges near Eastwood heavy with rain as they had been on the day of the accident. She had got up and walked around the flat putting her thoughts into at least conscious order before returning to bed. The next thing she had been aware of was the grey light of early dawn flooding coldly into the room.

Below her Elizabeth Quinn's sitting room on the ground floor of Silverlawns was laid out for inspection. A large picture window and glass door looked out over the lawns that ran away from the house for fifty yards or more. From her vantage point, three or four feet above the level of the lawn, Jane could see almost every detail of the room. There was the small wooden table her mother kept near the window, the floral patterned armchair, and the not so comfortable easy chair to which Jane was inevitably ushered on her visits. Then there was the display cabinet, the television, the tea-making set. Only her mother's writing bureau was obscured from view from this angle.

Jane rubbed her hands together and her breath exhaled in a slowly moving cloud of white water vapour. It was desperately cold but the air was heavy and still and there was no immediate danger from wind chill.

Elizabeth Quinn appeared immaculately dressed in a navy suit, with her hair pinned neatly back. Jane watched for a moment. Her mother was standing stock still in the middle of her sitting room. She stood in the same position for what seemed an eternity and then simply lowered herself into a chair and picked up a book.

There was a cracking sound close to Jane, and a small branch dislodged itself from the tree above her and landed at her feet. It was time to move. Mark Mandell had promised to do all that he could to help sort out where the missing money was and then he had kissed her, his lips warm against her cold skin.

"Jane," her mother said as she opened the flat door. "I wasn't expecting you. You should have rung."

"I did Mother, this morning. Besides this is the day I always come."

"Oh," her mother said looking surprised. "But I've got nothing for you. Except perhaps you might like a glass of sherry."

Elizabeth Quinn led the way into the sitting room and picked up the bottle but made no move towards the silver tray that held the sherry glasses. Sometimes Jane waited half an hour or more for her drink. On this occasion her mother was looking past Jane out of the window. All Jane could see at first was the face of herself and her mother reflected back at her, a picture of family normality. As she looked harder she saw there was another image, a rectangle of garden illuminated by the light from her mother's room.

"The flat is being watched," her mother announced.

"Mother, you can't see anything out there."

Elizabeth Quinn favoured her daughter with a slightly pitying smile.

"Of course I can't see, it's dark. But I can see when it is light and besides I can feel when I'm being watched. I was being watched just before you came in."

"That was probably me," Jane said. "I walked up into the trees. I wanted to think for a second and I saw you come into the room. There's something I want to tell you -"

"That doesn't explain it," her mother said. "I know when my own daughter is watching me. But I could feel somebody else."

"There was only me out there, Mother."

"No, there was somebody else. Somebody who had been there for a long time. Longer than you."

Elizabeth Quinn seemed quite determined about it. The features on her face were frozen into certainty.

"But why should anyone be out there in this cold? They would freeze. Besides I should have seen them."

"Not if they were hidden. Besides he is still there. I know."

"Mother," Jane said imploringly. "Why should anyone be watching you?"

"I didn't say he was watching me. He is watching this flat."

"We could turn the light out," Jane continued looking at the reflection of the two of them staring out into space.

"Why ever should we do that?"

"It would be easier to see anyone."

"He is hidden," Elizabeth Quinn said firmly. "Besides if we turn the light off he will know we are on to him."

Jane put out a restraining hand to calm her mother's fancies and had the effect instead of galvanising her into adding the sherry bottle to the tray. She poured two glasses of sherry and handed one to her daughter.

"You really should have told me you were coming," Elizabeth Quinn scolded. "I would have got something for you."

"This is fine. Really. It's my favourite. Dad used to buy a couple of bottles every Christmas."

Elizabeth Quinn looked rather blankly at her daughter as though Jane was making up a story that couldn't be possibly be correct, but she had stopped staring out into the dark.

Jane reached for the brown paper envelope beside her handbag. "There are some papers for you to sign. The last formalities on Dad's will. Richard dropped them off at the office yesterday as he knew you would want to deal with them straightaway," she added encouragingly. Richard's name was one of the magic levers that could sometimes stir her mother into decisive action.

"Ah yes," Elizabeth Quinn said. "I was expecting them." She was reaching into the bureau for her glasses. She found them and propped them efficiently on her nose. Then she sat in her favourite armchair and started to work her way through the papers with what appeared to be genuine interest. After a minute she looked at Jane and said, "Your father would have made more orderly provision if he hadn't died."

There was something mildly reproachful in her mother's tone as though John Quinn had recklessly disregarded his obligations in the area rather than suffered a fatal heart attack.

"I must tell you something Mother," Jane said as her mother checked through the documents. "It's someone I've met. Mark Mandell. He is really rather interesting. I don't know why. He finances films."

"That's good dear," her mother said without apparent interest.

Elizabeth Quinn got to her feet and pulled down the front of the writing bureau. She put the documents in an orderly row and reached into the back of the bureau for what turned out to be a ancient ball point pen. She inscribed a precise signature in thin ink on all of the documents and then neatly piled them on top of each other.

"It was only three I had to sign." It was more of a statement than a question.

"Only three."

"Good. I'm going to make some tea. Would you like some?"

"Yes," Jane said. Normally she would have refused but somehow simply to walk out of her mother's flat now was inappropriate. She collected the neat pile of documents and put them back in the brown paper envelope. She would have preferred, she told herself, rather more of an active reaction from her mother to what she had said about Mark Mandell, even though she knew that, by the time of her next visit, Elizabeth Quinn was almost bound to have no recollection of Mark Mandell at all.

Jane wondered whether she would have got a more positive reaction from her mother if she had talked about Robert Stuart's earrings. Elizabeth Quinn was normally better with objects than people.

Jane heard her mother filling the kettle in the kitchen, cups being put on a tray, and then the hiss of boiling water. There had also been another sound, a slight rustling of paper, which Jane could not explain.

Elizabeth Quinn came back into the sitting room carrying a tray set with the bone china that Richard had bought her for her birthday and for which she had expressed unfettered delight to Jane every time she had made tea. She also had a parcel lodged precariously under her arm that explained the rustling of paper that Jane had heard from the kitchen. Elizabeth Quinn put the tray on the small table with the parcel next to it. Jane saw that the parcel was a little over a foot long and rather irregular in shape. The wrapping paper was bright blue like the sky and tied with string.

Jane looked at the parcel for a long time, trying to control the building sense of dread within her. Her mother looked at the teapot. They might, to the mysterious outside observer, be sharing the silence of families who know everything about each other, but they weren't. Jane looked at her mother and asked herself what it was she really knew about Elizabeth Quinn.

Her mother poured tea into two cups and they drank it in silence, a silence penetrated only by her mother asking her if she wanted milk. Jane refused, as always. Somewhere from an adjoining resident's room came the noise of screeching tyres and gunfire, the nightly life of television violence.

Eventually Jane got to her feet and prepared to leave. She almost forgot the brown paper envelope with the documents her mother had signed and Elizabeth Quinn had to hand it to her with an understanding smile. Jane was standing in the open flat doorway when her mother also picked up the sky blue parcel.

"I thought I should give it to you now -" her mother said.

Jane took the parcel. Under the wrapping paper she felt something yielding with arms, legs and a head.

"Thank you," she said.

Her mother was looking at her as though she was behaving strangely.

"It will be all right for him," Elizabeth Quinn said. "It is mohair, but they are so much nicer I think. After twelve months it is no problem anyway. Look at the label. It specifically says for children of twelve months or more. I checked."

"That's good," Jane said. She took a step backwards through the door.

"It's a nice one. Make sure it gets well looked after."

"Goodbye Mother."

Jane kissed her mother on the forehead and waved from the end of the corridor as the door closed. Outside she had difficulty in aiming the electronic key in the right direction to undo the central locking system in her car. She told herself it was the cold but knew she was lying. Even when she was in the car she managed to drop the brown paper envelope on the ground and had to get out again. Then she almost slipped on the icy surface and had to cling to the top of the car door to stop herself falling over.

As she steadied herself she thought she saw a movement in the screen of trees her mother had been pointing at when she said she was being watched. She looked again but saw nothing. She told herself that she must not get involved in her mother's imaginings. She started the car engine. It coughed a little and blew some toxic gases into the night before settling down to a steady rhythm.

Jane eased her way down the slippery drive back to the main road. At the traffic lights at the top of the hill she had to brake sharply. The sky blue parcel toppled for a moment on the edge of passenger seat and then fell from view.

CHAPTER EIGHT

By the time she got back to the river her pulse had slowed to near normal. She had told herself that she shouldn't be affected any more by her mother's vagaries and inability to live in the same segment of time that everyone else inhabited. Most weeks her lecture to herself worked, but today the sky blue parcel had destroyed her defences. The rapidly freezing roads on the way back had helped a little, as she had had to concentrate hard to prevent the car sliding off the road on the black ice that was forming as the night got ever colder.

She coaxed the Peugeot round the last bend and down to her underground parking space and switched off the engine. There was silence. She waited for a moment in the car, unwilling to move and get back out in the cold. She told herself that she knew what her mother was like, and that nothing real had changed.

There was a figure in the shadows by the service lift, a burly, reassuring male figure in a long navy blue overcoat. It was a figure that Jane thought she recognised, but then she realised that what she had imagined wasn't possible. Whatever was in the Silverlawns tea that was affecting her mother's memory was getting to her too. It was a simple concept she had to hang on to. Time travel wasn't possible, not now, not anytime. Her father was dead, not here to comfort her any more as he had always done, from the stories he had read her in bed every night when she was a child, his voice acting out the characters as she dropped into the comfort of sleep, to the last time he had spoken to her, reassuring her about her mother's ability to cope.

"Jane?"

She knew who it was now.

"Minister."

Kenneth Ormond was walking over to her.

"It's good to see you. Sorry about this cloak and dagger stuff. I was driving past and thought there might be the opportunity to talk. I didn't want to 'phone you from the office, so here I am. Acting on impulse Jane, you always used to advise me against it. You're probably right but I thought we needed to talk."

Jane looked round. Ormond's ministerial Jaguar was in the parking space for visitors. A shadowy figure stood to one side. A match flared throwing a face into sharp outline – Ormond's driver.

"You'd better come up to the flat. How long have you been here?"

"Just arrived."

"How did you know I lived here?"

"The party when you moved in. A couple of years ago. I was hoping to come but there was a late night debate in the House. Illegal immigration out of control and a three line whip to keep MPs under control. I had Charlie work out a route and he reckoned we could get here in less than ten minutes, but duty prevailed in the end – a great mistake. I'm sure the Government wouldn't have fallen if I had been absent an hour. But I allowed myself to get roped in to talk to the usual malcontents before the vote. So I didn't come."

"Was that Charlie?"

"No, it's a new man. Just out of the forces. Nice enough, but only just getting plugged in to the driver network. I've never been so short on intelligence on what is really going on."

Inside Jane's flat the remote controls on the heating system seemed to be behaving themselves and the air was warm to the touch. Ormond took his coat off, accepted a whisky, and subsided on to the sofa.

"So how are you Jane? You look well."

"I've been away. A holiday in Ireland. Simon's father's house. I spent a few days there between Christmas and the New Year. Very relaxing."

"Sounds wonderful," Ormond said. "I should have done something like that myself."

Jane found it difficult to disagree and said nothing. Ormond looked exhausted. His eyes were hooded with fatigue and his movements were heavy and lacking energy. She had seen him tired before, but nothing like this.

Ormond could see her studying him.

"It's been a bad week. I thought Christmas would calm things down but it hasn't. The party is at each other's throats on this schools business the PM announced, and the *Mirror* is inviting people to write in to vote whether I should resign. A worse than usual dose of mid-term blues, but we'll get over it." He paused, seemingly considering whether he believed his own words. "At least the party will, albeit with its usual bad grace, although I'm not so sure about myself. It's this Mandell business. There's one thing that I didn't tell you. I'm a shareholder in Mandell Holdings. A significant one. That shareholding is collateral for loans shoring up a company my wife set up which is going through a rocky patch at the moment. We need cash badly and I need to sell some shares to raise funds. I should have done it months ago but I didn't. My realisable assets are 90% in Mandell Holdings and that whole avenue is blocked until this KM business is sorted out."

"Surely the banks?"

"Aren't going to foreclose on my wife and me?" Ormond rubbed his hand over his forehead. "I wish that were the case, Jane. But I'm afraid I haven't made myself popular in the City. In fact I haven't made myself too popular anywhere. Half the backbenchers in my own party would like to see the back of me. The Mandell connection could be the final piece of ammunition if it doesn't get sorted soon."

"It's not that black is it Kenneth? I mean the PM.."

She hadn't called him by his first name before, or his second. The ubiquitous 'Minister' had always inserted itself in her side of any conversation between them. She thought a flicker of surprise crossed his face that, a moment later, turned into a wry smile.

"Yes," Ormond said slightly more brightly. "There's always the PM. According to the papers he can't afford to lose me."

"And he wouldn't want to."

It was a statement rather than a question but Ormond seemed to be considering the point in detail before replying.

"No," he said, "Tom wouldn't want to. We are both committed to the reform programme; we can't go back to where we were. I am sure he would do anything he could to help."

Ormond's promise that she would receive the closest co-operation across Government seemed to have firm foundations.

"Another whisky?"

Ormond nodded.

"So tell me a bit more about David Mandell."

"What do you want to know?"

"Can you see him running off with £250 million?"

"No."

Ormond was emphatic.

"You seem very sure."

"David may have had his faults but he was basically straight."

"Faults?"

"Faults is probably putting it a little too strongly. I suppose he's always needed to be in control. That's probably why they can't find the £250 million. He's never been able to trust people too far."

"There must be some people he needed to trust. What about this Finance Director he has had for years, Geoffrey Chorley?"

"Chorley? Geoffrey was very good at getting things into order after the event, not before.

"Somebody else then – his son for instance?"

"He's never been close to Mark. There was a row when Clare – David's wife, Mark's mother – died. Clare had breast cancer. Too far advanced to be operable. David had a mistress. He had her before Clare became ill, before anyone knew Clare was ill. David has a weakness for *femme fatales*, always has had, ever since I've known him. I thought Clare had cured him of it, but it was only remission. Clare was lovely, laughing, jovial, fun, but, after a time simply not young enough. They had ten good years together, maybe more, before David started straying. I don't think Clare ever knew he had, and there's some blessing in that, I suppose. But Mark found out about it and blamed his father for Clare's illness and her death. I'm not sure they ever quite made it up. If they didn't it's too late."

Ormond took a thoughtful swallow of the whisky.

"And did you tell Mark Mandell to talk to me? It doesn't sound as though his father would have confided in him."

"I didn't think he would but I thought it was worth a shot. You probably need all the help you can get."

"Why?"

"There's something wrong Jane. That's the other reason I wanted to come round to talk to you. I can't quite put my finger on it, but somehow I'm not getting everything I asked for on this."

"Are you sure? It's hardly a normal situation."

"Perhaps not, but yes, something is wrong. And I don't know what. And if I don't know I'm not sure it's right to involve you."

"It's on my desk whatever, so there's no real debate. Tell me anything you know about the other people close to David Mandell in the company. Hasn't he got a secretary, Eve Jackson?"

"Yes."

"And could she be mixed up in this?"

"Hardly. Eve is tremendously loyal and hardworking, but she is there basically to take orders and sort out his domestic arrangements. She's efficient enough but not wildly bright."

"This personal assistant he has then, Paula Black?"

"Never met her. Geoffrey and Eve were around from the old days, or at least when I had more direct dealings with the company. She may have had some influence on David. Is she blonde? Young?"

"Certainly good looking from what I've heard."

"Sounds like another to add to David's collection then. He has had a string of glamorous PAs over the last few years. It is a habit he got into after Clare died. It's always been platonic as far as I know. He just seems to like to have a glamorous personal assistant around, sort of at his beck and call, available at all hours. He likes showing them off. It's not admirable behaviour, but not unexpected."

"I suppose not."

Ormond glanced at his watch, and heaved himself to his feet. "I'm sorry Jane. I need to go. I have an overseas trip to prepare for. Take good care of yourself, that's the most important thing."

Five minutes later Kenneth Ormond had gone and there were only the lingering exhaust fumes from his car to prove to her that he had ever been there.

She added Paula Black to the priority list of people she needed to speak to. Somebody at David Mandell's beck and call, Jane thought, seemed somebody she should talk to. No man, as the saying goes, is a hero to his servants, and Paula might have some ideas on what David Mandell had been planning to do.

CHAPTER NINE

When Jane had fallen asleep images of David Mandell floating past a brightly lit pleasure boat on a dark river had filled her mind. Mandell was on the surface, the bright lights of the boat eliminating all shadow and detail on his face and making him look years younger. Jane had got tangled in the strings of white fairy lights and when she had freed herself and was able to look again Mandell was floating into the shadows, his face and his white shirt still distinct, but the rest of his body merging with water and sky and then retreating into the complete blackness beyond.

Jane's dream might have been prompted by an ill-considered supper of cheese biscuits and wine that she had resorted to after Kenneth Ormond had left. Whatever the reason, once the dream had passed away she had fallen into a deep sleep that left her surprisingly refreshed, if a little short of time to prepare herself for Robert's arrival. She had meant to give herself an hour on some more material the Bank had sent over about Mandell Holdings but had decided that she didn't have any confidence that a deeper knowledge of the intricacies of the Mandell companies, that others had already crawled over, was the key to unlocking the fate of the missing money. Discussions in the following week with Christopher Bellmore, Geoffrey Chorley, or Paula Black were likely to be far more productive. So she had spent the time until Robert's arrival trying, inconclusively, to find an explanation that fitted the known facts on Mandell.

Robert was smiling, two cups of coffee and a white paper bag in hand.

"The Portuguese place down the road," he said in answer to Jane's questioning glance. "You did say the cakes were exceptionally good. I thought it would set us up for the journey. It's still freezing out there. And we should drink these before they get any colder."

"I didn't think they did take-away coffee there."

"I don't think they do exactly. I said you were an invalid and trebled your age, and they took pity on me."

"Robert, that's dreadful."

"I know but we're on a reasonably tight schedule and if we're to get the benefit of some daylight down there we need to move on before the traffic begins to build up. We won't have time to stop for refreshments."

"Well the coffee is delicious," Jane said sipping it. "It's really very thoughtful of you Robert. And I'll have one of those cakes as well."

They were a few miles from Eastwood on a long straight stretch of road before the mood of domestic bliss that Jane had dropped into suffered a setback.

"I hear Kenneth Ormond is in trouble over this Mandell business," Robert Stuart said.

"There have been some rumours," Jane said. "What have you heard?"

"He needs funds urgently that are tied up in Mandell stock which is essentially worthless until the loan or whatever it was is sorted out. It must be difficult for him."

Robert Stuart pulled the Range Rover out to overtake a lorry.

Jane said nothing. It was certainly not likely that a potential bankrupt, which seemed to be Kenneth Ormond's position, could survive unless some sort of financial rescue package could be put together, and from what Ormond had said, that didn't seem likely.

She wondered for a moment if what Richard had told her about Robert Stuart being a member of MI5 could be right. Kenneth Ormond was the strong man in the Prime Minister's inner circle, and a man who had always ruled himself out as a successor. If he fell the whole balance of the Government would be threatened and the Prime Minister exposed. Sorting such a crisis out would be an important feather in any organisation's cap and a valuable bargaining chip when it came to talking about budgets and spheres of influence. The police and the security services were both trying to get the lead in the fight against large-scale crime. Perhaps Robert was feeding her information. Maybe it was this jockeying for position that was causing Kenneth Ormond's disquiet.

The traffic was thinning as they got deeper into Suffolk and nearer the sea. Eastwood was only a few miles away. Jane hadn't been to the house since November.

"Don't turn here," Jane said quickly as Robert signalled at the crossroads. "I think we should keep on the main road. I never go that way."

Robert Stuart nodded.

"Of course, I'm sorry."

"No really Robert," Jane said as they drove past the signpost. "I'm just being silly. I must drive that way again, sooner or later, but not today."

Eastwood was a ramble of a house with woodland behind. Half a mile away, past the church, the road to the sea ended in an abrupt drop of thirty feet to the wild beach below.

There was a curl of smoke hanging over the main part of the house. Mrs Smart had said she would light a fire and had been as good as her word. As Robert pulled the Range Rover in to the side of the road, Jane thought that the house had every appearance of being lived in. She didn't know if she found the thought reassuring or threatening.

In the drawing room a wood fire was glowing deep red and the sunshine of a winter midday cast a pale glow over a red patterned carpet. The windows of the room had been newly cleaned and the surfaces were dust free and smelt of lemons. Jane knelt in front of the fire and added a couple of logs and was greeted with a sudden spurt of yellow flame.

"Somebody is looking after the place rather well," Robert Stuart said. "I can see why you are fond of it."

Jane looked round. He was standing by the doors leading out to the garden in a green countryman's jacket. He and Eastwood might have been designed for each other.

There was the sound of footsteps upstairs. Mrs Smart had been insistent that the house needed airing and was opening a window. The floorboards squeaked as they always had. Once the squeaks had been a source of concern to Jane, denoting the possibility of displaced joists and collapsing walls.

"I should have invited you down before, Robert."

Robert Stuart lived in a flat in Chelsea that was furnished in clean and exquisite modern taste with nothing either superfluous or redundant. Jane had only been there once. They met in town and went to shows, theatre, exhibitions, and restaurants. Robert fitted in naturally everywhere, as he did here among the fading furniture, some of which was ripe for retirement.

"Are you going to show me round?"

"Of course."

"Is there anything I can do Jane?" Mrs Smart was standing in the doorway. She was much more of a dominant personality than her husband. If she had been totally in charge Jane had no doubt that the contract for the renovation of the Eastwood roof would already have been signed.

"No thank you. I'm very grateful for you coming in at all."

Jane saw that Mrs Smart was giving Robert a full appraisal. There would no doubt be a detailed report circulated to the village before the end of the day. The new Range Rover would go down well. Jane had noticed there was a certain respect for conspicuous resources in the village, and a certain disappointment that she did not possess them.

They took the staircase from the hall to the first floor. The bed that Jane had ordered from Heals was still in the corner of the large room that had windows looking out two ways. The sea was grey and still in the distance. Mrs Smart had made up the bed as Jane had asked with the white cotton sheets that had never been used, but hadn't turned the cover down.

"It's a lovely room," said Robert Stuart. "What's next door?"

"That was Simon's study," Jane said. "We were going to change it into a bathroom but we didn't have the money. So Simon took it over. He liked the view of the forest."

"Do you mind if I look in?"

"No," Jane said sitting on the bed and idly fingering the smooth sheets. "Carry on." She felt suddenly weary and could have lain down and slept.

There was a crash from the next room. When she went in Robert Stuart was standing rather helplessly with the contents of a box file and two containers of index cards intermingled on the floor.

"I'm sorry," he said. "I tripped on something and this happened."

"There's no problem," Jane said. "The room needs putting into order. I've never had the heart to sort out Simon's papers. I need to."

Robert Stuart was picking up objects from the floor. The first two were photographs. Mrs Smart's magic duster had also been employed here as well as the bedroom and the whole place, Jane noticed, was miraculously clean, far cleaner than anything she and Simon had ever achieved.

"Do you want to put these somewhere safe?"

The photographs in Robert Stuart's hands were head and shoulders portraits of two young women. Both the women were classically beautiful and exuded poise. They both had shoulder length hair and were probably both wearing off the shoulder evening dresses except that the angle of the photograph showed no evidence of any such garment at all. The portraits - for that was what Jane supposed them to be - seemed either curiously dated or timeless. If the two women had been going out to some social event the photographs might have been taken recently. The technical quality of the pictures and their general gloss suggested they were not old.

Jane took the photographs from Robert Stuart. She had never seen them before. She turned them over. On the back of each photograph was a cross and a date written in black ink.

"Probably the remains of the blonde and redhead address books," Robert Stuart said lightly.

"Yes," Jane said. "Perhaps they are."

Jane tucked them into the top drawer of Simon's desk. Robert Stuart was looking uncomfortable in the middle of the room. She didn't know how long she had been staring at the photographs. "I think we should go down. I really would like to get your opinion of the state of the outside of the building. Ken Smart tells me it's desperate."

"Lead the way!" Robert Stuart ushered Jane out of the room.

They took a walk round the outside of the house. The brittle stalks of plants crackled underfoot and the light was already dimming a little as the sun faded and the sky darkened. Robert Stuart made critical observations on the state of Eastwood's roofs that would have encouraged the business aspirations of Mr and Mrs Smart.

"I'm cold," Jane said eventually. "We should go inside."

In the drawing room the fire was blazing. Mrs Smart had left tea and biscuits on a tray in front of it. Jane unbuttoned her coat and took it off. The fire had warmed the room.

"Tea?"

"Thanks."

Robert Stuart sat down on the floor beside her. The light of the flames blazed brightly in the fading light of the afternoon. The lamp in the corner of the room that Mrs Smart had turned on threw a yellow pool of light down onto the carpet. Robert Stuart took a meditative sip of his tea and looked round the room.

"This is a wonderful place Jane. I don't think you should give it up whatever happens. It needs some money spending on it of course but this sort of old house always does, particularly if the maintenance has been neglected a bit over the years. If you were to go to America that wouldn't change anything about this house. Look, why not come out with me? Just for a couple of days. We could fly tomorrow. I know it's short notice but I need your views on what I'm getting into.

"That's very sweet of you, Robert, but I'm afraid I just couldn't get away at the moment. There's the Mandell business on top of everything else."

Robert Stuart nodded. "I'm sorry, I'm just being selfish. But is there any chance of Mandell being sorted out quickly and the money found? I could change the dates."

"You must stick to what you've promised Robert. There's a bit of a chance that Mandell can be sorted. I've got my brightest person on it and I have a sense he may be on to something, but the more likely solution is everything will take weeks, if the money is found at all. You need to go the States and report back and we'll talk when you get back."

Robert Stuart nodded reluctantly.

"I suppose you're right."

"Look," Jane said after a moment, "about tonight.."

But Robert's mobile had started ringing, high pitched and insistent. He pulled a mock grimace and moved to the other end of the room. A second call followed the first and Jane retreated into the corridor.

She walked the length of house and up the end staircase to the second floor, past the bedrooms for the children, past the echoes of Simon's and her plans.

In Simon's study she rested her hand on the top drawer of his desk. She was motionless for a moment, undecided. Then she took her hand away. There were a hundred explanations of why the photographs could have been there, none of which needed to be understood today. She had to stick to her plan. She had come to Eastwood to look forward, not back.

In the bedroom she turned down the bedcover and looked at the smooth white sheets, slightly cold to the touch. Mrs Smart had laid the fire as she had asked. The box of extra long matches had been brought up from the sitting room. She had only to stretch out her arm and the room would be alive with enticing yellow flame. She did not move. She had thought she could see the future but whatever mix of her and Robert's limbs she had imagined warmed by the fire now seemed impossible to summon up. Instead she had a mental picture of Mark Mandell she couldn't rid herself of.

She had become Robert's lover in April in a rather gloomy looking, but otherwise hospitable, hotel near Lulworth Cove. They had ended up at the hotel by accident after Robert had had to change a punctured tyre. The hotel had a room free and they were disinclined to carry on back to London. She couldn't quite remember precisely how, or if, they had taken the decision to sleep together. However she could remember the slightly squeaky wooden furniture in the dining room and the enquiring looks of the middle-aged woman at the next table.

There had been a little chill in the night, Robert had ordered a Dover Sole and she thought she had had the same. The wine had been surprisingly pleasant, a bottle of Sancerre decorated with a turret, and Robert had been at his calmest. Part of her had been excited and part of her relaxed. They had been walking earlier, and she remembered the tiredness of her limbs as they had gone up the stairs, perfectly clear in their intentions.

In the drawing room the flames of the fire had died away and only the glowing embers remained. Robert Stuart looked up as she came in, as handsome as ever. There had been a scar on his chest, a little line where the skin was whiter. She had awoken in the early morning with moonlight filtering through a gap in the curtain. She had run her finger in a matching line below the mark and thought, before she fell into the forgetfulness of sleep, that she must ask him how he had come by it.

"I'm sorry, Jane," Robert was saying, "it's this problem at the bank. I thought it was sorted but it seems to have a few legs left. The people in New York aren't entirely happy. I need to get back to London."

She saw he was looking at her waiting for her to say something to him.

"That's a shame, Robert," she said. She wondered if he expected her to start arguing with him, but she suddenly felt without energy, or any sort of plan. She looked out of the window into the dark shadows of night falling over the forest.

CHAPTER TEN

Jane slept late on Sunday morning. When she awoke from a dreamless sleep she saw that it was already ten o'clock and that Robert would already have taken off for New York. He had finally decided to take the morning flight when they had got back to London the previous day. On the return journey from Eastwood he had talked lightly about possible futures that seemed to involve both of them, but not made any further request for Jane to change her plans.

She drank coffee looking out over the freezing river and idly considering the possibility of telephoning someone. It was, for an hour or so, a pleasantly idle existence enhanced by periodic wanderings through the apartment and a sense of expectation that things in the future might be different.

Then she found that there was no food left in the flat, at least nothing that was not protected by tin. A trip in the Peugeot across the river to the supermarket was long overdue.

She drove up the ramp and out of the underground parking and pulled into the road and on down to the traffic lights, which turned red as she approached. She put her foot on the brake pedal and started worrying about Kenneth Ormond. He hadn't just been exhausted when she had seen him on Friday. Somehow, now she could think about it, he had seemed dangerously near to being beaten as well. It wasn't something that she had ever expected to see and she knew she had been right in refusing Robert's requests so that she could ensure that everything possible was done to help.

She wasn't slowing quickly enough and she pushed the brake pedal harder down but her foot met with no resistance and the Peugeot kept on moving towards the red traffic lights and the three lanes of traffic racing towards Vauxhall Bridge. Jane cursed the car and the icy road and pulled the hand brake hard. There was no appreciable effect on her forward momentum and she slid serenely on towards the vehicles in front of her.

Afterwards she could always remember each of the vehicles with which she could have collided - the white van, the oil tanker, the black taxi, the red bus, the Volvo estate, the BMW with the long gash down its side, and the motorbike accelerating in the middle of all of them. They couldn't be aware of her. She might conceivably miss one or two but not all of them, and none of them would see her, not until far too late, and all they, or she, might gain would be a few micro seconds to prepare themselves for the shock of impact.

There had been nothing on the road when she had driven out on to it from the flats, and it was a reasonable supposition that there was still nothing behind her. She also didn't want to crash into anything that was moving.

Jane swerved the Peugeot across to the nearside lane and into the metal railings stopping jaywalkers crossing the road. The car came to a juddering halt against a lamppost.

It was the noise that was more frightening than the smashing glass and the crumpling metal. It was shockingly loud and very, very close. The car came to a thunderous halt. Jane was thrown forward and then back. Something, she didn't know what, hit her on the side of the head and there was sudden physical pain to add to the assault on her other senses.

The noise of impact stopped as suddenly as it had occurred, and was replaced by something much more distant, the traffic streaming past her towards Vauxhall Bridge. She felt very sick and saw that the knuckles of her hand showed white where she was still gripping the steering wheel.

Jane pushed open the car door and got out. A man on a bicycle went past at speed and for a moment braked slightly, but then continued.

The air flowing in through the broken passenger window was cold and unreal. She stepped out of the car and pushed the door shut and walked round to the front of the car. The whole of the nearside wing was buckled and the front bumper had split into two. Where the headlight had been there was now an empty socket. The metal round the socket had been shredded into thin strands and this part of the car looked as though it had been dissected in some crude mechanical autopsy. The front wheel was bent at an unnatural angle.

The lamppost had escaped any serious damage. The only sign of the collision were two green streaks of paint on the concrete base and half the number plate of Jane's car and some metal fragments on the ground. The railings were buckled at the top at one point but otherwise unscathed.

A police car came driving past but did not stop. Jane started to walk back to her flat. Her whole journey had been less than half a mile. She numbered off the vehicles that had been streaming across the gap in front of her. It was the shock she told herself. It would wear off. No one else had been involved and she had only been shaken. She just needed to hold herself together and make arrangements for the car to be picked up and fixed. She wondered whether her insurance firm would think the car worth repairing.

She was shivering when she got back to the flat and her teeth had started to chatter. When she was in the warm, she told herself, she would be better. She would get the car sorted out and ring her brother. Richard was always reliable in a crisis.

There was a cream envelope wedged between the top of her door and the doorframe. She was surprised. The mail was always left downstairs for each resident to pick up. She couldn't quite see how the envelope had been inserted either. There was no obvious gap. She opened the door, let the envelope fall into her hand, and walked into the kitchen area.

She poured herself a glass of brandy to steady her nerves. The garage where she had the car serviced also did repairs. It was the obvious place to start.

The envelope puzzled her. It was blank. Perhaps it was a message intended for somebody else that had been left in her door by mistake. It was easy to mistake one floor for another. It might be a message between two residents. That would explain how whoever it was who had left the envelope had got access to the building.

When she opened the envelope she saw that there were only three lines to the message that had been neatly printed in an ornate font on a word processor. Jane found herself reading -

Drop the Mandell business now.
Otherwise you could get hurt.

A Friend

CHAPTER ELEVEN

The accountants arrived at Mandell Holdings (UK) at eight-thirty in the morning on the day after Jane's accident. They politely said that they were in charge and asked that nothing be removed from the offices. Geoffrey Chorley, who had taken control following David Mandell's death, protested that many of the papers were confidential and that he couldn't agree to their being released. The leader of the team, a small lean man with intense eyes, called Frank Lee, asked Geoffrey to sit down and said that he didn't quite think Mr Chorley understood the situation. Mandell Holdings and all the companies in the group were now in administration, and under Mr Lee's control, in accordance with the provisions of the Insolvency Act 1986. KM Investment Bank (London) and the other banks that had loans outstanding to David Mandell had asked Mr Lee and his firm to investigate the situation.

Geoffrey Chorley said that David Mandell had always paid his bankers and Frank Lee smiled and said that he agreed that David Mandell always had, but David Mandell was dead, and that, unless Geoffrey Chorley could tell him otherwise, a great deal of money could not be accounted for. It was his job to find out what had happened to it and he and his team would be grateful for full co-operation. They would want to interview everyone in the office who had any relevant information.

Jane was told of the development at nine o'clock. A man with an American accent, called Scudder, telephoned her on Frank Lee's behalf. Mr Lee, said Mr Scudder, would be willing to extend full co-operation to her under the circumstances. He was aware of her interest in the matter.

Jane put the telephone down. She would have expected co-operation from the administrators but this was surprisingly helpful. Kenneth Ormond's contacts seemed to have been put to good effect. Scudder had been bubbling with energy and Jane could almost see him - an academic financial analyst eager to pursue the intellectual challenge presented by the disappearing finances of the Mandell companies. He would get on well with Ian. Quite who had briefed Lee and Scudder about her and the Government interest was another matter. She had thought for a moment of asking. Theoretically there was nothing uncomfortable in her position. Public servants did not take sides and were not partial.

But Jane did not feel impartial about her involvement in the least. The car crash and the message from the "friend" had temporarily put paid to her normal equilibrium.

She dialled Mark Mandell's number and counted the rings. She had hoped that he would ring her but she had heard nothing. After twenty rings she put the telephone down.

She looked at her watch. The garage had said that they should be able to give her a quote for repairs by eleven. It was lucky, she supposed, that they had been willing to turn out on a Sunday and that the car was now safely stored away out of public gaze. Richard had been sympathetic and had come round for an hour. The message from her "friend" had been folded on the coffee table. She had meant to mention it but she hadn't. If Robert Stuart hadn't gone or if Mark had telephoned it would have been easier to talk to them. But what could Richard have done? She had started talking instead about Elizabeth Quinn and her trip out to Silverlawns. She had talked about her mother seeing things, or imagining she did, and she had thought of talking about the sky blue parcel her mother had given her, but before she could do that the accident had come back to her and the sight of herself spiralling forward towards oblivion. Richard had come across the room and hugged her, the way he had just after their father died. She had just said she was tired and had mumbled something about the shock of the crash.

She got a mirror out of her handbag and looked at her face. The cut high on her forehead and the slight bruising were the only signs of the accident. They would be hidden by her hair. The headache following the collision was slowly ebbing away.

There was a knock at the door and Suzanne came into the room with coffee and chocolate biscuits.

"You should have something to eat. You'll feel better for it."

Jane felt like disagreeing. Ever since the crash the thought of food had produced feelings of nausea and she had only managed to eat some toast. Suzanne put the coffee and biscuits in front of her.

"Brian said he would like a meeting. I said you were free later in the week. Is that alright?"

Jane nodded.

There was a tantalising aroma in the coffee that persuaded her that if she were not sick she might enjoy it. She took a sip of the coffee and reached out for a biscuit and bit into it. She felt the nausea recede and a faint sense of well being begin to creep back into her. That morning had been icy and she had been cold even before she had stepped outside the apartment block. She missed her car as well.

"Thanks Sue, this is lovely."

Suzanne was leaving the room when Jane added, "But I do want to see Ian. I have got an urgent job for him. Do you know if he is in yet?"

Suzanne nodded. "He was in early this morning. About eight."

"What? Couldn't he sleep?"

"You will have to ask him," Suzanne smiled.

"If you can find him I will," Jane said. "If he is around could you ask him to come along here now. There is an immediate job I want him to do. I need him to go down to Mandell Holdings."

"Any particular reason?"

"The Mandell Group has been put into administration," Jane said. "And if they are not pretty careful the whole group will go into liquidation."

Suzanne raised an enquiring eyebrow.

"In administration they generally try to keep the company or companies trading as they are normally worth more that way. The companies concerned may even be able to trade their way out of any financial difficulties they are in. In liquidation the companies are simply closed down, or sold off for the best price that can be got, and the proceeds paid to the creditors. My guess with the Mandell Group is that keeping the companies running isn't going to be particularly easy without David Mandell, and their whole future hinges on whether they can find this £250 million or not."

Suzanne nodded and disappeared.

Jane found Suzanne curiously calming. She was in the brightest of spirits that morning and had had her hair cut over the weekend, into a shorter, more sophisticated, style. She also had the happy knack of finding people at very short notice. Ian Hart appeared in Jane's office two minutes later and was despatched to find out what he could from the accountants.

By the time Ian Hart returned in mid afternoon the dull throbbing in her head had disappeared. Ian was looking enthusiastic.

"Sit down," Jane said, "and tell me how it was done."

"That might not be easy. But I think we are making progress."

"O.K." Jane said. "What have you found out?" She could tell from Ian's eager expression that there was more than one area of development to report on.

"In addition to the £250 million loan from KM that has disappeared there is also £5 million missing from a private account that David Mandell had."

"Interesting."

"Isn't it? Particularly as the £5million doesn't seem to have got mixed up in the flurry of transfers on Christmas Eve involving the KM funds."

"Are they making any progress on tracing that money?"

Ian shook his head.

"It's not easy. Money was paid out of an account before other monies were paid in. The account became overdrawn. The same process was repeated with a number of accounts which all had transactions with each other. The overall effect is that it is almost impossible to say which accounts were overdrawn and which were not at any given moment. It makes it extremely difficult to know what happened."

"Is there any explanation of what has been going on with these movements?"

"The actions were taken to make it difficult or impossible to trace the money."

"And you think David Mandell was behind all this?"

"He authorised all the transactions."

"Motive?"

"I don't know. I don't think it was connected with any share holding he was building up. You said he liked puzzles and was secretive. Perhaps it's as simple as that."

"Doesn't seem a sufficient reason."

"I can't think of anything better at the moment."

"What about this Finance Director, Geoffrey Chorley? What did he have to say about it?"

"He didn't seem to know any details at all."

"Could he have been involved in anything shady?"

"Hardly. His finances are sound; he is on the brink of retirement. It's not him."

"So what did he think was going on?"

"He wasn't offering any explanations except that he didn't think David Mandell could have done anything wrong. It was apparently not in his nature."

"So what is his version of events on Christmas Eve?"

"He doesn't have one. He was visiting his very elderly mother in Devon. He always goes for Christmas."

"Mmmh," Jane said. "Not very helpful. But then nothing else in this has been, so I suppose that is not unexpected. Who else was around today that might throw some light on this?"

"There is a woman called Eve Jackson who was David Mandell's secretary. She must be nearly sixty. Apparently she has been with him for thirty years. Hair done up in a bun. Rather proper manner but probably quite tough. She seemed to respect Geoffrey Chorley. She was very frosty with the accountants. She also doesn't believe that Mandell was capable of doing anything wrong despite the evidence."

"Looks like that is going to be the HQ party line. Was there anything else useful?"

"I looked at the register of directors' interests and the register of substantial interests in shares. Prepare yourself for a shock."

"Why?"

"Kenneth Ormond owns 10% of Mandell."

"The Home Secretary?" Jane found the right note of surprise in her voice. She wondered where Robert Stuart had got hold of the information.

"It presumably explains why this man Lee was being so helpful to us," Ian suggested.

"More than likely. Are there any other major interests?"

"David Mandell was still the majority shareholder. His son, Mark, was left some stock by his mother but sold it some years ago."

"So was Mark Mandell in the office on Christmas Eve?"

"Nobody I spoke to was quite sure. Neither Geoffrey Chorley nor Eve Jackson was there that day. The receptionist downstairs was there for part of the time but the only people she remembers seeing were Paula Black, Mandell's personal assistant; oh, and according to Paula some businessman called in early to see Mandell before the receptionist arrived. He didn't stay long."

"And does Paula Black really qualify as one of your company danger signs?"

"She is certainly a stunner," Ian Hart said enthusiastically. "I only managed to talk to her for a couple of minutes. I was trying to get some information out of her for our trip to KM. When I finished the conversation she got into a row with one of the accountants and left. Apparently she comes from the East End. At least that is what Eve Jackson told me but she may not be entirely reliable. I rather gathered Eve feels she has lost out in the influence stakes with David Mandell. Paula Black's roughly your height - about five foot seven. Curvy sort of figure, blonde hair."

"Could David Mandell have lost his senses over her?"

"From what Eve Jackson was saying Paula had cast something of a spell over him. They used to stay in the office for late night meetings"

"So what do you think?"

"It's pretty clear that none of them know where the money is."

"I thought you said we were making progress."

"We are. We've got the information on the £5 million transaction involving David Mandell's personal account that I mentioned. It happened later than all the others. It was a straight transfer to a company called Dellmark in Liechtenstein."

"Dellmark?"

"That's what Lee said."

"Didn't anybody question it at the time?"

"Everybody had gone home apparently. Then, of course, David Mandell died and they were too busy trying to find the £250 million."

"If it is based in Liechtenstein I suppose we are not going to be able to find the ultimate beneficiaries. I imagine Dr somebody or other will turn up in Vaduz to tell everyone that he can say nothing or that even, in accordance with Liechtenstein law, he does not know who the beneficiaries are."

"That's probably right," Ian Hart said. "Liechtenstein pretty much guarantees complete anonymity. I'll see if the Bank has any way in. Perry may be able to help, but I doubt it."

"In the unlikely event they can find something let me know first. It might need careful handling."

"If there is the slightest hint of anything substantial I'll beat a path to your door."

"Good. Are you set for this visit to KM tomorrow?"

"I may need to do some more work on that."

On the way out Jane noticed Ian smile at Suzanne.

CHAPTER TWELVE

Jane and Ian were shown into a room at KM with a round meeting table and a modern landscape on the wall. Coffee, orange juice, mineral water, napkins, cups and glasses had been left on a side table. Jane looked out of the window onto a view of flat roofs decorated with ventilation shafts and fire escapes; the clutter of service functions plugged randomly into the backs of buildings.

"Do we know why KM were being difficult about the meeting?" Ian Hart adopted a conspiratorial whisper.

"Not entirely. Not convenient, too early, nothing to say, that sort of thing. Perhaps they just wanted the administrators in."

"What about the guy Mandell did the deal with?"

"Karl di Rocca?"

"That's him. Is he around?"

"In Singapore, according to his secretary, and she didn't volunteer that he had any plans to return to the UK. Bankers seem to be rather averse to discussing deals that have gone sour. Di Rocca was apparently not involved in the mechanics of the transfer in any case. That was overseen by Bellmore."

Next to the refreshments a pile of magazines was spread out in a fan. Jane flicked open the pages of 'KM PEOPLE'. Various clean-cut executives in white shirts were shown concluding deals worldwide. Most of them appeared to be about Ian Hart's age and verging towards the androgynous in looks. Jane dropped two copies into her briefcase.

A slightly plump man in his late thirties in a well-cut suit walked into the room. Behind him was a precise looking woman in fastidiously co-ordinated clothes who Jane instinctively knew was a lawyer. A look of unshakeable seriousness was etched on her face.

"Christopher Bellmore," the man said extending his hand. He pointed to the woman beside him. "Catherine Powers of our in-house legal team."

"Jane Quinn," Jane said. "And Ian Hart."

"I understand," Bellmore said when they were seated, "that you are interested in the loan to David Mandell."

Jane nodded.

"So," Bellmore said clasping his hands together, "what can I tell you?"

"Ian, why don't you lead off?" Jane said. Bellmore was clearly nervous about something and could repay careful observation. It might simply be the reflection of the tension that anyone involved in losing their employer £250 million might feel, but she wasn't sure. She needed time to work it out.

"We understand that you were directly involved in the transfer of funds from KM to Mr Mandell."

Bellmore nodded. Catherine Powers started writing notes in an A4 notebook.

"Did you know David Mandell well?

"I'd met him on a number of occasions, mostly business, one or two bank social occasions, never privately."

"Would you say you were on good terms?"

"David Mandell was a respected client of the bank. Our relationship was a cordial one but not particularly close. David Mandell did most of his deal making with the bank's senior partners. I was involved with the logistics but the basic deals were agreed at board level."

"But you authorised the transfer of KM funds to David Mandell?"

"Technically yes, but the deal had been already been agreed. One of our senior partners had finalised it earlier in the week. Our word is essentially our bond but we were waiting on David Mandell to confirm the details were acceptable. I had a call from his office first thing saying there were one or two matters he wanted to renegotiate but I said I couldn't help. David Mandell finally telephoned around noon to say the terms were acceptable or, perhaps more accurately, that he accepted the terms."

"He wasn't entirely happy with the terms then?" Jane found herself asking.

"He was never very happy with our terms and may have been feeling a little bruised. But we thought he needed the money and had a deal going."

"Was there any suggestion at the time that the Mandell Group finances were not in order?"

"There were rumours that Mandell was short of cash but nothing serious. One of our New York partners, Fred Santini, was a little concerned after the deal was made, but there was nothing we could have done then anyway. There was a celebratory drink in mid afternoon where he expressed a few doubts about Mandell's set-up."

"But you weren't worried?"

"Not at the time. I thought it was a good deal for the bank and David Mandell had a reputation for always paying up. Besides, we thought the Mandell group businesses were sound."

"But he was borrowing a large sum relative to the size of his businesses?"

"Not excessively so."

"Was that the last contact with David Mandell on Christmas Eve?"

"Not entirely. His office confirmed that the money had been received safely."

"Who actually confirmed that?"

"I'm not quite sure. A woman. I'm not sure who she was, although I must have spoken to her before. Her call was merely a confirmation so I didn't pay too much attention to it."

"And that was the last contact?"

"Yes."

Christopher Bellmore stopped for a moment's reflection and then nodded his head. The lawyer stopped writing.

"Do you have any view of what happened?"

The lawyer twitched.

"Mr Bellmore has just told you what happened. I understood you were interested in the regulatory lessons of this. I can't see how any conjecture on Mr Bellmore's part can help you."

"Trust is one of the areas that we are looking at," said Jane. "I was trying to establish the background to the transfer taking place. I simply wondered if Mr Bellmore could help me with any view on whether the money could have been misappropriated by a third party in some way."

"I'm happy to answer that," Bellmore said decisively. "I am afraid on the basis of what I know there can only be one explanation. The bank's funds were misappropriated by David Mandell. Nobody else could have done it. There was nobody else who could have been involved. In my view only one person could have stolen the bank's funds."

"It was rumoured, wasn't it, that David Mandell was planning a takeover bid?"

"There were rumours certainly."

"And you think they were just a smokescreen for David Mandell's real intentions."

"I don't think there can be any other explanation now. A couple of weeks ago David Mandell had a reputation for integrity. I think that reputation was mistaken. But a number of businessmen with high reputations have subsequently been convicted of this sort of fraud."

Jane looked out of the window. Bellmore's last point was unarguable. He looked altogether more confident than he had done at the start of the meeting. Outside the sky was as grey and static as it had been the previous day.

"Do you think he overreached himself?"

"I don't know."

"So when was the basic deal agreed?"

"David Mandell met Karl a couple of days before Christmas Eve. They had half an hour together."

"And that was it?"

"Apart from Mandell's slight quibbles over the terms."

"Did anyone come with Mandell?"

"No."

Not entirely unexpected, Jane thought, nor helpful.

"I'm not sure I can help you any further." Bellmore said.

"We might like to look at your records of the transactions."

Bellmore nodded. The KM lawyer remained motionless.

"Anything else?"

"Not at present. This has been very useful. I am grateful that you could find the time to see us."

Bellmore nodded and got to his feet. The lawyer wrote a couple more words and closed her notebook.

"I'll get your coats," Bellmore said and walked out of the room. The lawyer picked up her notebook, nodded, and left.

"I see you noticed he was lying," Ian Hart said.

"What?" Jane said.

"Oh, c'mon Jane, it was obvious."

"I suppose so," Jane said.

"Do you have any explanation?"

Jane shrugged her shoulders.

Bellmore was back in the doorway with Ian's coat.

"We have other lady visitors," he said to Jane. "I am afraid I don't know which your coat is. If you could show me. It is just outside."

Bellmore led Jane out of the room while Ian Hart was putting his coat on. On the dark panelled wooden walls Jane saw a dark etching on a white background that seemed to be a symbolic representation of some of the murkier and despairing events of the century. She saw that there were a row of them stretching down the passageway, testifying to the bank's conscience and support for the arts.

Bellmore had pulled back one of the wooden panels on the facing wall to reveal a hidden cupboard in which a single coat - Jane's - was hanging.

"The other visitors must have gone," he said. "This is yours I hope?"

Jane nodded.

"It does give me the opportunity," Bellmore said softly, "just to tell you something." He looked around to see if there was anyone in sight but the corridor was deserted.

"It is just this. Something quite nasty is going on in the Mandell business. I would advise you not to get too involved. I am certainly going to get out of it as soon as I can."

"I - ," Jane said, but Ian Hart had emerged from the meeting room.

Bellmore was helping her on with her coat adopting a slightly reserved smile so that Jane almost wondered whether she had imagined the events of the last few seconds.

"The lifts are just here," Bellmore said.

Jane pulled on her gloves. The lift doors opened projecting whiter light into the slightly dim passageway.

"We really could do with something more cheerful up here," Bellmore said pointing to an etching close to the lift, which was now revealed in detail. A dark hammer and a slender knife were competing to destroy an amorphous living object below them and had already cut and flattened half of it.

"It is very good I suppose," Bellmore said. "But I always think there are some things not worth revealing. Straight down, the ground floor is clearly marked."

In the few seconds that the lift spent travelling down to the ground Jane almost convinced herself that she must have imagined Bellmore's words, or misunderstood them in some way. She had for a moment thought he had been alluding to the other warning she had received. But that could hardly be possible. Only she knew about it and she hadn't told anybody. There was, of course somebody else who knew - whoever had left the message in the first place.

Outside in the street she announced to Ian Hart that she must make a phone call.

For a moment she thought that Richard was not in. He had said he was taking a few days off before starting his next assignment but there was no particular reason to suppose he would stay in London.

"Mmmh," a voice said at the other end of the line.

"Richard?"

"Yes." the voice said as though it might have been a little unsure.

"It's Jane."

Jane's announcement was greeted in silence.

"Your sister."

"Ah."

"Look Richard -"

"Jane," the voice was returning to full volume, "is this important? What time is it?"

"Ten thirty. You should be up."

"I didn't get to bed till six."

"I'm sorry," Jane said, "but I need a favour."

"What?" Richard sounded bored.

"I want you to follow someone."

"What?"

"I want you to follow someone."

"That's what I thought you said. Who?"

The boredom, at least, had vanished.

"A banker. I want to find out something about his personal life."

"I knew you were going off Robert Stuart. Who is he?"

"A man called Christopher Bellmore. He works for KM in the City."

"Good looking? Young? Old?"

"Late-thirties, nothing special in looks."

"Never mind, they all earn a lot of money in banking."

"Look," Jane added, "I've just remembered that you said that you and Melinda -"

"Miranda -"

"Were going away together."

"We were, but as of six this morning we're not. So I'm very happy to work on your love life instead."

"It's not my love life."

"I know, really, I do. You're doing it for a friend. Sally Fry probably. It's about time that she got rid of that accountant husband of hers. Anyway that's your business. I don't want to know. But rest assured that your happiness is my chief concern. But I've still got my money on Mr Reliable, Robert Stuart."

"Richard!"

"I know, I know. I will say no more. I'll get you a report as soon as I have tracked Bellmore down to his lair and mistress. How do I know him?"

"I've got a photograph," Jane said. "A company magazine. Until recently at least Bellmore seemed to be doing well. His picture is a quarter of the page in the magazine. Sort of faintly cherub like."

"Are you sure you don't fancy him? I would have thought you

might like to wake up next to a cherub. I always think Heaven is near us when we sleep. Unfortunately Miranda left before I could find out. I suppose you want me to pick up the photo from your office."

"That would be ideal. I'll be back there in fifteen minutes."

"What I do for your love life," Richard said resignedly. "I'll be seeing you.

Jane saw that Ian Hart was coughing. She could smell the petrol fumes heavy in the street. She waved her arm and a taxi drew in beside them. She had no intention of venturing underground.

In the back of the taxi Ian Hart's cough subsided and he started looking absently out of the window.

"What is it?" Jane said.

"Bellmore knows more than he is saying. I just wonder how much more."

"Maybe they missed some checks at the KM end. I can't imagine that being involved in losing the bank £250 million is going to be good for the career of anyone concerned."

"I think it is more than that. He makes me uneasy."

Jane trusted Ian Hart's intuitions. She wondered what he would make of the additional information about the warning Christopher Bellmore had uttered. She might have told him if she felt she could have found some words to accurately describe the moment. But it had all happened so quickly that she could scarcely trust her memory. Richard would produce something.

There was something that didn't make sense in the whole Mandell affair and she was rather afraid that it was somehow centred on her. There was a whole series of things – the note in the door, Kenneth Ormond's message, Mark Mandell, Christopher Bellmore's warning, the car crash. She felt she was being sucked in but she couldn't see any reason for it. Why were Bellmore and whoever had stuck the note on her door so eager that she should stop her involvement in Mandell? What were they afraid that she might find out and why did they know so terribly much about her?

CHAPTER THIRTEEN

"I could do with a drink," Richard Quinn said that evening. "I've been running on brotherly love all day and it's not enough. I need a fee as well. I'm frozen."

Jane poured a large measure of brandy into a glass. "I only said follow him. I only wanted to know something about him, not his whole life. It's nearly ten o'clock. What on earth have you been doing?"

"It's a long story," Richard said. "Besides there was a reason why I couldn't get back. I nearly froze to death then comforted myself that your love life has always been my chief concern. I couldn't let you down. Anyway it got quite interesting, fascinating really." Richard Quinn sipped the brandy appreciatively.

"Before you really annoy me," Jane said, "why don't you just start at the beginning and tell me what happened? Chronological order will do. I'll contain my curiosity about the reason you couldn't get back."

"Before I do," Richard said. "Just tell me one thing."

"Just one."

"You went down to Eastwood with Robert Stuart on Saturday. How did it go?"

"I told you I was going to. It was very pleasant."

"So when are you seeing him again?"

"When he gets back from New York."

Jane had the satisfaction of seeing her brother's irritatingly calm expression severely disrupted.

"New York? What is he doing there?"

"Investigating a job."

Richard made approving noises.

"I thought you said he was dull. New York doesn't sound dull."

"I have never said anything of the kind. Now I've answered your question, will you please tell me what happened with Christopher Bellmore?"

"I just wanted to know where your affections stood." Richard continued in his reasonable voice. "Frankly I think Robert Stuart would be infinitely better for you than this Bellmore character."

"Why?" Jane said. There was no point in trying to argue Richard out of his assumption that the whole matter revolved around her love life.

"The first thing is his name. Did you know his second name was Orson? Christopher Orson Bellmore. I mean Orson Welles is a great film director, I admit, but *Citizen Kane* was a long time ago, and that last film of his *F is for Fake*, simply didn't work."

"Never mind about his name, what happened?"

"You had better sit down," Richard said in a kindly tone. "You may find the next part of what I have to say a little painful. No, please, sit down and hear me out."

Jane sat down.

"Bellmore went out to lunch. I was lucky to catch him. I'd just arrived outside the building. So I followed him to a wine bar. It was a bit of a distance from the office and a pretty discreet sort of place. You'll see the importance of that in a moment. He was at a table hidden away in an alcove. He got a bottle of wine and drank half a glass. He looked round from time to time but I was hidden in the next alcove. A young woman appeared. She was rather attractive, a good figure and about your height. Blonde hair."

"A stunner." Jane said decisively. Richard was exhibiting the same after shocks that Ian Hart had shown after describing David Mandell's personal assistant, Paula Black.

"As a matter of fact she was."

Richard Quinn was looking at her curiously.

"Do you know her?"

"Not for certain, but I have an idea. Your description matches another one I heard. It's probably coincidence though."

Richard looked unconvinced. "Are you sure you're not stuck on this man? You seem to know a lot about his likely mating habits."

"They might be of interest. Tell me more."

"She turned up. They talked for a bit. He drank most of the bottle. She hardly drank anything. He seemed upset about something. Nothing too dramatic. He was just a lot more animated than she was. They disagreed about something, probably something that she said. He was reasonably calm when she came in. Perhaps they are splitting up. When she left she didn't seem too heartbroken. He seemed moodier. She brushed past me on the way out and smiled. She has quite an effect."

"I can see that. Then what happened."

"You said follow him so I repressed my natural instincts. He went back to the office. He didn't come out till about six. Went home by taxi. I wasn't expecting it and I nearly had a problem following him. Luckily the bike was fairly nearby and there was a snarl up in Blackfriars. He lives in a big house in Wimbledon with a drive and a large garden. The whole place is fairly secluded. There was a new BMW in the front and a Volvo Estate. There was a woman in the house and a couple of children. I presume it was his wife and the children were his. Whatever you think about Robert he is single. No complications. Although I suppose you might say his judgement was weak. With you in this sort of mood he shouldn't be leaving the country."

"Richard!"

"All right. I know you are not personally involved and there is some other good reason why you send your closest and only sibling off into the freezing night. I suppose some day you will tell me."

Richard struck a pose of unflinching nobility.

"Some day I will," Jane said, "but not now. I can't. Honestly."

"I suppose I have to believe you," Richard said reluctantly.

"So what took you so long?"

"The reason I couldn't get back in reasonable time," Richard said, "was nothing to do with Christopher Bellmore, or his family. It was due to someone else. I was hidden in a fringe of trees to the side of the garden. It gave me a good view of the house, but I wasn't planning to stay. It was too cold for that and I had accomplished what I thought you wanted. I had established the fact that beyond reasonable doubt Bellmore was a married man and that he might also be fooling around with another woman. I was just about to go when I realised I was not alone. Somebody else was also watching the house. I think he must have arrived after I did. I heard a movement in the bushes near me. It was only a slight noise which wouldn't have been detectable from the house, a faint crackle in the undergrowth no more than twenty feet from me. He stayed there about an hour while I didn't move. I thought he would never go and I simply couldn't work out what he was doing. They had pulled the blinds down in the kitchen about five minutes after he arrived and there was nothing to see. It didn't make any sense at all."

"What was he like?"

"I only really saw him from the back when he left. Tallish, about six foot. Well wrapped up against the cold but quite slim and athletic looking. I might have tried following him but my feet were quite numb, so I just waited a couple of more minutes and then went to the bike. There was no sign of him. I stopped off at a pub to fend off hypothermia and then I came back here. If you want the address I can give it to you if you like."

"Three Church Lane isn't it?"

Richard looked nonplussed.

"How did you know that?"

"Bellmore is in the telephone book."

"I hardly need to have bothered then."

"No, no" Jane said. "It has been very valuable. Particularly knowing the people he met."

"But you seemed to know this young woman anyway?"

"Perhaps, perhaps not. Look Richard, I really can't tell you anything more at the moment."

"The Thirty Year Rule?"

"Not exactly, but something like that."

"You haven't joined MI5 have you? Aren't half of their operatives meant to be women these days? I could understand that I suppose. You might even be able to talk about your work to Robert Stuart."

"It's a nice thought," Jane said. "But I haven't."

"That's quite a relief. I thought I might have just been subsidising the Government by doing work that should be carried out by their own operatives. I mean I know they are very keen that the voluntary sector should pick a lot of responsibilities up."

"Richard, you're quite impossible."

Jane found herself by the window gazing out on the black river making its way down to the sea. There must have been an edge in her voice, but not the one she had meant to insert. In the reflection of the glass she saw that Richard was looking at her.

"I was thinking of going to Paris."

Jane turned round.

"Why?"

"That's where Miranda has gone."

"Paris is a good place for a holiday, even if you don't make it up with Miranda."

Miranda was leggy, moody, and as far as Jane could see there was no possibility of a long-term relationship.

"But I could just as easily stay. There is something going on isn't there? Not just your love life?"

"No, it isn't just my love life."

"So what is it?"

"I'm probably just working too hard."

"C'mon Jane, you don't expect me to believe that do you? If you were working too hard you would never admit it to anybody but yourself. What's the real reason?"

"There's a bit of an entanglement. Kenneth Ormond is a big financial loser in the case I am working on at the moment."

"*The* Kenneth Ormond? The one you used to work for."

"Yes."

"You were fond of him weren't you?"

"That's probably the problem. I think I may just be getting too involved. I'm going to clear it with my boss."

"Make sure you do. Not that I'm entirely in favour of all this hierarchical stuff but that's where you are I suppose. And if there are any problems give me a ring. I'll let you know where I'm staying. I'll be back at the weekend anyway."

"No problem." Jane said. There was something faintly ridiculous about Richard being employed to spy on people in his holidays.

"In fact I could take the train." The normal note of mischief had returned to Richard's voice.

"Before you start, the Channel Tunnel is not a subject that is ever mentioned here."

"Whoops," Richard said unconvincingly. "I forgot. Plane it is then - at least as far as you are concerned."

"There is a very relaxing service from London City Airport. I recommend it."

"I might give it a try."

When Richard had gone, Jane spent ten minutes wandering round the apartment. It was not entirely a successful exercise in convincing herself that everything was really familiar and normal. The sky blue parcel was still at the back of the wardrobe. The earrings were still in the velvet case at the bottom of the bread bin. There was, however, some comfort to be found in both the hidden objects, slightly strange though both of them were. She knew, at least, that they were not connected in any way with Mandell. Part of the stress she was feeling was because of dealing with Robert Stuart. Her mother's present of the sky blue parcel wasn't helping either.

She sat down and poured herself a brandy from the bottle that had been placed next to Richard. There was another problem as well if she was being absolutely truthful.

Dellmark - the Liechtenstein company that had been favoured with a £5 million transfer of funds from David Mandell's personal account on Christmas Eve. She had thought about what Mark Mandell had said about his father's devotion to puzzles and his own indifference to them. Then there had also been what Mark Mandell had said about similarities between his father and himself. In that moment Dellmark had become clear to her. Nobody needed to go to Vaduz or anywhere else to find out who the beneficiary of the £5 million was. One just had to apply Mark Mandell's disregard for puzzles with a desire to mimic his father. Dellmark. Easily convertible into Mark (Man)Dell - (Man)Dell Mark - Dellmark. It was the sort of foolishly thin, almost provocative, disguise that Mark would use.

The note in the apartment door, her car crash, Bellmore's warning, had all happened after her meeting with Mark Mandell at the Pompadour. Mandell knew more about her involvement than anyone else. After the meeting with him a lot of Mandell Holdings events had become centred on herself.

She shook her head. She could telephone Richard and at least arrange that she would be able to contact him immediately if something did turn up. Paris was, in travelling time, no further away than the North of England. If she left it for him to contact her it was likely, despite his promise, that he would forget to do so. She needed to know his new mobile telephone number. He would be home in the next ten minutes. She would telephone him then, arrange something definite, and then spend an hour relaxing and getting her brain properly into order. She sat down.

The telephone rang.

CHAPTER FOURTEEN

Jane picked up the receiver. There was a faint crackle on the other end of the line that sounded as though the call might come from a long way away, and then silence. Robert Stuart had said he would telephone from New York if he could.

"Hello."

"Jane?" Mark Mandell said. "I'm sorry to call you at home but I need your help."

She had been expecting him to telephone but the call still came as a shock. The evening they had spent in the Pompadour now seemed to belong to a different time. Her life was assuming an unreal texture. Jane was missing her normal evening feeling of tired oblivion when she could sit utterly exhausted on the sofa and forget about the pressures of the office and be too tired to think about anything else, a limbo land to inhabit with a glass of chilled wine.

"Jane? Are you there?"

"Yes."

"Can we meet?"

"Now?"

"Yes."

"Where are you?"

He was ten minutes away.

"You'd better come here."

When she put the telephone down she wondered quite why she had suggested that Mandell could invade her home territory. The flat was where she was used to hiding. It was her private place. It had been sparse and white when she bought it and she had welcomed the anonymity and hadn't changed anything. But now Robert Stuart had chosen it as the setting to hand over diamond earrings and Mark Mandell was on his way over.

She stopped in the middle of the little hallway and put out a hand to steady herself against the wall. She saw the line of vehicles across her path, any one of which she could collide with. For a moment she felt attracted to the Volvo, then to the red bus. Mark Mandell was probably walking past the place at that moment. She could feel her foot press down on the brakes. There had been nothing there, nothing at all. She hadn't wanted to remember that. But it had been true.

Eventually she went back into the living room and sat down on the sofa. Her heart was thumping against her rib cage. She was cold, but there were beads of sweat on her forehead. Normally she felt nausea when faced with a crisis. This was something different. Her whole system was in a panic overdrive. The outer world faded into a white, buzzing, haze.

The buzzing stopped and then started again. She ran the back of her hand along her forehead. The sweat was cold like her skin. The haze cleared a little but the buzzing wouldn't go away.

Then she knew it was the buzzer on the main door of the apartments and she found herself walking back into the little hallway, a slow motion progress towards the entry phone by the front door. She saw her hand reach out to it. It buzzed again. She pressed the intercom button.

"Jane?" Mark Mandell said.

She remembered she hadn't had to give him any instructions how to get to the apartments. He knew where she lived. She found herself counting ten before she replied.

"Yes."

"Can you let me in?"

"Of course, sorry for the delay. This system doesn't seem to be working very well."

"The door is stuck" Mandell said.

"I'm pressing hard Mark," she said. "I am sure it will all be fine."

She reached up and lightly touched the release button. The whirr of the door opening came up the intercom. She counted the seconds till he would appear.

At one second more than she had expected there was a gentle knock. She looked through the spy hole. Mandell's distorted face loomed down at her through the lens. He had a slight bruising under his right eye and a long thin scratch had traced its way down his cheek. He was only a few inches away from her. She didn't feel danger now, but then she hadn't felt anything when she had got into her car.

She opened the door.

"I'm sorry," Mandell said. "It's very late."

"You've been in the wars," Jane said.

"I fell over a luggage trolley at the airport."

He was looking at her. She started to move backwards down the hallway.

"You'd better come in."

"Thanks," he said.

She led the way back to the main part of the flat. The oblong space stretched out in front of them.

She kept a distance from him.

"Are you all right?"

He was looking at her.

"Why do you ask?"

"You look a little tired."

"I am. The office."

"I shouldn't have come. I'm sorry. It's late."

"No," Jane said moving closer towards him. "Don't go. It's fine. Sit down. Where have you been?"

"New York. Trying to raise money to keep Mandell Entertainment in being."

"Successfully?"

"No."

Mandell was dressed in a green Burberry jacket, cord trousers, and a pair of heavy-duty boots, the sort that would be appropriate for spying duties in Wimbledon but hardly for raising finance in New York.

"Do you mind if I take these off?" Mandell indicated his boots. "They're killing me."

"There is a cupboard in the hall, next to the clock. You can put them in there."

She heard Mandell slide the cupboard door back. She took the bottle of brandy and put it on the coffee table and sat down.

Mandell was wearing thick woollen socks that would keep the cold out. They were different colours.

"I need to ask you a couple of things. I thought it would be easier to come over. But we could talk in the morning."

"It's fine," Jane said. "Really. Help yourself to a drink."

"These administrators that have taken over my father's firm," Mandell said as he poured, "who do they take their orders from?"

"They will probably report to a creditors' committee but they are quite independent on what they do day-to-day. The creditors will be interested in how much money they find, how they go about that is their business. I imagine KM is leading the creditors."

"So they are trying to find the missing money?"

"Of course."

"Would they tell me if they did?"

"I can't see why not. They would probably tell everybody."

"But they would certainly tell you?"

"Yes, I'm sure they would."

"It would be helpful to know immediately if they do find anything. They can't do that a moment too soon as far as I am concerned. Mandell Holdings restored to financial health would help the family reputation for financial probity. Everything is on a knife edge at the moment. It could be a lifesaver."

"Would you benefit directly?"

"Only reputation. I don't have any financial interest in the business now."

Mandell stared into the depths of his glass of brandy. Somewhere, from across the river, there was the faint sound of a bell striking twelve. It was muffled and unconvincing.

"You didn't come here just to talk about the administrators did you Mark?"

"No. There is another problem. I wondered if you could help."

"If you let me know what it is I could tell you."

"There's a police car outside my house. I don't doubt it is waiting for me. But being held for questioning or whatever it is they have in mind is not on my agenda. I've got forty-eight hours to come up with some extra money or the film is dead. I can't waste any time."

"It could just be something routine."

"Whatever it is, I haven't got the time, not at the moment. I had to go in at the back to get a change of clothes without being seen. I don't like breaking into my own house. Can you tell me what they are up to? Ormond said there were connections that could be used."

"That might not be so easy."

If she were in charge of Ormond's office there would have been no problem. She would have just asked a general question and the information would have come flooding back. The chief representative of a Secretary of State needed to know the complete picture of any event. But she was removed from that information base. There were other contacts she could use but there was not the same certainty of being successful. And there was also another problem. Suppose the police wanted to charge Mandell with something? What should she tell him if she did find something out? She hoped it was a theoretical problem. Looking at Mandell there was no hint in his manner that he thought he had done anything wrong.

She found his account of breaking into his own house to change his clothes reassuring. The unmatched socks seemed to bear the story out. If he had been in America he could not have had anything to do with either the letter in the door or her car; and he certainly had had nothing to do with Bellmore. There was one thing that she needed to find out about though.

"Look," Jane said, "I might be able to help on the police and what they are interested in but something else has happened at Mandell that I need to ask you about. There was a late transaction a couple of hours after the main movements of money had been completed. £5 million was transferred from your father's personal account to a company called Dellmark registered in Liechtenstein. It seems a completely separate transaction to the main money movements. As the company is based in Liechtenstein however, I suspect my chances, or anybody else's, of ever knowing who actually controls Dellmark are strictly limited."

"There's no problem about Dellmark," Mandell said to his reflection in the brandy glass. "It's my company. But you have guessed that already haven't you?"

"It seemed a possibility. Why Liechtenstein?"

"It's not illegal and it can help in tax management. The tax position for filmmakers in this country is not entirely favourable. One needs to avoid tax if one can by any means that is legal."

"So you still have £5 million?"

"I wish I had. But I owed three. I've injected all the money to try to keep things going. I need some more."

"What sort of mood was your father in when he agreed to lend you the money?"

"He seemed his normal self. In a good mood if anything."

"Did he mention any deal he was engaged in himself?"

"No."

"Did you see him?"

"Briefly." Mandell paused. "Look, it wasn't totally philanthropic. He wanted a couple of things. Mandell Entertainment was to change its name, and he wanted a part of the action on the film. I hadn't really got any choice. I agreed."

Jane started to shiver slightly.

"You look tired," Mandell said, "I should go."

"It's nothing."

Mandell looked at his watch.

"I need to go to Paris. There's a chance I can pick up the finance I need. If you can tell me anything about the police I would be grateful."

Jane giggled.

"I'm afraid I don't quite share your amusement about officers of the law."

"It's not that. You can't go to Paris in odd socks. It's not exactly chic."

"I have a change of clothes at a friend's."

"That's good."

Mandell was putting his coat back on.

"You're not going straightaway?"

"Needs must."

"Take care."

They faced each other in the hallway of the apartment. Jane took a step forward so that she was close to Mandell. His eyes and mouth were now only an inch or two away. She could feel the slight exhalation of breath gently caressing her skin.

"Seriously Mark."

"They're only French bankers. It should be a good lunch even if they are not prepared to cough up any more financing."

Their lips had touched accidentally, a fleeting contact as they had both lent forward together.

"Are you sure you are OK Jane?" Mandell said. "Has something happened?"

"Nothing serious," Jane said. "Nothing that should delay you."

When Mandell had gone she looked at the clock in the kitchen. It was not yet twelve thirty.

She pulled the curtains back and looked down on the dark river. Why were the police so interested in questioning Mark Mandell that they had a car stationed outside his house?

She checked the lock on the glass doors out to the balcony. When Mandell had been in the apartment the sense of apprehension that had gripped her before he arrived had evaporated. Now he was gone another thought struck her about the letter that had been left in her door. The door was so tight fitting to the frame that she could not see how the letter had been jammed in. It was more likely that someone had opened the door, put the letter in place and then pushed the door to. She couldn't be entirely sure, of course, but it was the best explanation of events.

She shivered again. This time it was not through tiredness or the cold.

She fastened the bolts on the top and bottom of the door.

It was only the next morning that she realised that she had not remembered to telephone Richard.

CHAPTER FIFTEEN

Peter Green called into her office five minutes after she arrived. It was unusual for him simply to drop in. Jane, and everybody else in the Directorate, usually got a request to go to see him. Jane glanced at the weekly movement sheet that Suzanne had prepared. She had a meeting with Peter scheduled for that afternoon.

"Peter - this is unexpected."

"I happened to be passing."

He sat down on the chair in front of her desk, his long legs stretched out in front of him and his body at an angle midway between the horizontal and vertical. A bright smile crossed his cadaverous features.

"Found out anything about this Mandell business yet?" The tone was casual but Peter Green never indulged in idle gossip. Jane wondered who he had been talking to.

"We're making some progress," Jane said. "Ian Hart is completing an initial analysis."

Peter Green was nodding.

"I spoke to Ian. He said he was convinced it was fraud, or at least some form of wrongdoing. Any hope of bringing it to a conclusion? Any leads from the SFO or the administrators?"

"Not that I'm aware of."

Peter Green slid round ninety degrees in the swivel chair. He

111

seemed light-hearted at the rather dismal prospects for success. Jane couldn't quite understand it. This sort of mood in Peter normally followed utter disaster to one of his colleagues or the resignation of a Minister. The news didn't seem bad enough to justify such extreme good humour.

"It's difficult to get a grip on what actually happened and who benefits. If the chief suspect is dead I don't quite know where we go."

Jane was about to make some reference to Kenneth Ormond's personal approach and establish some cover for what she had been doing but she held the words back. There was something deeply unattractive about so much jollity in adverse circumstances. All that would really appeal to Peter in his current mood was a larger disaster. For her to register a personal appeal from Ormond would probably convince him that that was precisely what was in prospect. It wasn't an attractive option. Perhaps she could get the matter on record in a general way.

"As you probably know," she said calmly, "Ian and I found out from the company records that the Home Secretary is a major shareholder in Mandell. His financial losses could prove embarrassing -"

She stopped in mid sentence. Peter Green was beaming ever brighter for some reason that must be connected with what she was saying.

"Haven't you heard? It was all over the morning news. Ormond had a heart attack in Singapore. Nothing too serious apparently, or so they are saying, but he has been ordered to rest for three months. No chance of anybody raising anything in the House about his financial affairs while he is sick, and the P.M. isn't going to replace him unless it proves necessary. As far as I can see anyway the Home Office will run a lot more smoothly with Ormond confined to his bed."

"I missed the news this morning -"

"I thought you were a Radio Four addict -"

"I am," Jane said. She was going to explain further but checked herself. There was nothing that she could say that she wanted Peter Green to hear. When she had awoken that morning she had not turned on the radio but devoted the time to thinking about Mark Mandell instead. A week ago she would have run a mile before associating with someone who conducted his business affairs with the aid of

Liechtenstein-based companies. Somehow, this morning that had not seemed quite such a barrier.

She looked up. Peter Green looked as though he expected her to complete the sentence.

"It's just that my radio is broken."

"That's a shame; I've rarely heard hypocrisy at such a peak."

Jane summoned up a wintry smile.

"I did hear one interesting rumour about the Mandell business though," Peter Green continued enthusiastically.

Jane gathered that there was further bad news for someone.

"Apparently there is some suggestion that Mandell didn't die a natural death."

"Mark Mandell?" Jane said foolishly.

"He wasn't called Mark was he? Surely it was David?"

"Oh yes - David."

"That's him - the fellow who drowned, or so they thought. They are not so sure now. The chap who did the autopsy is a neighbour of mine, Michael Crane, reasonably eminent in his profession but not exactly first class. Probably trust him on this though. He was pretty sure at first that it was an accidental death. They thought he might have had a heart attack. There wasn't much water in the lungs. Mandell had been drinking which is apparently quite usual in accidental drowning. According to Crane it is remarkably difficult to prove anything one way or another with drowning, you just have to look at the attendant circumstances."

"I don't follow; I thought you said there was nothing that suggested the death might have been suspicious."

"I'm coming to that. Apparently there was nothing to suggest foul play except one thing. The body seemed to have been in the water a lot longer than it could have been. It's to do with the temperature of the water and the onset of *rigor mortis*. In this case Crane couldn't really explain it. It's not impossible that David Mandell died on Christmas Day but the facts don't really fit. Crane thinks he must have died earlier than that. Not that his is an opinion I would put any money on."

"But how do they know when he died?"

"The last person to have any contact with him was his son, who also found the body. Apparently they are trying to interview him at the moment but he is proving elusive."

"Interesting," Jane said with as much calm as she could muster. She felt the bottom of her stomach falling slightly away.

"Isn't it? Particularly with the money missing. There must be a motive for murdering David Mandell surely?"

"I am sure there is always a motive for murdering anyone," Jane found herself saying without conviction while Peter Green nodded vigorously. Luckily he seemed focused on possibilities of general mayhem rather than anything in particular. Jane was encouraged when he looked at his watch and got up.

"You used to work for Ormond, didn't you?"

Jane hesitated for a moment. Peter's tone had softened a shade. He knew perfectly well that she had been Kenneth Ormond's Private Secretary. His innocent sounding question was more, she judged, an invitation for her to confide anything that might be troubling her about Ormond and Mandell. It was the opportunity to cover herself, however obliquely, for anything that might subsequently be judged irregular in her approach. There was, however, one major change in circumstances. With a fit and powerful Kenneth Ormond backing her actions she had no doubt that Peter would have nodded approvingly of her sense of initiative. With Ormond ill she didn't know which way his advice would fall.

"A few years ago now," she said airily.

Peter nodded and then he was gone.

"I need some coffee," Jane said. "Please."

Suzanne nodded.

"Ian is here."

"Thank goodness for sanity," Jane said. "Can you offer him a cup as well."

"Of course," Suzanne said.

"Has the Vulture left?" Ian said provocatively as he walked in the room.

"Yes."

"You're not going to defend him?"

"Not today."

Ian sat on the edge of Jane's desk.

"That's an improvement."

"That's as maybe. Have you heard about Ormond?"

"Who hasn't?"

"No one but me, clearly. Have you got anything more on Mandell?"

Ian slid off the edge of the desk and into the swivel chair that Peter Green had occupied.

"Perry can't find out who controls Dellmark and doubts if anyone can. There is a rumour, however, that Mark Mandell may have something to do with it. He has been pumping money into Mandell Entertainment to try and keep his film afloat. It may be too late. There are some rumours that the film is going to be a turkey anyway. Straight to video release, that sort of thing."

Suzanne appeared with the coffee.

"So how is Mandell Entertainment doing?"

"Badly as far as I can see. Like other parts of the Mandell businesses."

"I thought the others were basically OK apart from this loan business."

"A lot of the performance is sluggish."

Ian Hart sounded slightly distracted.

"Did you tell Peter?"

"No. I stuck to the headlines. He didn't seem to want any in-depth analysis."

"Fair enough. Anything else?"

"I've got a hunch but I need to think it through."

"What sort of hunch?"

"I can't explain it at the moment. I don't really know myself. It is something about the transactions that doesn't make sense. Actually, that is not quite right. It is something about the transactions that does make sense."

"I thought you said they were designed that way to obscure how the money had exited from the system. As far as I can see they have been remarkably effective in meeting that purpose."

"They have. It's just that there's no logical reason for the accounts that David Mandell used to transfer the £250 million into. At least on the face of it, except-"

"Except what?"

"You said David Mandell liked puzzles."

"Yes, why?"

"There's something about the account numbers we know, the first ones the money was transferred into. The numbers are too low; they're not random. There is some sort of sequence if only I can find the key."

"I don't get it – are they in code?"

"Not exactly, they are the real account numbers, they haven't been turned into anything else, if they had that would have been coding. No, it's some sort of sequence I think. If we knew what the sequence was based on we could generate some more account numbers."

"And find the money?"

"If it's still there."

"Sounds the best lead we have. It should be the priority."

"There's the final Kuopio report for the Minister."

"That can wait for a day or two. This can't. I'll let them know there will be a slight delay."

"Fair enough. I'll get on to it."

"Remember to come back to me first when you have," Jane said.

Ian Hart waved assent from her doorway. Jane noted 'Kuopio' on the pad in front of her as one of the things she needed to keep in mind. If Ian Hart sorted his intuition out quickly it was possible that she could still meet her target for delivering the report. If not, she no longer considered that it would represent a significant failure. Anyway, the detailed performance targets no longer seemed so important.

She reached for the telephone.

The cheery voice of her brother announced that, as he was on holiday, it might take him a day or two longer to get back to the caller but they could rest assured that he would return the call.

"Richard, if you are there, pick the telephone up!"

At the other end of the line the machine whirred on for a few seconds, gave a beep, and lapsed into silence. Richard had departed on his sacred pursuit of Miranda. Unless he had fallen in love with someone on the way he was probably already over the Channel or under it. She swore to herself. She couldn't see why Richard didn't adopt her own more level-headed approach to matters of the heart.

She also needed him in London. He was the one person she could trust implicitly who would also be prepared not to inquire too deeply into her reasons for doing anything - at least for the time being. Now there was likely to be no prospect of being able to contact him for three or four days at least. She 'phoned the number again and left a further message for him to get in contact with her the moment he returned.

She flicked through the papers that Suzanne had assembled on her desk. There were interim budgetary returns and requests for her forecasts for the next Financial Year. There were job objectives for each of the members of her staff for her to agree and countersign. Below them was a mass of EU briefing papers.

She got up and walked into the outer office. Suzanne was typing with her usual rapidity.

"I'm going out," Jane said.

Suzanne stopped in mid sentence and consulted Jane's diary, which lay open on the desk in front of her.

"I don't have an appointment. I had better put it in."

"No appointment," Jane said. "I just need a breath of fresh air to think about things. I'm going for a walk in St James's Park."

"Oh." Suzanne looked slightly bewildered. "How long will you be?"

"I'm not quite sure," Jane said. "There are a couple of problems I need to get to grips with. I might take an early lunch as well."

"I've got your sandwich."

Jane stopped on the route to her coat.

"Sorry, of course you have. Look, do please eat it yourself. My treat. It is just one or two things have come up."

Suzanne nodded understandingly. Jane had the curious feeling that Suzanne had decided that her best course was to humour her boss. She had a slight brainwave.

"It's Peter Green," she said with a slight sigh. "I really do need to think through the implications of what he was saying."

"Of course," Suzanne looked brighter with an explanation to hand. "There is nothing in the diary until 2.30."

"Good," Jane said.

In the reception area Jane borrowed the security guard's telephone and invited a surprised Diana Vere to an early lunch. Jane thought for a moment that the security guard gave her a slightly odd look, much the same as Suzanne had done when she had announced her sudden exit. She smiled at him and he nodded reluctantly. Accounts of her unusual behaviour might start circulating round the building but she doubted whether they would get to Peter Green who, anyway, had little time to listen. Besides she had not wanted to use the telephone in her room, or her mobile for the call to Diana. She had a suspicion that both might be being tapped. Robert Stuart and Peter Green had been remarkably well informed of developments on Mandell and Jane wanted to break the links and have a bit of free time. It was ironic perhaps that she had actually been telephoning a member of MI5 if it was they who were doing the tapping. But she would have broken one of the circuits. Whoever was listening to her could not be listening to all the other lines out of the building. She had moved a little ahead of a part of the game, but only if that was the game that was being played. Perhaps she was just becoming paranoid.

CHAPTER SIXTEEN

"So what did the garage say about your car?" Diana Vere asked.

She was curled into a chair in the corner of the restaurant, her long and languid form instantly adapted to the space she found herself in. Diana Vere had smoky eyes and an inclination to accidentally break men's hearts. Even today, out of the corner of her eye, Jane could detect more than usual passing interest from the businessman in the sharply defined blue and white striped shirt at the next table.

"I went there on an impulse," Jane said. "There was a taxi outside the office and it isn't far. I wanted to find out if it could be repaired and how long it would be off the road. I wondered if I needed to hire another one. It all came as a shock. That's why I was late getting here. I spent ten minutes walking round trying to clear my head."

"I wondered why. Being late isn't like you. But what did he say?"

"The first man I spoke to seemed to think it could have been accidental. Stones."

"Stones?"

"Or gravel, perhaps."

"Sharp gravel?"

"I would think so."

"You don't get a great deal of sharp gravel in London do you?"

"No."

Jane found there was a slight tremor running through her leg. If somebody had tampered with her car they would have had plenty of opportunity. The Peugeot had been in the basement garage at her apartment from late on Friday evening when she had travelled back from her mother's flat to mid afternoon on Sunday. On Saturday she had been at Eastwood with Robert Stuart. There had been more than enough time for somebody to tamper with her car. And that somebody clearly had access to the apartment building. There was no point in simply assuming the note that had been left in her apartment door was some accidental connection. Somebody had intended it as a serious warning.

She had already told Diana about the note. She had needed to tell someone. With her brother away and Robert Stuart in New York Diana had been the obvious choice. As reliable old friends went the only other alternative was Sally Fry, and Sally, whatever her other qualities, was hardly discreet.

"So perhaps it could have been accidental?" Diana Vere suggested.

"I don't think so," Jane said. I am not sure the first man's opinion was worth anything anyway. His foreman was perfectly definite about it. The hydraulic lines had been severed."

"So what did the foreman think?"

"He thought I was keeping bad company."

Jane drank some of the wine. It was a little cold, and she found herself shaking.

"Jane," Diana Vere said. She had a protective hand outstretched over Jane's arm.

"It's nothing," Jane said. "Nothing at all really. Delayed shock."

And anger, she thought to herself. Because somebody is frightening me off and is quite prepared to kill me if it turns out that way. I could have been killed and they must have known that. If she had been crushed under the oil tanker they would probably have come back to the apartment door and removed the envelope. She was angry too because it was now all so obvious and yet she had resolutely refused to face up to the logic of events. Her brakes had failed and there had been a warning note in her apartment door, yet she had been unwilling to connect the two and face up to their implications.

Diana Vere had lit a cheroot and was looking at her. Diana's skin, always pale, was unusually white in this light. She might have been wearing make up for a mime performance, the role of a ghost waiting to escort her hapless friend downwards.

"C'mon Jane, there's more. What is it?"

"It's this Mandell business. I'm meant to be looking into it from the regulatory angle, but I seem to have got a bit close to something."

"There's a lot riding on Mandell."

"You know about Ormond?"

Diana nodded.

"Some people are very anxious that it gets sorted out. Then again," she added, "there are others who would be perfectly happy for Ormond to have to resign. But maybe, in view of this morning's news, that is all a bit academic." Diana seemed to be considering another point. "You used to be quite close to Ormond didn't you?"

"That was some time ago, but yes."

"So why don't you tell me more about it?"

"As a friend?"

"I'll stop you if I think there is anything I wouldn't feel comfortable in knowing."

Diana Vere seemed comfortable in knowing most things. But then MI5 agents probably did feel comfortable in knowing things. They were used to listening. It was what most of them did for a living. It had its own dangers. One of Diana's first jobs, or so she had confided to Jane, had been dealing with a series of claims for industrial injury. 5's electronic eavesdroppers had been suffering hearing loss from tuning in to crackly foreign radio transmissions. Hour after hour of whistles and bangs had led some to have a permanent ringing in the ears. Nowadays personnel didn't retire early from 5 with a gunshot wound in the leg but tinnitus in the ear.

That was what 5 were like now, just another part of the Government organisation with problems no different from anyone else, or so it seemed to be being claimed. Gone were the spies of yesteryear, the buccaneers and amateurs, to be replaced by people who listened and watched and who were infinitely anonymous. There weren't any clear rules for the competing team in the great spy game anymore. These days things were much less certain, the enemy less clear, every citizen potentially involved.

Jane found herself talking quite calmly. The tremor in her leg had ceased. She edited her feelings for Mark Mandell and the details of Dellmark. She simply asked Diana for any details that could be provided on Christopher Bellmore. 5 had access to the police computer. Her request, although a little unorthodox, was clearly for the public good.

"You will want anything we have on David and Mark Mandell as well I suppose?"

Diana's question was rhetorical. The only logical answer could be yes. Jane nodded.

"That would be useful."

"And this woman you mentioned, the one who was with Christopher Bellmore?"

"Paula Black. Yes, anything you have on her."

Diana blew a smoke ring into the air.

"I'll see what I can do. Twenty-four hours?"

"Twenty-four hours would be fine."

"I'll telephone," Diana said. "We should meet up if there is anything to pass on."

"Yes, of course."

Jane didn't know quite why they were close. They had not got a great deal in common. Diana came from a wealthy upper middle class family who lived in Kensington and Hertfordshire. She was conducting a long-term affair with a married MP. Jane had met him once, at a reception. She didn't know for sure whether Diana had any brothers or sisters. She knew she loved opera and went away to France in August - probably with the MP. That was about the extent of it. She and Jane also met, on some infrequent pattern, for lunch.

"You should be careful," Diana Vere said. "You really ought to go to the police. Whatever is happening doesn't quite sound suitable for amateur sleuthing."

"But what would I say if I did go to them?" Jane said. "I think they would think I was just being hysterical and I can't really start telling them anything about Ormond or the political implications. Besides I'm not sure there are any. I destroyed the note in the door and the garage aren't totally clear in their view."

"But getting Richard to follow people around!" Diana shrugged.

"I mean you're not us Jane. It seems crazy really. Maybe you should just forget the whole thing. Whether the money is found next week or not isn't going to make any difference to Ormond's career now. Make it clear to everyone - Peter Green included - that you're not interested. Take a holiday like Richard. That would be safe."

"Just get me the information and perhaps I will. If there is something on Bellmore that could be all I need. If he has got a record for something then if I point the police in his direction they can take care of it."

"That would be best. I'll get back to you tomorrow."

"There is one thing," Jane said.

"Name it."

"I could do with some advice."

"On what?"

Jane gave a little laugh that she hoped didn't sound too mad. "It is just this: how would I know if I was being followed?"

"By us?"

"That would be a start."

"You wouldn't. Not unless you were an expert. Our people are anonymous. Medium height, medium build, nothing unusual about them at all. And they are all very patient and they work in teams so even if you did suspect one of them you would probably never see him or her again. If you are being followed by us the chance is that you would never know."

"Could you check that for me?"

"I'm not sure I heard that," Diana said. "I think I may have heard another question that I might just be able to answer. Remind me to let you know yes or no."

"Thanks. The police?"

"They very rarely tell us anything. I can't help you there. Anything else?"

"No," Jane said. "I am sure that is more than enough. I appreciate it."

"Please be careful," Diana said. "There is nothing you have to prove."

"I know," Jane said. "Coffee?"

"What are you going to do with Eastwood?" Diana said when

the coffee had arrived.

"I thought I might keep it."

"I thought you said the finances were impossible."

"Robert thought..," Jane stopped. "They are. The truth is that I can't bring myself to sell it just yet. I need to spend some time there to get rid of the ghosts. I thought I might do that in the summer, if we ever get a summer."

CHAPTER SEVENTEEN

Jane hurried back to the office. It was not quite two thirty, just in time for whatever appointment it was that had been included in her diary.

One of the security guards waved her to a halt.

"There's a message for you, Miss Quinn. A gentleman called in, asked me to give it to you personally."

He smiled at her, a friendly smile, and gave her a long white envelope simply marked "Jane Quinn."

"Did he leave a name?"

"He said you would know."

"When was this?"

"Shortly after you went out, Miss Quinn. He asked if you were in and when I told him you had gone out, he left this."

"Well - thanks," Jane said.

"A pleasure, Miss Quinn."

The guard was new, and enthusiastic. Jane remembered he had joined just before Christmas.

She walked quickly along to her office. The afternoon coffee was brewing comfortingly on the machine like it would on any normal day.

"The two-thirty is off and Ian would like to see you," Suzanne said. "As soon as he can."

"Just give me five minutes."

"He says he thinks he has solved it," Suzanne said. "He told me to tell you. And there were a couple of other calls. They are on your pad."

Jane looked down. Robert Stuart had telephoned. He had told Suzanne that he would call again later. Knowing Robert's precise mind it was probable that he had deliberately called in the lunch hour knowing that that would normally be a good time to catch Jane in her office. Jane wondered if Suzanne had given any indication that the reason she was not available was that she had abruptly taken to leaving the office in order to think.

The other message was business, a submission that she needed to sort out by the end of the day. She glanced at the draft. It had been typed in the standard Treasury format of wide margins and one and a half spacing. She had been surprised when she had transferred to the Treasury about how few words they managed to get on an A4 page.

She sat down and slid the envelope open. There was a single sheet of paper folded into three. She left it lying in front of her for a moment. Her father had always said that it was always best to consider the worst that could happen. She picked it up.

Mark Mandell hadn't left for Paris. Instead there was a short note that looked as though it had been written in a hurry -

> Jane,
>
> Things are getting sticky. Paris is a non-starter. I need to go to Frankfurt, perhaps New York again. My only problem is that there is a policeman following me around but I don't suppose you can do anything about that. At least it means that if any of my creditors get close, there is likely to be someone on the spot to intervene. I thought I would call in as I think I have shaken him off for the moment but you are not here. I'll contact you again as soon as I can.
>
> Love,
>
> Mark

She slipped the note into her handbag and looked out of the window. The clouds had turned leaden overhead but the promised snow had not materialised. She took the envelope, looked at it for a moment, and tore it in half and threw the two pieces into her wastepaper bin. On one of the bits of paper Mark Mandell's handwriting was still uppermost. She bent down and turned the piece of paper over.

She took the note out of her handbag. Mark Mandell had written 'Love' at the bottom of his note. Robert Stuart might have invited her to America but he hadn't managed to use the word to her directly or even on a birthday or Christmas card. She shrugged. Mandell probably scattered the word in all his communications while Robert would only use it entirely seriously.

There were voices from the outer office, a curious low murmur of sound. She walked across to the office door, which was slightly ajar. Ian Hart was handing something to Suzanne. Their hands were locked together. She was aware of words floating in the air -

"If you get there early you can let yourself in.."

She stepped back a pace so she couldn't be seen. It was a private conversation and normally she would have turned on her heel. But she had seen the way they were looking at each other and there was something transfixing about it. The look was quite clear. Ian and Suzanne were madly in love with each other. She wondered why she hadn't noticed. Now that it was being spelt out in a way that even she couldn't miss, she remembered other little events that should have led her to the same conclusion on her own. Why couldn't she see the obvious at the moment?

Their hands parted and Suzanne put something in the top drawer of her desk and closed and locked it. Jane took another silent step back and retreated into her office. She picked up the top paper from her in tray and started reading it.

There was a knock at the door and Ian slid discreetly into the room. Jane put down the papers she was holding and motioned to Ian to sit down. He seemed no different from normal.

"Suzanne tells me you've solved it."

"That's a little bit of an exaggeration. More that I'm convinced I can solve it."

"Where the money is?"

"Where it went next. Whether it is still there is another matter."

"Finding the sequence you were talking about."

"Low numbers."

"You said that before."

"I think I know why now. I'm pretty sure they're football scores. Find the ones we have and you'll see what comes next. You said David Mandell was a supporter of Nottingham Forest didn't you?"

"Lifelong, apparently."

"I probably don't need to look any further then. Brian is a bit of a football fan isn't her? Given his love of statistics he's ideally placed to tell me where to look."

"So you think the money could still be there?"

"I thought that was your pet theory. It may be that you're right. Perhaps there are no black holes currently in Mandell finances because the money has already been transferred to prop things up. It sort of makes sense."

Except, Jane thought, if David Mandell had been working alone and the money was simply untraceable until Ian worked his magic, that didn't explain the note in her apartment door or the brakes on her car.

"Except," Ian said, "why was Bellmore so unhappy?"

"There could have been dodgy elements to the deal that Bellmore was aware of, but his employers were not. Perhaps he was in league with David Mandell in some way. Perhaps he has already got a kick back from David Mandell and doesn't want anyone to find out about it. If the money were traced a bit further we would have a much better idea of what our friend Bellmore is concerned about.

"I understand he's been talking to Paula Black."

"Bellmore said a woman confirmed the money had been transferred. It might have been Paula. They were probably trying to work out what had happened."

"That sounds plausible enough," Jane said, "but I'm not sure this is getting us anywhere. You need to come up with the accounts where the money is."

"Or was," Ian Hart added. "Although I may just be going loopy. It is always possible that I am simply suffering from overwork exacerbated by the lack of a compensating large financial reward."

"The work is its own reward," Jane said. "They must have told you that when you joined. Besides you look fine. So how long might it take before you come up with something?"

"I need to sleep on it. And I need some statistics. I'll go and see what Brian thinks is available on the net. Then maybe I'll have something in twenty-four hours, or I can tell you that I've got it wrong and I can't solve it. I sort of sense I'm close. Once I've spoken to Brian I might go back to the flat if that is OK with you. I just need some peace to think."

"Seems the best plan we've got," Jane said. "Twenty-four hours and then get back to me whether you've solved it or not. And don't tell anyone about this - not even Perry. We need to be sure. This is sensitive. There are too many important people involved. Besides, we want to be able to catch the perpetrators."

"No problem. I'll be like the grave." Ian Hart assumed Peter Green's lugubrious expression when faced with a Directorate success.

"And don't work too hard," Jane said as Ian rose to his feet. "All work and no play make Ian a dull boy."

"If only there was some play," Ian said regretfully.

"You must have some distractions," Jane said. "Even Treasury officials are allowed them."

"If only -" Ian said, smiling.

He stopped in the doorway. His body was momentarily lopsided as it always was when something new occurred to him. It was as though his brain froze all movement the better to concentrate on the new insight that was occurring.

"Yes?"

Ian Hart was in motion again.

"I don't know. I'll tell you some more when I have actually worked it out."

"I look forward to it."

Jane sat down. She was finding it difficult to weigh up any of the things that were happening. She seemed to be getting wound ever closer into Mark Mandell's business affairs. She hadn't expected to encounter the scene between Ian and Suzanne. If she hadn't seen Ian with Suzanne she would have believed the line about all work and no play. Curious how easy it was to be deceived, however innocently, by two people she felt very close to.

She wondered what she should do next. Perhaps she should sort out her own life and make a decision about Eastwood. She could leave Mandell to Ian for the moment. Ian's hunches invariably produced results. It seemed from what he had been saying that he simply needed some key piece of the jigsaw and then everything would fall into place. The way he was bubbling probably meant that the solution could come to him at any moment. That he was so obviously enraptured with Suzanne might give him such a strong distraction that his unconscious brain might be free to work through all the number patterns he had stored. She wondered if he was seeing Suzanne that evening. She looked at her watch. Five minutes to three. She had not been back in the office for more than half an hour.

Suzanne was in the doorway.

"There is a call for you," she said. "An Inspector Norman."

"What does he want?"

"Something about the Mandell business. He wasn't too specific."

"You had better put him through."

"Jane Charles," Jane said.

There was a slight pause at the other end of the line.

"Miss Quinn?"

"Yes," Jane said. "Jane Quinn."

She had forgotten for a moment that she was in her office.

"I am telephoning about David Mandell. I am looking into the circumstances of his death. I have reason to think that his business affairs may be relevant. I would like to make an appointment with you to discuss them. I believe you have an interest."

"The Treasury certainly has an interest in the regulatory aspects," Jane found herself saying smoothly. It stopped her having to indicate that her own interest was slightly more personal than usual.

"And you represent the Treasury interest?"

There was something painfully pedantic about Inspector Norman's sentences. Jane could almost see him holding a notebook at the other end of the line.

"Yes, I suppose I do."

"Would Friday morning about ten be convenient for an appointment?"

Jane looked at her diary. Friday morning was inconveniently free.

"Yes, that would be fine."

"Good. Can I call at your office?"

"Of course."

Jane was about to ring off as she thought the Inspector was about to finish the conversation. Then Norman started speaking again. There was now a pant in his voice as though he might have been running before he picked up the telephone and finally his lack of breath had caught up with him. It was unattractive.

"There are a couple of things you should be aware of Miss Quinn."

"Which are?" Jane sounded more collected than she felt. The curious tremor in her leg flickered momentarily to life.

"There used to be a time when white collar crime was a bit of fun," Norman said. "Some people, to judge by the sentences passed, still consider it is a gentlemanly activity in which the worst punishment is social exclusion or a spell of community service. But that is really no longer the case. Where there is big money involved, as with Mandell, the rules have been changed. Things have got a lot tougher. Professional criminals are very unpleasant."

"I am sure that may be true in some cases Inspector but are you sure this applies to Mandell?"

"Yes." The voice at the other end of the line was quite definite.

"Why?" Jane's leg was starting to tremble freely.

"Because it is perfectly clear to me that David Mandell was murdered Miss Quinn. I have no doubt about the matter at all."

"Is there any evidence, Inspector?"

Jane sounded calm but she was really far removed from that state. Her pulse was racing again.

"I'll find it," Norman said in a voice that suggested that he had no doubt at all that he would. "Remember if there is anything you want to tell me, call me straightaway. Anything that might be relevant."

"Of course."

Jane put the telephone down. She couldn't make up her mind. There was something about Norman that she had taken an intense dislike to. And there was something in his warning that was chilling. It was probably just a tactic. But an effective one. She was still thinking about it half an hour later when the telephone rang again.

It was Mark Mandell. He gave her an address and suggested a meeting that evening.

She agreed. She could, if she wished, pursue the question of how David Mandell had died.

Mark Mandell had spoken quickly and with urgency. Something had obviously happened. She would need to leave the office early again. She looked at the pile of papers in front of her that would normally have tethered her to the spot. She looked round her office. For a moment she felt like a stranger intruding on somebody else's life.

CHAPTER EIGHTEEN

Three hours later Jane adjusted her reflection in the mirror of the hired Peugeot the garage had come up with. The car had done a little over 700 miles and everything worked perfectly, including the brakes. She put the lipstick back in her handbag. She had seen no one since she had turned into the street. As far as she could tell she was entirely alone. She needed a moment to think. Richard's answer phone had still been delivering the same cheery pre-holiday message and there had been no response from Edward Charles in Ireland. No one knew where she was or what she was doing. A call to Kenneth Ormond's office had produced nothing beyond the news that the Home Secretary was incommunicado on doctor's orders and convalescing in a hospital in Singapore. Jane shrugged. She had one last look behind in the mirror and opened the car door.

Number 15 was a large double-fronted Victorian house that had been converted into flats. She walked up the wide stone steps to the front door. Her fingers touched the 15E bell and there was a faint ring from within. She was about to press the bell more firmly when the door was opened by a man in a long blue overcoat. He moved back to let her enter and then stepped out into the street. He was in too much of a hurry, she thought, to notice anything. The door closed and the immediate cold was cut off. She was in a carpeted hallway with white striped wallpaper and a dado rail running up the stairs in front of her. 15A was to her right and 15B to the left. She walked up the stairs. The top floor of the house had a single door marked 15E. She looked at her watch. It was a few minutes off seven. She knocked.

The door opened ten degrees and she saw Mark Mandell look out at her, and past her to see if there was anyone else. Then he pulled the door open wider and ushered her inside. He was dressed in casual trousers and a thick green pullover. His feet were bare and one was scratched and bruised.

The apartment behind him opened out into a sunken area where two sofas guarded the approach to a long sloping glass window stretching down to floor level. A single table lamp with a yellow shade despatched warm light across the polished wood floor. An open bottle of Scotch and a glass stood on a low round table. The curtains were open and Jane could see the lights of neighbouring houses showing through the bare branches of trees in the garden. Whoever had converted the building had had a flair for the dramatic.

"You're early," Mandell said.

"You said you were desperate. I came as soon as I could. Who does this belong to?"

"It could be mine."

"The furnishings aren't right for you, nor are the pictures."

"I rather like horses."

"I don't believe you."

"No," Mandell said after a moment. "I didn't think you would."

Jane looked at him and then at the open bottle of Scotch.

"I gather your film financing prospects aren't improving?"

Mandell shook his head and followed her eyes.

"That comes with the premises. I'm not sure I can afford a bottle myself. Do you want a drink?"

Jane nodded.

"I'll get you a glass."

Jane sat down. Most of the back roof of the building had been turned into a giant glass-roofed conservatory so that, particularly in summer, it must seem like living in the treetops.

She looked round. The two side walls were brick, and supported a variety of pictures and trailing plants. A large collection of drinks occupied the top of a sideboard. A low bookcase had a long run of yellow Wisdens and some thrillers. There were no ornaments. Mark Mandell's friend was clearly male.

Mark Mandell had returned. He had a tumbler in his hand and was now wearing thick blue socks.

"It's easier to find the booze in this place than something to drink it out of."

"What did you do to your feet?"

"I fell off a wall."

"Any particular reason?"

"Yes. I thought there was somebody after me. I didn't wait to find out."

"You are going to have to talk to the police sometime soon. I've just had a Chief Inspector call me up, a man called Norman."

"What did he want?"

"You said there was something you wanted to ask me that was urgent. Perhaps we should get that out of the way first."

Mandell poured whisky into the tumbler and gave it to her.

"As you like."

He sounded as though he thought Jane was being unreasonable.

Jane found her eyes drawn up to the sky. Despite the light pollution the brightest stars were visible. If she could get away from the Earth she could see them as they really were. Bright fires burning in endless empty space.

Mandell was speaking again.

"Do you know when the main transactions transferring money from KM and the other banks into my father's accounts on Christmas Eve were completed?"

There was an edge to his voice.

"Two thirty, three o'clock. I'm not sure precisely but no later than that."

"And who signed the deal off?"

"I can give you the official version of events. Your father was in the main office at Mandell Holdings in the morning. There were a few people around but not many. He spoke to Christopher Bellmore, who was looking after the KM end of the deal about ten to try to get a bit of movement from them. It was his normal tactic. But Bellmore wasn't giving anything away. Your father agonised over the deal for a time but decided early afternoon that the conditions were acceptable. The money was passed by electronic transfer to bank accounts under the control of his firms and was immediately split up and transferred into a series of accounts and then moved again until it became effectively untraceable. That process was completed by the time you telephoned your father and he agreed the separate refinancing deal for the film. The next day you found him."

"Do you know for certain that my father spoke to Bellmore?"

"According to Bellmore he did."

"Ah."

It was the least authoritative word that Jane had ever heard Mandell utter.

Jane felt the silence between them; stars and galaxies moving further apart, waiting for their fires to die. Perhaps it was more real to be in London than Edward's house in Ireland. There the stars filled the sky, but that was how it had been in the past, now many of them, in reality, would be extinguished. Eventually, wherever one was, the whole sky would be an unremitting black.

"I had better tell you," Jane said decisively. "This policeman, Inspector Norman, thinks your father was murdered."

"I thought he might."

"You're not surprised?"

"Not entirely."

"Then," Jane said. "You had better tell me why."

"Promise to hear me out?"

Jane waited for a moment and then nodded.

"My father didn't authorise the £5 million loan to keep my film alive. If I had asked him to do so I don't think he would have agreed. I had sounded him out on it a few days before and he had said there was no point in throwing good money after bad. It wasn't quite a closed door but he wasn't a man who changed his mind much."

Mandell, agitated, walked over to the window and looked out. He spoke more quietly, weighing every word.

"I did find my father dead, but not at the time I said. I didn't telephone on Christmas Eve. I went to see him. I suppose I thought if I turned up in person there was just a chance. At least I thought there was no harm in giving it a try. I had sensed there was some deal he was engaged in. The only times I had seen him in December he had been preoccupied. There was intensity about him when he was close to lining something up. He normally had a high after completing a deal. I thought if I caught him at that moment there was just a chance. I didn't have any other options anyway."

"And he didn't want Mandell Entertainment to change its name?"

"No. I made that up. I'm sorry. If you have the heart to, I suggest you treat it as a white lie."

Mandell returned to the table and picked up his drink. He didn't meet Jane's eye.

"I rang the bell but there was no reply. That didn't mean anything particularly. He often walked across the common to buy a newspaper. I helped myself to a drink and then I went down to the basement. I told you the rest."

"I seem to remember that in the version you told me in the Pompadour you found your father on Christmas Day."

"Yes. I needed to get the £5 million transferred. It probably wouldn't have mattered in the normal course of events. Besides I didn't know you then."

"What time was this?"

"Not much later than noon."

"So your father was dead two or three hours before the money from KM was wired over to him?"

"At least, I would have said. I said it was colder than I expected. My father always used to fiddle with the heating controls in the house. If it got too hot he would turn the heating off completely and then turn it back on again when it got cold. He was quite dead when I found him. I am sure it hadn't just happened. And it was cold."

"So if your father was murdered, as Norman suspects, you have succeeded in giving whoever did it an alibi?"

"Pretty much, if he was murdered."

"Maybe it is just the fact that somebody is lying about when he died that is confusing Norman. You've got to go to the police, Mark."

"And turn myself into the number one suspect?"

"I suspect you are that already."

"It's no good, Jane. If I go to the police they will only arrest me.

I lied about my father's death and I have a motive for killing him. Taking the £5 million would also have been completely pointless. It's given me some breathing space. There's still a chance with the film. I can't turn myself in just yet."

Mark Mandell was speaking with more energy. Jane looked at him.

"Why did you leave him floating in the pool, Mark?"

"There was nothing I could do. It was like a stranger dying, not my father. I had gone there with the single idea that I must save the film. It was a shock finding him dead, but even when I was walking back up the stairs from the basement I was thinking what effect it would have on my chances of saving the film. It is not pretty, but I am afraid it is true. Sorry, Jane, I would have liked it to be different. No, I had better be truthful about that as well. Up to the time we met in the Pompadour I don't think I was too bothered about what I had done. I don't feel like that now. I just told myself that I was solving my problem with the film and may be I thought my father owed me something. The only cost would be a few hours delay in reporting my father's death. It wasn't something that worried me at the time. My father would be found and they would work out that he had died of a heart attack or whatever. No problem."

"And you didn't kill him?"

Mandell met her gaze. The mental image of David Mandell bobbing up and down in the water came to Jane's mind from her dreams, but when she looked into Mandell's eyes it dissolved away.

"No, I didn't."

She could feel herself falling into those eyes if she was not careful.

"You do believe me, don't you?"

"Yes."

She turned away. She could feel Mandell behind her, his arm on her shoulder. She took a step forward.

"I need to think."

"I'm sorry."

"Not about that. How we are going to get you out of this?"

She felt Mandell's arm relax.

"I'm not sure anything can."

"The money," Jane said. "There may be a lead. There are patterns in the account numbers the money was transferred into. It is just possible that it is possible to find out where it is. If we can find out where it is we can find out who is controlling it. Then you can go to the police in safety."

"But who?"

"One of the people who works for me, Ian Hart. He has just got a sixth sense with numbers. He thinks there is some sort of progression in the transactions. If anybody can work it out, he can."

"That could take months -"

"No, I've seen Ian in this sort of mood before. I'm sure he is on to something. I've given him some time off to work on it. It will only be a day or two."

"Surely they could move the money on at any time?"

"At least if we knew where it had been we would have an idea of who is behind all this."

"I suppose so, but it sounds like a long shot."

"It is, but he can do it if anyone can."

Jane sounded surprisingly confident to herself. She realised that she did have faith in Ian. Mandell looked as though he thought she was trying to cheer him up. Perhaps she was. But there were other possibilities; Diana Vere might come up with something on David Mandell's entourage. There was another lead as well, the obvious one.

She turned round. Mark Mandell was in front of her, six inches away. She could stumble and fall into him. Much had been settled. She knew why the police were following him, she understood Norman's suspicions. She could see how detached Mark had been from his father but how vulnerable he was, and how much still alive. Diana and Ian might solve everything, might be in the process of solving it at that very moment.

"Don't go," Mandell said.

"There's somebody I have to see."

"Not now, surely?"

"The sooner the better."

He was looking into her eyes.

"Don't go."

139

"I have to Mark. I have a feeling that we don't have much time."

"I don't have much time. You needn't get involved in this. There's no point in dragging you in. It's too dangerous."

"I am involved."

"No."

"Yes, deeply."

He moved an inch closer. She felt her mind and her senses going to scramble. But there was something else too that was to one side of the exploding neurons. Her instinct for danger was hoisting a little flag on one side of her mind. On the flag was a reproduction of the picture that Bellmore had pointed to when she left the KM building, the hammer and the knife destroying life. She knew time was running out, that the stars were already much more burnt down than anyone realised, that events elsewhere were rushing forward too quickly. Something told her that if she relaxed now the time for action would have passed.

"I have to go Mark."

"I can come with you."

"No, I have to do this alone."

"When can I see you -"

"Soon, but be careful."

She was sure that she hadn't been followed that evening. That was another reason why she knew she had to act now. She was off the map for a moment, able to act freely. Mandell was still in front of her, embarking on a slow backward movement towards the front door.

"Jane, I was wondering."

"What Mark?"

"Are you seeing anyone?"

Jane stopped.

"Are you?"

Mandell seemed to be considering the question.

"The short answer will have to do."

"No."

"We're much the same then," Jane said, "as you ask."

She let herself walk away from Mandell, let him open the door for her, and stepped into the outside world.

CHAPTER NINETEEN

Directory enquiries had no problems locating Mr C Bellmore's number but the telephone box offered no protection against the cold. Jane stamped her feet. She could have used the mobile from the car but she wanted to be as untraceable as possible. She looked at her watch. Eight o'clock. What would she say if his wife answered? Not that that was really the problem. She was becoming convinced that Bellmore was the man who had left the warning note at her flat. Had he also tampered with her car? Whatever he was responsible for he knew something and she had to find out what that was, and quickly. Particularly if she was to save Mark from the consequences of stealing £5 million to support a film that seemed bound to sink. The telephone continued ringing. She was about to put the receiver down when a voice answered.

"Bellmore."

A distant voice that sounded unreal.

"It's Jane Quinn. We met the other day."

When had it been? It seemed an age ago. No, it had only been yesterday.

"Yes." Bellmore acknowledged the fact with reluctance. "I remember. What do you want?"

"I need to talk to you. Could we meet?"

"When?"

"As soon as possible. How about now?"

The freezing breeze caressed her as she waited. There is a temperature at which the cells of the body start to die. She wondered how long it would be before she reached it.

"I don't think we have anything to talk about."

"There are a couple of loose ends from our talk about David Mandell."

"I have told you everything I know about Mandell. I am not interested in discussing it any further."

"I am."

"You don't want to get involved in this."

"I only want to ask you a few questions," Jane said. "I'm five minutes away."

There was a long silence at the other end of the line. She knew Bellmore was going to turn her down, but she was wrong.

"You'd better come round."

The telephone clicked and went dead. Jane glanced both ways as she went back to the car. There was nobody else foolish enough to be out. The car burst eagerly into life when she turned the key.

Number three was bigger than she had imagined from Richard's description. The drive that led up to the house was wider and there were large grounds beyond. The tall fringe of trees where Richard must have stood were on the right. Church Lane was only two roads down from Sally Fry's house and Jane must have travelled along it at some time. She had remembered the houses as exclusive and ones on which Sally had extended an envious eye. Any prospective purchaser would have to find most of £2 million, although if Bellmore was involved in the swindle that sort of figure would now be loose change.

She was about to press the bell a second time when the door opened. For a moment she thought that there was nobody there. The hallway of the house was in darkness and lit only by a stream of light from a room somewhere in the interior. Then she saw that Bellmore was hanging on to the edge of the door and beckoning her in. She stepped forward.

"You look as though you need a drink," Bellmore said colliding lightly with what, in the gloom, looked like an oval side table. "I used to drink Gordons but they don't make it as strong as they used to so now I drink this." Bellmore waved the bottle in his hand in Jane's direction. "But come in here and you can choose for yourself."

The lit room was being used as a study. A wooden desk with a computer was in one corner. There was a long sofa and a built in bookcase, the shelves half full. Dominating everything was a large sideboard with a massed collection of bottles on the top.

A cigarette was burning down in an ash tray leaving a trail of smoke in the air. Bellmore was clumsily scooping ice from a pineapple shaped container into a large tumbler. The room was surprisingly warm and Bellmore had discarded his jacket over the back of an armchair. The overhead light was off but three lamps with blue shades in the corners of the room created pools of light and shadow. Music, a jazz dirge with deeply recessed drums and woodwind, was emerging from a sound system in the corner of the room. Bellmore had turned the sound so low that it was barely audible.

"So what do you want?"

Bellmore was pouring generous measures of gin into two glasses, and looking round for something to add amid the crowd of bottles.

"Just some questions about KM."

"You know the thing about bankers?" Bellmore slurred at her. "I know about bankers. I am a banker. The thing about bankers is this. They seem to think they are worth the money. They really do. All of it. It doesn't matter how many millions it is, they are absolutely convinced they are worth it." Bellmore laughed satirically. "They might just as well steal it. At least then people would know what is happening to them."

"You don't like bankers?"

Bellmore looked at her as though he was trying to get something into focus.

"They don't like me."

Bellmore pushed a glass of gin in her direction.

"Cigarette?"

Jane shook her head.

"Did you talk to David Mandell personally on Christmas Eve?"

"Maybe, maybe not. I don't remember."

"Try. You said you checked various things with David Mandell's office. When was that?"

"Around lunchtime."
"Who did you speak to?"
"One of Mandell's secretaries."
"Paula Black?"
"Yes, I think it was."
"Do you know Paula personally?"

There had been an increasing gap before each of Christopher Bellmore's responses had started. Now Jane thought for a moment that he had stopped altogether.

"Why don't you answer some questions for a change?"

Bellmore was swaying slightly but his tone had a new belligerence to it. He looked as though he needed appeasing.

"I'd be glad to," Jane said lightly.

Bellmore took a large gulp of the gin in his glass.

"They haven't found the money have they?"

Jane shook her head.

"Has Mandell got it?"

"Mark? What makes you think he could have it?"

Bellmore didn't reply but sat down heavily on the sofa. His eyes closed. He was either considering the point or falling asleep. The air was heavy with alcohol fumes and smoke.

"He was about on Christmas Eve wasn't he?"

Bellmore dragged the sentence up from somewhere and the effort seemed to have used up the last of his energy. Jane saw that that he was slowly listing to a horizontal position on the sofa.

"Wake up," Jane said patting his face and removing the cigarette from his fingers. She couldn't understand quite how Bellmore could drop asleep so quickly. There were some small yellow pills next to his glass of gin. She tapped harder at his face.

"What could I do?"

The words were faint, almost unintelligible. Jane lent forward over Bellmore.

"Chris, what did you do?"

There was no response from Bellmore and his eyes had closed. Jane looked round. There was no way of judging precisely how much he had drunk because of the profusion of bottles in the room.

Jane loosened Bellmore's tie round his neck. She could feel his heart beating strongly and he was muttering something that she could not make out.

"Chris! Chris!" she said loudly, but Bellmore, apart from a rasping breathing, had lapsed into silence. Jane disentangled herself.

With one eye on Bellmore she reached for his jacket and was about to search his pockets when she stopped. Something in the room had changed and she had to work out what it was. The jazz dirge had stopped and the room was more silent, but that wasn't it. There was something else.

She looked up and saw a pair of eyes watching her from the doorway of the room. A woman was standing in the shadow looking at her.

"Well," the woman said softly, "you didn't take long to show up did you?"

Jane dropped Bellmore's jacket.

"I must say," the woman said as she moved closer to Jane, "I do think you are more than dear Christopher deserves. Perhaps he really has got the hidden depths he goes on about. I do assure you his charm quickly fades and he really isn't very good in bed. But then," she said, after a slight pause, "I suppose you know that already."

She turned away from Jane and started circling round the room like an estate agent.

"None of this is his you know," she pronounced. "It all belongs to me." She stopped. "No, that is not quite true. Chris collects decanters. A perfectly reasonable hobby but one I find intensely irritating. You can have those–" she indicated an array of glass in the drinks cabinet below the assembled bottles. "I would be glad to get rid of them. Take them to a car boot sale or something. Except that poor Chris doesn't have a car either, not even a company one as KM have just sacked him. But perhaps he hasn't quite managed to tell you that."

"Look," Jane interrupted. "I do assure you that it is not what you think it is–"

"Please don't bother. All the women who fuck my husband say that. I think that it the right way of putting it, isn't it C.B.?" She favoured Jane with a patronising smile. "I don't really need to know anything about you. I am afraid you are just a statistic attached to a loser. My lawyers will be in touch. Oh, by the way, I would be grateful if you

145

could tell my husband that I expect him to leave the house tomorrow. I can see he wouldn't be capable of leaving tonight."

Bellmore's wife was buttoning the top of her coat. She picked up a heavy plain glass decanter that was on the top of the drinks cabinet and walked out of the room. Jane could see through the small window in the corner of the room that there was a BMW in the drive. She heard the front door close. She wondered how she had not managed to notice the car driving up. Outside there was the sound of smashing glass.

The noise seemed to rouse Bellmore. She heard him stirring behind her.

"Bitch!" Bellmore was muttering. "Bitch!"

In raising himself to the vertical he had knocked over one of the blue lamps. It lit the way into the hall like a searchlight. Jane moved decisively towards the door. The stream of light lit a picture on the oval table. Two adults and two children posed in a sunlit Tuscan landscape. The sky was the dazzling blue that only holiday photographs ever seem to capture. Two adults and two children with a selection of bicycles posing outside a white painted villa with terracotta roof tiles. Christopher Bellmore and his family stared happily at the camera. They were different people in a different land. In both the faces of the boy and girl Jane could recognise the faint imprint of a cherub's features.

Behind her the original cherub was swearing ever more loudly. Jane closed the front door behind her.

The curtains next door were twitching as Jane hurried down the drive. She thought she could see a face in the window of the house opposite. There would be no difficulty in recognising Jane's car either. It would be the most modest in the neighbourhood.

"Damn," Jane said. "Damn."

She started to run.

CHAPTER TWENTY

"It was a pretty crazy thing to do Jane."

Diana Vere put the coffee she had made down on the table. "Mind you, judging by your appearance, all this seems to agree with you. It has got the colour back in your cheeks. I thought you might just dry up in the Treasury. People do. It would have been a great waste. I'm glad to see you haven't lost your capability to surprise."

"It was a stupid thing to do."

"That's undeniable. But at least you know more about Christopher Bellmore. It might be useful."

"Yes," Jane said. "I suppose so."

She would have gone on to say how disappointing she had found the expedition. It had really added nothing very much to her knowledge except that it was clear that Bellmore couldn't have access to the £250 million. Apart from her initial admission she didn't really want to talk about it. When, if, Bellmore sobered up she could try to speak to him again. She couldn't talk about her meeting with Mark with the police on his tail. She looked up and smiled.

"But what are you doing here?"

"I said I would drop round if I found out anything. Besides I was worried. They said you had left the office and there was no reply from this number. I had just parked across the road when you came roaring up wild-eyed. I don't think you are quite safe to be let out on your own and as far as I can see there is virtually nothing to eat in the flat. I'm seeing Toby later. Why don't you join us for supper? We're meeting at that rather nice restaurant behind the National Theatre. Toby is going directly there when he has finished in the House. It will be a bit after ten. Do come."

"I'd like to, my appetite seems to have become voracious in the last few days. But are you sure? If you were planning a simple supper just for the two of you -"

Diana Vere laughed. "Really, Darling, it is not as though we have just started going out together. Toby would love to see you. He always appreciates female company, particularly the good-looking kind. In fact I won't take no for an answer."

"In that case I'd love to come. But what information have you got for me? Why don't we get that out of the way?"

Diana Vere curled herself into the sofa.

"I am not sure it is anything too startling but you may have other ideas. Let me get my thoughts in order. Do you mind if I smoke?"

"No, not at all."

Diana produced her usual small flat tin of cigars.

"It concentrates the mind. But Toby hates it."

"You could give it up, or smoke on the sly."

Diana Vere looked rather pained at the suggestion.

"It's addictive as far as I am concerned. And I don't want to deceive him, just to keep the inconvenience to a minimum."

Toby had a constituency in the Midlands, with a wife and three children in residence. He spent Sunday night to Thursday night in London when the House of Commons was sitting. On those nights, as he had done for five years, he slept with Diana. On Friday and Saturday he slept with his wife.

Diana lit the cigar and puffed contemplatively into the air.

"It's probably best to start with Christopher Bellmore. KM has suspended him. Two reasons. The main board in New York are distinctly upset about the Mandell fiasco and need a victim to be going on with. The other reason is that they have just found out that he has a criminal record. A car export business he was once involved in - high performance cars for export to the Middle East. Most of the cars were stolen as it turned out. Bellmore was very co-operative with the police and got a suspended sentence. He didn't tell KM when he was employed by them. If he had they wouldn't have touched him."

"Do they think he had anything to do with the money going missing?"

"I don't think they are very happy about his role. His dubious past connections also don't help. Why?"

"I am sure he knows more than he is telling, that is why I went to see him. But there is something I don't understand. The house -"

"Belongs to Mrs Bellmore as she said. She runs a business from it. It was inherited."

"So what has Bellmore been doing with his money? Even if he hasn't got access to the £250, million bankers are hardly underpaid. If his wife had money in the first place that should make him better off."

"Bellmore is something of a high roller. So is Jackie Bellmore if it comes to that. Bellmore also still dabbles with cars, stocks and shares, futures, anything that might turn him over a quicker buck. He is a gambler. Recently, however, he has been on a slide, a whole series of deals that have turned sour. He owes money everywhere and his wife is anything but keen to bail him out."

"No car, and down to his last decanters-"

"I wouldn't know about the decanters but he does have a car or two left. Not that they are going to help his overall situation and not that his wife knows anything about them. Bellmore has been trying to create a back pocket over the years that his wife knows nothing about."

"Any girlfriends?"

"A couple of the secretaries at KM. That was another thing they were not keen about."

"What about Paula Black? Is there anything on her?"

Diana shrugged. "We can't find anything at all. No mortgage records, credit cards, offences, nothing at all. On the records she doesn't seem to exist. I even checked whether she was on benefit, but nothing. Ultimately anonymous. Any special reason why we should be particularly interested?"

"Maybe. I don't know. She was close to Mandell."

"Mark?"

"No," Jane said icily, "David."

"You do need to be careful," Diana Vere said with an amused smile. "Mark Mandell is an attractive man but you shouldn't let that suspend your judgement. There are some question marks around him. We think that at least some of the money that disappeared from the Mandell companies may have landed up in his hands offshore and the police want to see him about his father's death."

Diana looked at her curiously.

"What about David Mandell?" Jane said firmly, anxious to cut off the debate about Mark.

"Tough businessman, important connections, important enemies."

"And any involvement in a major fraud would be totally out of character?"

"From what we know at present."

"Anything on the time he died?"

Diana raised an enquiring eyebrow.

"My Director knows the police pathologist," Jane explained. Apparently there is some dispute about the time of David Mandell's death."

"I didn't know that. The Met are never very co-operative. Less now that there is this move to get us into the fight against organised crime."

Diana Vere blew a smoke ring into the air and watched the frail structure ascend to the ceiling before disintegrating.

"I am trying to give up," she said after a moment. "I've got it down to about five a day."

"It's fine," Jane said. "It just reminded me. Simon liked small cigars."

"We used to smoke them together, before he met you."

"I didn't know that," Jane said.

"No reason why he should have told you. It wasn't anything serious. It might have been something, most probably a fling. I specialise in those. But whatever it was, it wasn't to be, because you appeared on the scene. I remember when he first saw you. He had been holding my arm and then he wasn't. He was probably feeling guilty because he was very attentive for the rest of the evening when he wasn't trying to speak to you. You were wearing that dress you had asked me to advise you on, the one I thought you looked gorgeous in. He was looking pretty OK as well. I had recommended the shirt he was wearing. It had particularly finely stitched cuffs. You made a perfect couple."

"Simon didn't tell me you had been going out together."

"Nothing to tell. He only had eyes for you. He was right anyway. I wouldn't have had the commitment he was looking for."

"I'm sorry."

"No need. It wouldn't have worked. I would have been too detached for him. Years of selective breeding I imagine. Large cold houses without proper heating. It makes one curiously self-reliant. If one encounters an unsuccessful love affair, or more of a rebuff as in this case, one retires glass in hand with a good book in front of the fire and lets the world exert its mellowing influence. It's quite pleasurable really. The weight of history can be summoned to smooth over the particular cares of the present. Aesthetics drowns us all in time."

"I didn't realise."

"It's tunnel vision isn't it, or love? I envy you the experience. Something that holds the rest of the world at bay must be very pleasurable."

"It is," Jane said, and then she added, "it was."

"So what about Robert Stuart? Sally seems very keen."

"Robert had a difficult relationship he was coming out of. A lawyer in California. We've needed a bit of time."

"What for?"

"Sorting things out."

"And have you?"

"There were some earrings he gave me."

"The ones in the bread bin?"

"Yes."

"They're rather splendid."

"A family heirloom. Robert lent them to me. He said they ought to be used. It was a generous gesture."

Diana was looking at her closely.

"I think it's a bit more than that."

"Robert had planned a romantic dinner, or at least I think he had.

We got interrupted by Sally and Martin, and then he got a business call, a problem at his bank. So he had to go. It probably wouldn't have come to anything anyway. Part of me was glad to see Sally. I'm not sure what I would have said if I had thought Robert was really being serious."

"I think he was."

"I don't see how you can say that."

"The diamond earrings. They're fairly recent for an heirloom. I'm certain they were designed by a woman called Fay Goodwin. She has a shop in Glasgow. She was in *Country Life* in November. Distinctive design, really rather good, mostly noted for her platinum settings and the intense white light she produces when they sparkle. It's just that she is in her late twenties. She is something of a prodigy but she didn't make her breakthrough more than four years ago. I can't see that they could have been handed down so quickly. Perhaps generations are speeding up, but not to that extent. Robert Stuart is more serious than you think. He didn't inherit them. He bought them for you."

"Are you serious?"

"You can check it out for yourself. Fay's establishment is just off George Square. About five minutes from the station. I have rather dull relations there. Shopping make the visit bearable."

"If we are going out I need to freshen up," Jane said.

Jane walked into the bathroom. She splashed cold water on her face and looked at herself in the mirror. She didn't know whether she found Diana's revelations about the earrings comforting or not. If Robert had judged they would have been too much to accept as a simple present he was probably right. Perhaps he had had an overwhelming desire to buy them for her and this was the way he had decided to manage the situation. She didn't doubt that Diana was right but somehow it didn't seem to make the situation with Robert any clearer.

More helpful was Diana's information about Christopher Bellmore. He had a clear motive for a major fraud because of the financial difficulties he was facing. That, at least, was reassuringly straightforward. More disturbing was the fact that Christopher Bellmore, unless he was a master of deception, bore very little resemblance to a man who had any successful part in swindling anyone out of £250 million.

She turned out the bathroom light and opened the door. For some reason Diana had extinguished the lights in the small hallway so that for a moment she was lost in shadows.

"Diana?"

There was no answer but Jane was aware of a form close to her and a restraining arm that turned into a comforting one.

"What is - ?"

A hand appeared out of the gloom to lightly cover her mouth.

"Shhh-" Diana Vere whispered. "Keep quiet and do as I say."

"Diana, what on earth are you doing?" Jane found her own voice had adopted the same strangled whisper as Diana Vere. Even then the words were scarcely audible through Diana's long elegant fingers that were splayed warningly across her lips. It was a curiously intimate gesture. It was as though this was the past and they were engaged in some undergraduate prank.

"Jane," Diana hissed. "Just do what I say. Please. This is important."

She dropped her hand from Jane's mouth.

"I want you to go back into the living room. Go and stand by the window. Pretend you are looking out over the river or something like that. Then pretend you are looking at something and move to the very edge of the window. Oh .. And stay relaxed."

There was an edge in Diana's voice that was unfamiliar. The normal languor with ironic edges had been replaced by a definite and positive purpose. Diana also had something in her hand, something like a pair of elongated opera glasses.

Below Jane the lights from the globes on the towpath shone round and clear on the river. The water was black and static and there was nothing moving across its flat and unwelcoming surface. Jane looked for the brightly lit boat of her dream, lights reflected on the water, on its endless journey to forever. Then she started her imaginary examination of a mystery document on the small table. As though in deep concentration, she moved to the edge of the window, took one long last abstract look out across the river and turned and retraced her steps across the living room. Diana appeared in the doorway of the bathroom with her finger across her lips and then a thumbs up sign.

"Diana-" Jane said warningly. "What on earth was all that about?"

"There was somebody outside. There was a flash of light I saw. It looked as though it came off a pair of binoculars. I needed to find out if there was anybody there."

"And was there?"

"Oh yes."

"Who?"

"More difficult. Whoever it was, probably a man, was down by the riverside, hidden. I couldn't see much more than a shadow."

"I don't get this. Why all the whispering?"

"Whoever it was might have had sound equipment with them as well so that they could hear what we were saying, but I am pretty sure they didn't. Anyway they've gone now. Could have been the Met. Have you upset them?"

"This isn't a joke?"

"Oh no, perfectly serious. But there is nothing we can do now." Diana Vere looked at her watch. "You'd better finish freshening up otherwise we'll be late for Toby."

*

Toby Jessop was an elegant man with immaculately groomed hair and a well fed, affluent, appearance.

In the warmth of the restaurant Jane relaxed. The events of the day faded to a distance and there was something infinitely calming about Toby Jessop's manner.

"How about a pudding?"

Pudding was one of the words that sprang naturally from Toby Jessop. There was a natural urge in him not to take life too seriously and always to have fun. Jane could see what attracted Diana to him. He was also meant to have refused ministerial office more than once to be able to devote himself wholeheartedly to the interests of his constituents and to the lucrative series of appointments that a well connected and senior backbencher on the Government side could expect.

"Yes, and perhaps some coffee."

Toby Jessop beamed benevolently at her and looked around for a waiter. Diana had disappeared to make a phone call.

"Diana tells me you have been working on this Mandell business," he said conversationally. "What is going on? Nobody seems to know but there are rumours that the money will never be recovered. Is that true? You Treasury people always seem to know everything. Did you see that story in the FT? They seemed to think it would affect the willingness of American banks to run their European operations from the UK."

"As far as I know there is nothing definite at the moment."

"Didn't Ken Ormond have something to do with Mandell?"

"Apparently so," Jane said in a neutral tone. "I'm sure he would be very pleased if it can be sorted out. I can't believe he would want to be associated with anything like this. It can't be good for his career." Jane weighed up the understatement.

"He hasn't exactly got a career left," Toby Jessop lowered his voice a tone or two and looked round to check the surrounding tables were free of anyone who might resemble a journalist. "The heart attack he suffered was rather more serious than they are saying. Apparently there is no chance of him resuming his duties at all. He may even have to give up his seat. The story about him convalescing and then resuming his duties is just to give the PM a breathing space to find somebody to fill Ken's shoes. That won't be easy. The police liked him. I can't see any of the contenders quite managing to strike up the same relationship, which could cause problems. All the Chief Constables I have ever met have always been terribly touchy. It must be having to go round in those ridiculous uniforms. Have you ever been to one of those ACPO conferences where they all meet up? They are always trying to give you ceremonial truncheons. I've got about six in the flat. I would get rid of them but if I ever got burgled and I didn't report them missing they would know. I suppose it is the perils of politics."

There was a sheen of goodwill that seemed to cling to Toby Jessop together with an energy that was compelling and attractive. Jane found herself looking at him foolishly for a moment. This was the first time she had been alone with him. It was probably just good manners or a knack that he had that suggested all his attention was focused on her to the exclusion of everyone else. Diana, she remembered, had once told her that Toby Jessop's wife did not entirely disapprove of

155

the fact that in London during the week he lived discreetly with his mistress. At least, Diana had said, Vivienne Jessop knew where her husband was. Jane could see that Jessop, only in his mid-forties, with consultancies here and there and a good reputation in the House, would be attractive to any number of women.

"But I'm boring you," Toby Jessop continued. "I promised Diana that I wouldn't talk shop but I do find it difficult not to sometimes. The great thing about politics is that it is the one forum where real personality does matter. You can't really be trained to deal with the pressure. In the end your true character comes out. Curious, really, but I do think it is an honourable profession." He smiled at her. "Like the Civil Service actually, although I don't suppose one is really meant to say that either."

Jane poured herself some more coffee. Despite the food she realised that she was a little light headed. She must have drunk more than she intended.

Diana had re-emerged and was talking to a woman two tables away. Jane had wondered what precautions she and Toby had taken at being seen together in public. To judge from the night's events they were relatively relaxed. Not, of course, that Toby was a member of the government. His potential to form part of the current debate about political sleaze and moral standards was limited. Besides, Jane reflected, it would be difficult for an observer to detect which of the two women accompanying him was his mistress. On the evidence of any observer to the earlier events of the evening in Christopher Bellmore's house, the most likely candidate was probably herself. She shivered.

"Are you cold?"

"Tired," Jane said, "but pleasantly unwound. It's been a long day."

"Yes. Diana told me how busy you were."

It was difficult to know quite where Diana's remarks might have begun and quite where they would have stopped. Jane found her infinitely mysterious. They were different people. Diana had said that the relationship with Toby satisfied her, and that, in most ways, there was nothing more she could ask for. Jane knew that she had been quite serious and that she, Jane, could never have settled for the arrangement that Diana had entered into with Toby. And Sally, of course, was always going to be the one of the three who got married first. The surprise in Sally's case was probably only that she had limited herself to three children.

"Sorry," Diana said as she returned to the table, "friends from Wiltshire."

Diana had a cottage there. Sometimes, rather than staying in London at the weekend, she drove there with a couple of books simply to relax and read.

"It is going to snow tomorrow," Toby said.

"You should know, Jane, that he is very unreliable in his forecasts. They are second only to his sense of direction, which he always gets wrong."

"Being invariably wrong in one's sense of direction could, I would have thought, be a rather valuable asset. One simply needs to head off in the opposite direction to the one I recommend. But never mind about that. I am absolutely certain it will snow tomorrow."

"They have been saying it is going to snow for about a week on the weather forecasts."

"Be that as it may," Toby insisted looking at Diana, "I guarantee it will snow tomorrow.

"I'm sure you are right," Jane said.

"At last," Toby Jessop said. "A true believer."

CHAPTER TWENTY-ONE

The seriousness of Kenneth Ormond's heart condition and its effect on government fortunes and the new policies on law and order was the first item on the seven o'clock news on the radio the following morning. Jane was barely awake. She had emerged from a deep sleep only at the promptings of her alarm clock. She had dreamt of snowflakes falling thickly to earth and covering everything in a blanket of whiteness.

For a moment she lay in the warm feeling totally relaxed. There was something reassuring and normal about the way the news, whatever its content, was presented on Radio 4. The same programme structure was followed every weekday and only a major war with the continent would overturn it. It increased the sense of security that she had built up during her sleep. The events of the day before had happened to a stranger, not herself.

She made herself coffee and found that there was fresh milk in the fridge and croissants on top of the stale bread covering the earrings. Diana had brought them round the night before. It was slightly shaming that Diana should assume in advance, rightly, that the apartment would be bereft of fresh food. She lay soaking in the bath as the journalists got to the really interesting part of the morning's programme - who would succeed Kenneth Ormond.

Toby Jessop's report had been borne out by the morning's

announcements. She had thought when the story first broke that Ormond might have overstated his illness to buy himself time while efforts were made to sort out the finances of the Mandell group. Even his direst political enemies could not be seen to be trying to unseat him while he was lying in a hospital bed. But she now realised this was fanciful. No politician as accomplished as Ormond who wanted to remain in the game would admit to physical weakness. Kenneth Ormond was obviously seriously ill.

It was unfortunate, but it did mean that there was not the same personal pressure on her to produce immediate results, and probably not quite the same backing as Ormond had been able to provide when he was well. Inspector Norman might be more difficult to handle under the new circumstances. She sipped her coffee and shuddered slightly. She did not wish to experience events such as those with Bellmore's wife again. She suspected too that the mystery watcher outside her apartment had been one of Norman's men. It was time for easing off and getting out, and not for getting mixed up in the proceedings of the Metropolitan police. Besides only Ian Hart's actions were going to solve the basic problem of what had happened to the missing Mandell millions.

She got out of the bath and wrapped herself in a large warm towel. She looked in the mirror and dragged the scales out from under the cupboard. Despite the increased wine intake her inability to properly equip the apartment with food meant that she had lost weight in the last two years.

Outside, little flurries of snowflakes were falling on the grey river, the forerunners of Toby Jessop's snowstorm that would drive away the polar cold that had frozen the ground and gripped London for the last two weeks. For five minutes she found herself watching the flurries but then they died away. Jane pulled the towel closer around her and went in search of clothes for the office.

The dress she had worn the night before was neatly hung in her wardrobe. It was almost as though somebody else had been in the apartment to hang up her clothes. She really had no recollection of doing it herself. She was getting like her mother and living in multiple time. There was a simple cure. All this amateur investigation had to stop. With Kenneth Ormond's illness there were no obligations on her. She would push the official investigation forward, but no more. She would raise no questions about Mark Mandell. A quick word with Peter Green and leave Ian Hart to make the running. If the money was found there was every chance that Mark Mandell's affairs could be sorted out relatively painlessly. Simple.

It still seemed relatively straightforward by the time that she got to the Treasury. She smiled at the security guards. She needed to have a further word with Ian before talking to Peter Green. Her boss was not discreet.

There were no signs of life in the outer office. She looked at her watch. Suzanne was always here by this time. Perhaps there had been transport problems. Perhaps she was ill. Jane walked down the corridor. The Treasury was bustling into life. If Suzanne was ill she was bound to have telephoned. She took a few steps further down the corridor to the office of her Grade 6. Brian would know what was happening or would be able to find out quickly.

He was looking at a single sheet of paper on his desk with a worried expression on his face.

"Hello Jane," he said.

He put the piece of paper to one side. Jane saw it was a list of names connected by questioning arrows.

"The reorganisation," Brian said following her eyes. "You asked me to make some proposals. It's easier when you can think about everyone together."

Jane looked at the list of names. She had thirty people working for her. Brian, who agonised endlessly about such matters, was obviously preparing to share the burden with her.

"We must meet up," Jane said pre-emptively. "We need to get these decisions right."

Brian looked a little more relaxed. "They do affect everybody's life."

There was a silence, which she saw Brian felt no compunction to fill. He clearly regarded it as a moment of rich reflection.

"How is morale?" Jane said. "It seems to me that we are on the right track," she added as she sensed Brian might be tempted to approach the problem from first principles.

"I think it is better," he said after a moment. "Ian spoke to me."

"I am sure it was not the only time," Jane said.

"No, no," Brian added quickly. "You don't understand. It was a purely social conversation, not business. About football."

"I didn't know Ian was interested in football."

"He might not have mentioned it to you, but he is. Particularly the statistical side of the game."

"That's very interesting," Jane said, and before Brian could develop his theme, asked "has anyone heard from Suzanne? She doesn't seem to be in yet."

"Isn't she taking leave? That was what I understood. But perhaps she has changed it?"

"No, no. Of course you're right, now I come to think of it," Jane heard herself saying rather foolishly. "I've just got the dates mixed up."

She backed out of the room and nearly collided with a trolley stacked with boxes of paper. How could she have forgotten? She supposed that it was because she had hardly been in the office the day before. Even so it was a little alarming. She needed some coffee to get her brain into gear.

Jane found a jar of decaffeinated in Suzanne's room but no sign of anything real. Jane couldn't remember whether they had run out or not and whether Suzanne was in the habit of locking it away. Suzanne kept her keys in the bottom of the box that contained the manuals for the computers. Jane fished out the manuals that detailed five hundred applications of the machine that she would never wish to use and of which she would probably never be aware. She picked out the keys and opened Suzanne's desk drawer.

This morning the keys to the filing cabinets were not the only ones. A Chubb and a Yale were attached to a square enamelled key ring that depicted Tintin and Snowy walking purposefully through a dark blue night. These were not Suzanne's keys and Ian Hart was a Tintin fan. She picked the key ring up. Attached to it, in Ian's small handwriting, was the address of his flat in Hackney.

"Jane!"

Jane dropped the keys back into the draw.

Brian was in the doorway looking worried.

"Yes?" she said rather sharply.

"I don't want to trouble you, but I would appreciate a word before Monday. I did mention it to Suzanne yesterday but she did say you were rather busy. It is just that I think it needs pushing forward."

"I'm sorry," Jane said. "Of course we must talk. Just let me find some coffee."

"It's behind the plant," Brian said. "To your right. At least you only have the caffeinated in the morning don't you?"

It was a rhetorical question. Brian clearly knew everything about the detail of the social side of her office habits.

"Yes I do. Thanks. How about ten o'clock?"

"Right," Brian said happily. "I'll be there."

Jane watched the smiling face retreat to the door. Brian would have made a good courtier. He had a natural aptitude for walking backward. She frowned after he had left. Was she that difficult to get to see? She had always thought of herself as accessible.

She looked back down into the drawer and picked the keys up. She tried to remember quite what handing over a set of keys signified in a relationship. Then she dropped them back in the drawer. Sue and Ian's private life was none of her business. Jane believed in clear water between the private and the personal. Ian and Sue were being discreet, as she would have expected.

More important was whether the approach Ian was following would come to anything. She rang his number. No reply. That was hardly a surprise. She had given him leave to stay away until he had figured the Mandell problem out.

She rang Ian again at two minutes to ten. There was still no reply. He was obviously working at home. She thought for a moment of telephoning his home number but realised that she didn't know where Suzanne kept her address book. She put the telephone down. She would contact Ian once she had completed her business with Brian Lloyd and then she would fix an appointment with Peter Green. She sighed. Brian was overwhelmingly thorough and did not speak quickly. Everything he said was well considered and unduly precise. When it came to the future careers of their colleagues he would be taking additional care in what he said. Jane shuddered. Meetings with Brian reminded her of eternity. Ten o'clock. There was a precise knock at the door.

"It's a bit tricky," Brian Lloyd said slowly by way of an opening statement. "Perhaps I could just run over a few points."

Jane nodded. The meeting would take at least an hour and probably considerably longer.

"Let's sit at the table." That way, Jane thought, she would be able to look out through the window and check on the progress of Toby Jessop's snow that was gathering into ever denser flurries. She needed a calming backdrop.

As Brian coaxed his scene setting remarks into a preliminary order she had no immediate action to hang her thoughts on and her memory banks started ticking over on other issues.

Why had she left Mark the previous evening? She had told herself on the way to the car that she should try to be fair to Robert Stuart. She had told herself that Diana Vere might come up with something. None of it was very convincing. Perhaps she had been afraid of what she might find if she had gone on. And what would that have been? That actually they were physically incompatible? That hadn't been the problem. There was guilt of course, although if she searched her heart of hearts she didn't really think that it was quite moral unease that had prevented her from staying.

She saw that Brian had stopped talking and was obviously expecting her to say something.

"Could you just run that past me again Brian," she said. "I need time to think it through."

Brian Lloyd nodded with satisfaction that Jane was not intent on tackling the meeting with her usual impetuosity, and started again, more slowly than before.

CHAPTER TWENTY-TWO

Brian Lloyd didn't leave until well after twelve and then only with some urging by Jane. Immediately he did go she dialled Ian Hart's number. There was no reply. It was possible that Ian had come in and gone to lunch. Jane walked down the corridor to Ian's cubby-hole of an office. There were reports of various kinds strewn round his desk but the central part of it was cleared of paper. Ian Hart hadn't been in. Some sheets of A4 paper had been thrown to one side. A whole series of figures had been written in pencil. The first group read 21012003210402. Underneath this group the same figures had been spilt up - 21 01 20 03 21 04 02. Down the rest of the page other figures, sometimes repeated, had been listed across the paper. The other sheets below contained similar runs of figures. On one page Ian had added an exclamation mark next to a seven - 7! It was the only figure seven on the page but Jane could get no sense of the significance of the exclamation mark. She looked over the pages of figures. Low numbers predominated but to no particular rhyme or rhythm that Jane could understand.

What was Ian doing? He wasn't just following up some sort of hunch. He was trying to detect some sort of systematic progression in the numbers in the transactions that had seen KM's money spirited away from them. That was clear. It looked to Jane as if he was seeking some sort of cipher that would be the key to finding out where the missing Mandell £250 million was. What she couldn't tell was how much progress he was really making.

The telephone rang.

She picked it up.

"Jane? There is a call for you," Brian Lloyd's voice said. "Somebody from the Bank. Wouldn't give his name."

"That's fine. Put him on."

Jane wondered quite how Brian Lloyd had known she was in Ian's office. Still it was possible that it was Ian calling from the Bank. Hadn't he said something about seeing Perry?

"Hello," she said eagerly.

"Jane?"

It wasn't Ian. It wasn't Perry. It was Mark Mandell's idea of discretion. She felt the slight nervous tremble in her knee again. This call wasn't going to deliver the magic answer.

"Yes," she said softly.

"I wondered how things were going. I'm not sure the film is going to get sorted. I thought things might be improving your end."

Jane looked at the run of figures on the desk in front of her. She saw that Ian Hart had scribbled two words on the bottom of one of the sheets. It was in Ian's small, neat, capital letters. And although one of the words was followed by a question mark there was a rather more confidence boosting exclamation mark following the second.

RANDOM? NO!

"I don't honestly know." Jane looked at Ian's words again as though there might be some hidden meaning to them. "I think there may be some possibilities. I hope to know more soon. Can I get back to you?"

"When?"

"I have to visit my mother. I can make later this evening."

"Any time."

"Ten-thirty then. My apartment."

"Fine." Mark Mandell hesitated. "Thanks."

There was a click at the other end of the line and the telephone went dead. Mark Mandell had sounded as though he was getting desperate but at least his call had been reasonably discreet.

She sat down in Ian's chair. There was perspiration on her forehead

THE SKY BLUE PARCEL

but when she wiped her hand across it, it was cold, unreal. She felt a little faint. Just for once she would need to be sensible about lunch. Why had she said she would visit her mother anyway? Richard always said her mother noticed, but she was not so certain. Sometimes she thought she could pay all her visits in the first fifty-two days of the year for all the difference it would make.

Jane walked to the front lobby. The efficient doorman confirmed that Ian had not set foot in the building. He was obviously still working on the problem.

In the outer office she checked the keys to Ian's flat in Hackney were still there. There was no telephone number, but Suzanne's address book was also sitting invitingly on the desk. Once Suzanne had a number she was always able to retrieve it. Jane flicked the book open and looked under H. Suzanne had not disappointed her. There was the number in the familiar clear round hand looking no different from all the others with which the book was crowded.

Jane hurried back into her office. Ian's number was engaged. She looked out of the window. The breeze had eased and the snow was falling vertically down. She pressed redial. The line was still busy.

It was two hours later that she decided she had to do something. Ian Hart's telephone had been constantly engaged. He might have left the receiver off the hook. It might be hours, or days, before he noticed. He might even have done it deliberately to avoid the possibility of distraction. If Suzanne were travelling home by train it would probably be the evening before she got to her parents in Carlisle. There would be no incoming calls he would need to take.

There was one obvious solution. She could drive to Ian's flat and speak to him face to face. Despite the snow she could be there in forty minutes if the traffic was reasonable.

She locked her desk drawer and walked into the outer office and, after a moment, removed Ian's keys. She needed, she decided, to get into Ian's flat. If Ian was out for some reason she could at least leave a message.

By the time she had threaded her way out of central London and parked the car it was nearly dusk. Ian had said he lived near the station, which she could see on the other side of the main road. She opened the car door. A Chinese girl in an open black coat revealing leather hot pants and a low cut red top moved forward towards her. When she saw Jane the smile on her face faded and she retreated into the shadows of a dimly lit grocery shop with a protective steel grill over the window.

There was a train pulling into the station. On both sides of the track long expanses of platform stretched back along a dead straight railway line. Overhead lights on long elongated columns shone down, illuminating people shuffling off the train so that some were now in light and some in shadow. It might have been a train arriving at the Gulag. She hurried on, breathing in the cold air.

The house on the end of the terraced row in which Ian's flat was situated had been extensively renovated. She remembered Ian saying it was where a gangland murder had taken place and his shock at seeing the house on a television programme and thinking it familiar before realising it was two houses along. They had had to line the walls with tarpaper because there had been so much blood. She stopped.

There was a slight collision with the man behind her.

"Sorry," he said and walked past her and crossed the road to a line of shops below two rows of council flats that had been built as local roads in the sky, but where the concrete was now stained and weathering. Despite the cold she felt that she was sweating, almost overheating.

The front fence to the house in which Ian lived was partly missing, broken planks lying carelessly against the trunk of a giant tree that stretched upwards into the evening sky, its branches black against the darkening grey. There was a faint light showing on the ground floor of the house, shining through net curtains. It was a promising sign. That was where Ian had said his flat was.

She moved forward down the path to the front door. Four bells were marked A to D, just discernible from the street lighting. A name, not Ian's, was marked as Bell C. She decided B was the one and pressed.

There was a ringing that sounded as though it came from the right flat but there was no movement within. She waited for a moment and then rang again. There was no chance of Ian not hearing. The obvious conclusion was that he had left for the office, and that he was probably trying to contact her. She hesitated. Her previous personal initiative had ended in the ludicrous scene with Christopher Bellmore and his wife, but she could hardly turn back having come so far. There was also a strange sense of foreboding that clung to the place. It was probably no more than the effect of the decayed surroundings, made worse by the fact that it was dark.

She looked behind her. Apart from a passing car and a knot of schoolchildren milling around in a bunch across the road, there was no one. She slid her hand from her glove and fished Ian's keys from out of her handbag. The Chubb key matched the Chubb lock on the front door. A second later she was inside.

There was a faint smell of old and musty carpet in the hallway. She switched on the hall light and closed the door behind her. By the dim light of a 40-watt bulb she saw stairs leading upwards and a door to her right. On the wall the hands in the dials of a phalanx of electricity meters connected together by bunches of black wires clicked round at variable speeds. She took the Yale and opened Ian's door. The 40-watt bulb expired on the time switch.

The light she had seen from outside was a in the small entrance hall of the flat, a bright 100 watts illuminating new pink plaster on the walls and a compact white radiator pushing out heat. Thick white waxed paper had been stretched over the floor under which the outlines of individual floorboards were visible. Ian was obviously keen to keep dust to a minimum.

"Ian?"

She opened the door to her left. A large rectangular room stretched in front of her, the light from behind throwing her shadow all the way to the large square windows at the end that overlooked a garden. She switched on the light and the garden disappeared into blackness. There was an elegant wooden table and chairs by the main window and a long comfortable sofa, pictures, books, a racked stereo system, and a television. She looked at the books. There was a collection of novels, philosophy, and some books about football. For Ian they were surprisingly neatly arranged. She wondered if that had had anything to do with Suzanne. Only on the dining table was there a slightly untidy collection of papers. This was presumably where Ian had been working on the problem. Leading off this room, down a few steps, was a small kitchen located under the main stairwell. Everywhere the new smooth pink plaster gleamed.

There was a sound outside. Anyone looking in would see her clearly. She switched off the light and returned the room to darkness. She backed out of the room and softly closed the door.

There were two other doors off the hallway, a small white bathroom with some antique chrome taps and every towel neatly folded and in place, and then what must be the bedroom, the front room of the house facing the road. The door was slightly ajar. She walked into the room and felt for the light switch. Even as she did so she saw that she was not alone. Somebody was sleeping on the bed.

There was no time, however, to stop herself and the light blazed forth illuminating the room and its occupant. In the brief moment in time in which the room was fully illuminated she saw Ian lying in the bed. When she switched the light off she was blind in the darkness.

As her eyes recovered she saw that Ian was in a deep and untroubled sleep. She probably had every chance of leaving without Ian realising that she had been there. The bell had not woken him. There was no reason to suppose that anything else would. There was no reason for him to know that she had ever been there. Although she had touched some of the objects in the living room, she had not moved anything.

Ian looked as though he had been working all night and that nothing would wake him. The white light filtering from outside through the gap in the bedroom curtain was falling across his face, making him seem for a moment quite ghostlike. She edged backwards. There was still the opportunity to leave unseen and unrecorded. It was a good plan. She still didn't know why he hadn't responded to her calls. She stopped. She smiled and then felt the smile freeze on her face. Ian looked as though nothing would awaken him because nothing would. There was no movement for a very simple reason. Ian was dead.

She held her breath. There was no sound of breathing or human life in the room. She moved forward. Ian's forehead was dampish but cold. Ian was no longer in the room. He had simply left his body as a reminder of who he had once been, but he had gone.

Jane felt sick. The acid in the pit of her stomach stirred and she found herself retching and fighting for breath. She put her hands to her face and massaged away the horrible grin that was controlling her features. Then she pinched herself as hard as she could. The new source of pain acted as a temporary distraction to the rest of her body. She gulped for air.

Moving as slowly as an invalid she pushed the door to the hallway closed and walked across to the window. She saw that the great bulk of the tree trunk cut out sight of the middle part of the bedroom from any passing car. There seemed to be no one walking past. She found a curtain pull and they glided into place, good, thick protective curtains against the cold and the outside world. The room was now totally dark and she had to feel her way back to the door and the light switch.

She switched the light back on. Ian Hart was lying face up on his own bed, dressed only in a pair of blue patterned boxer shorts that looked as though they were new. The duvet on the bed was drawn up a little above his knees. His body was slim and fit. He might have been a model of a young Greek God sleeping. His eyes, thankfully, were closed.

For a moment she willed herself to believe that Ian was sleeping and could be awakened. There seemed to be nothing wrong with him that waking would not cure. There was rigidity in his rib cage that made it seem that he was eternally breathing in, bracing his body for some athletic purpose. Although the expression on his face was calm the fingers on his right hand were clenched as though he expected there might also be trouble in Heaven.

Jane took a deeper breath than she had managed before and knelt over the bed. She could see no reason why Ian should be dead. There were no marks on his body that she could see, not even the faintest bruise.

On the bedside table was an alarm clock, a book by Camus, and Ian Hart's two Ventolin inhalers. She picked them up. They were both full and within easy reach.

She stood there for a moment. She supposed it was possible that it had been an accident. Indeed it was probably likely. Except that she didn't believe it. It was another sudden death to add to David Mandell's, another accident. And the accidents might have extended to her, mashed to a pulp underneath the wheels of a white oil tanker.

She put the two inhalers back where they had come from and walked into the hall where she switched the light on. The newly painted white door to the bedroom faced her unblinkingly. She probably needed to telephone the police, although she had no idea what she would say to them. She walked back into the main room, pulled the curtains and switched the light on. The papers on the table were the same sorts of lists of figures that she had found in Ian's office. He had also helpfully written on the top sheet of paper - again in capitals, normally a sign that he was getting close.

42 MATCHES!
MUST BE FOREST!

She put the paper down and then looked round her. The telephone was on a small black sideboard in the corner of the room. The handset was lying alongside the main body of the telephone, exactly parallel to it. It was inconceivable that Ian would not have noticed it and it hardly seemed likely that he would have calmly placed the receiver down in such a meticulous way if he had been overcome by an attack of some kind. Perhaps he had been talking to someone and had wanted to get something from the bedroom and had been overcome there. It was the best explanation she could think of if she wanted to believe he had died accidentally. The trouble was that it wasn't plausible.

She switched the light off in the room and walked back into the hall. She needed to go through the white door of the bedroom once more and satisfy herself that he really was dead. She pushed the door open.

She nearly closed it again there and then. There was nothing to be seen except the two Ventolin inhalers and the alarm clock. She had no stomach for rummaging through any of the fitted cupboards or the chest of drawers by the window. She would want to mourn Ian, but not like this - in secret and alone. Besides there was no reason why he should hide anything away. If he had found anything out he would have telephoned or come into the office.

But she didn't close the door. There was something about the whole situation that was profoundly wrong. Ian's death couldn't just be explained away on surface value. There wasn't sufficient cause for it to have happened. It didn't make any sort of sense. Whatever had happened to him, some sign was still operating this side of the line and beckoning to her.

Think, she said to herself. That is what you are meant to be good at and what you need to do now. Look - and think. There's something here that needs to be sorted. You owe that to Ian. This is going to be a still point in a spinning world. She started counting to slow the world down and get control of her emotions and then stopped.

His right hand was tightly closed. That gesture had not been needed for the next world. It had been needed for this. She tried to pull the fingers apart but they were almost rigid. It took her a minute to prise them open.

Inside was a small piece of paper screwed into a ball. She spread it out on the bedside table. On it two sets of numbers had been written. They were like all the other sets of Ian's numbers but for the fact that each had a single decisive tick at the end. She folded the paper carefully and then stuck it behind the Visa card in her wallet. She tried to knit Ian's fingers back together without success and the long tapering fingers lay apart like those of a man deciding to reach for an apple from a tree.

She stood in the small hallway as though it were some sort of airlock between two different worlds.

"I'm sorry Ian," she said.

She had difficulty closing the door to the flat when she left. The lock was stiff and it took her a moment or two. She hardly noticed the sound of another key turning and she was hardly prepared for the light in the hallway, dim as it was, to come on. She turned to find herself face to face with a man and a woman in the doorway who subjected her to a suspicious gaze.

"Just dropping something off," she said. "Ian gave me a key."

She waved the key in front of them to give extra credence to her story. The explanation hardly seemed to convince them until a sudden note of recognition crossed the man's face and he smiled at her.

"We heard you the other night," he said. "I'm Zack - this is Jazz. We live on the next floor up."

"Must fly-" Jane said, pulling her coat around her to conceal her features. The hall light clicked off but the woman pressed it on again. She hurried down the steps. They might not remember her, she told herself. It might be put down as an accidental death so no enquiries would be made. The light in the hallway had been very dim so there really was no possibility of a definite identification. She almost ran back along the road to the car until she decided that she would look less suspicious if she simply walked.

She looked behind her. A row of footprints in the snow stretched all the way back to the house she had just come from, a trail connecting her neatly to Ian's dead body. There was an obvious explanation, of course. Ian had been murdered.

CHAPTER TWENTY-THREE

She thought it through as she drove away.

Inspector Norman was coming at ten o'clock so she needed to have her explanation ready.

- And you say the body was naked when you found it?
- No, he was dressed in a pair of cotton underpants.
- Are you sure they were cotton?
- Yes.
- You looked at them closely?
- I am sure they were cotton.

Raised eyebrows.

And the rest would hardly be any better.

- This was late afternoon Miss Quinn?

Nodded assent.

- Can you think of any reason why Mr Hart would be in bed in the middle of the afternoon?
- No.

A pause.

- Why did you go there Miss Quinn? It is not an easy journey The weather was cold. The snow made driving difficult.
- I was concerned about a piece of work Mr Hart was dealing with. I couldn't get him on the telephone so I decided to drive out. It was an impulse.

- An impulse.
- Yes.
Another pause.
- You have a responsible job Miss Quinn.
- Yes.
- I am sure it involves a heavy workload.
- Yes.
- And yet you took time off to go to Mr Hart's flat on an impulse?
- Yes.
- And you had time to drive to East London?
- Yes.
- Not a short journey?
- Not a long one.

There was a warning car horn and Jane braked hard. The Peugeot slithered to a halt on the snowy road.

Her story wasn't looking too good even before she got to the question of how she had managed to have Ian Hart's keys in her possession. If the events with Christopher Bellmore's wife and her meetings with Mark Mandell were known to Norman she would be hard pressed to find an explanation that even she would find plausible.

She could have telephoned the police from Ian's flat and told the absolute truth. There had been a great attraction in the proposition. It would hand over the problem to the proper authorities, the police, Norman even. She could just stop, answer the questions, and not be responsible any longer. Giving up have never seemed so attractive. But somehow it wasn't an option. Not before she checked out the numbers that Ian had been working on when he died, and not before she had had a chance to talk to Mark Mandell.

She turned off the road into the grounds of Silverlawns. As she got out of the car the snow flurries that had accompanied her journey from Hackney and which had been filling up her retreating footsteps eased. When she got to the main door of the building they had stopped altogether.

Her mother was cooking bacon under the grill, protected from any assault from spitting fat by a plastic coated apron depicting a bottle of Guinness that she had taken to wearing. Richard had given it to her as a joke Christmas present.

"I'm having a late tea."

"No, mother. I'm early. Look at the clock."

Elizabeth Quinn glanced suspiciously at the clock on the kitchen wall.

"It's wrong."

Jane glanced at her own watch. The clock was virtually right but judging from her mother's expression there was no point in arguing.

"It's not very good quality," her mother said decisively. "It's Japanese."

Could I have some bacon? I'm hungry."

She felt faint, as though she might collapse. She needed to be strong to work out who had killed Ian. It was an unusual request for Jane. Eating with her mother would normally have been the last thing she would have contemplated. The only time they normally ate together was at her mother's birthday when they would go out to a local restaurant and Elizabeth Quinn would ignore her daughter if her son was present.

"Is the family coming?"

Instead of explaining Jane nodded her head.

"Probably later."

Elizabeth Quinn opened the fridge door and produced two extra rashers which she added to those already under the grill.

"Some fried bread would be nice," Jane added. "You know how they like it."

Her mother produced a frying pan from a cupboard without comment and Jane escaped into the sitting room.

"Can I 'phone Richard?"

There was little chance of Richard having returned home unless he had fallen in love with someone travelling in the reverse direction to his own but she needed to make some contact.

When she had left the message she smoothed out the paper she had found in Ian's hand and made a note of the numbers on a cheque stub. Then she looked up "storeroom" in her mother's 1929 copy of *Roget's International Thesaurus of English Words and Phrases* that she had never seen opened by anyone but herself and put the paper in section 636 'Store'.

Then she put the red book back on top of the writing bureau.

Her mother was putting two square place mats depicting Scottish Castles, that Richard had given her as a more serious present, on her round oak tea table. Jane could smell the bacon cooking and memories of the past come floating back to her. She would have preferred it to be a past with the last two hours missing. She could almost persuade herself anyway that she must have been mistaken, that Ian was only sleeping, but she knew it was not the truth.

Elizabeth Quinn was back in the doorway, hair neatly pinned back as usual, her skirt and blouse seemingly new and un-creased. She was holding a green wooden tray with an oval serving dish on which was bacon, fried bread, tomatoes and scrambled eggs. The eggs were well done, as always, but for once Jane was not going to object.

Elizabeth Quinn must have seen her looking at them for she gave a slightly admonitory shake of her head and said "You mustn't be selfish Jane; you know the rest of the family like them like this."

Jane saw that there were already two mats on the table and her mother also produced two sets of knives and forks. Whatever the problems with her mother's memory or expectations, some functions were still carried forward automatically.

When she had eaten most of what her mother had provided and drunk a cup of hot tea Jane started talking.

"A terrible thing has happened. A colleague of mine at the office is dead. I don't know whether it was an accident or something else. I think he was murdered."

Elizabeth Quinn nodded with something of the wisdom of an owl, but with no sign that she had understood completely what her daughter was saying.

"It is all rather difficult. You see there is this man I'm trying to help and I am rather afraid for him. He has really done something rather foolish - wrong really - but I still think I should do all that I can to help him -"

"Mark Mandell-" Elizabeth Quinn interrupted.

"Yes, yes that's right. I'm so glad you remember.

Her mother had adopted rather a pained expression that suggested that she would rather that Jane did not continue. It was an expression that Jane knew well. It had been applied at one time or another to all

Jane's boyfriends and even to her own husband.

"It is just that I am not sure it is the right thing to do; not now this has happened. I thought I knew what I was going to do but now I just don't. If I told the police what I know there is no guarantee that anything would be sorted out. Somehow I feel I have got to do something myself just when I thought I hadn't. I think that is the only way this is going to get sorted out."

"You probably know best."

Jane looked up at her mother.

"You were always very bright," Elizabeth Quinn added by way of explanation. "Your father always used to say so."

Jane couldn't remember the last time that her mother had said anything quite so complimentary - even if it was passing on a received opinion. The family past was always a bottomless well that had enough water to engulf her. Having left the family she had thought she had escaped that power but it always seemed to have the ability to return. And as she grew older the past did not disappear but more pasts - most of her own making - were added. Robert Stuart and Mark Mandell both had the potential to be turned from prospective futures into immediate pasts if things went wrong.

"You should be careful you know where your real affections lie."

"What mother?"

"You must honour your husband."

Jane ate the last piece of bacon. Some version of the past had established a temporary hold on her mother's mind as usual.

She told herself that Ian Hart's death had been accidental. The doors and windows of the flat would have been tightly locked against the cold and snow. There had been no signs of anyone breaking in and to judge from the report of the couple she had met there was every chance that anything violent that had occurred would have been heard. Besides, nobody would have known that Ian was in a position to expose whatever had been going on.

She walked across to the glass doors looking out on the lawn. The snow was pristine and white and glistening in the lights from the flats. The angles where the lawn encountered the flowerbeds had been smoothed over so there were now only gentle contours leading up to the trees.

There was the sound of a dog barking angrily quite close to them, a couple of deep-throated protests and then silence.

"He's still there," her mother said.

"Sorry?"

"The man in the garden. Can you see him? He's still there. He arrived just before you came."

"What man?"

"He is up in the trees. I think he is from the Council."

Jane looked casually out of the window. She could see nothing.

"I can't see anyone."

"Of course not. He keeps himself hidden."

"Why is he spying on you?"

"He isn't. Mrs Adams has made another claim for disability allowance. Of course she is not entitled to it. Everyone knows that."

"But don't you mind him being out there?"

"Oh no. They have got to catch them. They come quite often. They are very skilful. You can hardly see them. Sometimes I can feel them more than see them. You know I always knew when someone is watching me."

It had been a slightly uncanny talent of her mother's in the past, Jane reflected, but now she seemed to be seeing people everywhere.

"I ought to be going," Jane said.

Her mother made no protest and Jane was soon outside pulling her coat around her to keep as warm as possible.

She had parked the Peugeot in its usual position slightly up the drive. She walked towards it and stood with her car key in hand, ready to get in. Apart from the faint drone of passing traffic it was quiet.

She looked at the row of trees where her mother had claimed that the watcher had based himself. Here again the snow had softened the outline of the trees so that the branches were not so gaunt against the sky.

Jane took a step or two forward. She was eager to rid herself of the demon watchers from her mother's private universe who had become absurdly overactive in conditions that presented a serious chance of freezing to death. If she walked into the trees she knew she would find nothing but that at least it would put her mind at rest.

It was pointless but she knew that she needed to press on. She took a series of firm strides towards the trees taking care to walk as silently as the conditions would permit. She reached the cover of the trees in a few seconds and found nothing as she had expected. It was time to turn back, but something persuaded her that she might just as well check the whole possibility that the cover of the trees presented. If she walked on a few more yards there would be conclusive proof that nobody had been spying on Elizabeth Quinn, or her, or any of the occupants of Silverlawns.

The snow lay virgin white in front of her as she walked forward. She had to preserve her sanity for ten seconds and then it would all be over and she would be able to go back to her car and convince herself how foolish she had been. She walked on.

There were footprints, newly cut, the imprint of a pair of heavy-duty boots with sharply defined soles and heels that had cut deeply into the snow. On each of the heels was the imprint of a six-pointed star with the leading point a little longer than the rest pointing the way the boots were walking. Beside one tree trunk an area of snow had been trampled down and the stars were superimposed on one another. This was where he had watched the occupants of Silverlawns.

She bent down. The imprint of the boots in the snow was sharp and new. Whoever had been standing there had occupied the position after it had stopped snowing and it had only stopped snowing as she arrived. From where she was now standing one set of footprints led towards her and one away. If she followed the set that led away she stood a good chance of catching up with whoever it was that had been spying on her.

CHAPTER TWENTY-FOUR

She looked about her. It was simple. She could go back to the Peugeot, lock the doors, and drive down the drive at the side of the main house at Silverlawns and then go out onto the main road to central London and Mark Mandell. That was safe. Or she could follow the tracks of a man wearing commando boots leading uphill through what was, as far as she could see, a small wood. She turned her back on the car.

She came across the dog first. It was a young Alsatian lying on its side in the snow. There were tracks leading down the slope. The Alsatian lay where they ended and where its paw marks crossed the footsteps of the man. Jane knelt down. She felt the cold seeping through her coat and chilling her skin. From the outward appearance there seemed to be nothing wrong with the dog except it was unmoving. Jane took off her glove and felt in the dog's fur below its neck. There was faint movement and warmth. She got up. There was little she could do. If the dog were to survive it needed to revive itself quickly.

No, dammit, she thought. I'm not walking by. She started stroking the dog's head and found herself uttering encouraging noises. The dog stirred and opened dazed eyes that melted into something friendly.

"That's better. You'll be fine. Of course you will."

She rubbed the sides of the dog's face gently between her hands. There was movement in its legs and she found resistance to her stroking. The dog's tongue appeared and it gave a slight pant.

"Good dog. Good dog."

She didn't know how long she stayed crouched by the Alsatian. It seemed as though the dog was gradually emerging from some deep and deathly sleep. Gradually the slight rocking and stroking movement that Jane was employing was easing it back into life. The eyes were gradually getting brighter as life returned.

A giant snowflake drifted gently past her eyes and when she looked up she could see that it had started to snow again in earnest. The flakes were dropping vertically down. The view of London that should have stretched out before her had disappeared.

It was quieter. The snowflakes had begun to muffle the noise of the city, each engulfing its own little particle of travelling sound so that everything became muted and joined together in a subdued and mystical hum, the background notes of the musical universe. She stared at the bright square of light of her mother's window. It seemed to her that there was a square tunnel of light connecting her to her mother, a tunnel surrounded by air of which she need not be afraid.

She shook her head. She needed to break out of whatever spell had seized her. She had also for a moment become infinitely tired, as only snow can tire you, that comforting cold hand that desires only that you assume its own temperature.

The dog was moving in her lap and then struggling to get to its feet but more with its front legs than its back, as though the paralysis it was suffering from was clearing first from this part of its body.

"Gently, gently."

What could have caused that? Jane eased herself a little off the ground. The dog now seemed able to support the weight of its own head. The snow was increasing in intensity so that even the light from her mother's room that a moment before had seemed infinitely luminous was now dimmed. Sound was fading as well, so that she could only detect the immediate here and now, a slight intake of breath, a sigh. She had become cut off in her own separate world whose only other inhabitant was an Alsatian.

As she eased the dog gently to its feet she saw that the distinguishing impression of the six-pointed star on the footprints was scarcely discernible and in a few moments would have disappeared. Even as she watched it was dissolving into a blurred outline.

She got to her feet and so, with a protesting whimper, did the dog. She moved off determinedly in the direction of the disappearing trail, but then her conscience told her that she should first check that the dog had properly recovered. She ought to ensure that at least it could walk.

She turned round but the dog had gone. A new trail stretched uphill that would also not survive more than a few minutes. She hurried forward. The man had picked his way closer to the edge of the belt of trees as he had gone upwards but there was just enough light for her to follow the trail. If he had disappeared into the thicker part of the wood she would not have been able to see.

She was aware that she was not properly equipped for the task she had embarked on. Her shoes were sensible but they were not boots and every few steps she slid and slipped a little. Her clothes were warm but designed for the centre of town. Her exertions were also making her pant. She had embarked on another foolish venture that had little chance of success.

She walked on. Who had she told that Ian Hart was about to solve the problem? Bellmore? Mandell? Diana Vere? Who had Ian told? Perry at the Bank? Suzanne?

She knew she was hardly being honest in adding the extra names. If anyone had conveyed to a third party a good reason for getting rid of Ian Hart it was most likely to have been her.

She tried to dismiss it from her mind. She needed to turn to practical problems. If somebody was watching her, who was it? Whoever he was - the boots were far too big for a woman - what was his purpose? He had been inconspicuous enough to be one of Diana Vere's colleagues. Without her mother's sixth sense she would have been totally unaware of what was happening. Could it be someone she knew? Bellmore? Could it be somebody protecting her? Mark Mandell? Or someone who had only a negative interest in her well being? Who was he?

She stopped dead. Even in the dim light she could see that the footprints were now more clearly defined, a six pointed star in each one. But the conditions had not changed and she should only have been able to make out general indentations where X had been walking.

These footprints could only have been made a minute or two ago at most. Even as she watched the sharp lines were becoming less well defined. Whoever the watcher was he was very close. She turned slowly round through three hundred and sixty degrees. The snow was falling gently around her. She could see no one. She took a gentle step sideways and retreated into the shelter of two of the larger trees.

She thought she heard something moving and held her breath but the sound, if it was a sound, was not repeated and she started breathing again.

As she looked, and she did not know how long that was, she saw the snow was thinning until, in only a few seconds, it stopped altogether and she could see through the trees that London had reappeared below her and that her world, which a moment before had been limited to a few yards in each direction, had infinitely expanded. Then she heard the sound again. It was from the way she had come, a slight flurry of movement in the snow.

It was the young Alsatian restored to health and bounding along in her wake, his nose almost pressed in each of her footprints as he followed her trail. As the trail ended he stopped, saw her, and gave a little bark of greeting.

"Shh," she whispered. "Good dog, time to go home."

She looked back the way she had come. She had lost her appetite for going forward. The single track of footprints led on through the wood on the top of the hill that she drove past on the way to her mother's flat. X was probably still somewhere close at hand and there was no chance of following him without him being aware of it. The way she had come was back downhill. She might be seen going back to the car but there was less danger of her being cut off. If she waited a little there was the possibility that X would go, although she supposed that he would know until her car moved that she was still somewhere about.

The dog was panting happily at her feet. Then she noticed his ears prick up, and he gave a short bark.

"Please puppy - be quiet."

He looked at her, trusting but not understanding. Then he suddenly bounded off into the trees barking loudly. Jane tensed herself to move from her hiding place and prepared to start sliding her way downhill as fast as she could.

The barking stopped, suddenly, and without warning. Jane pressed herself back closer against the tree trunk. Now she could hear somebody, the sound of a person moving lithely through snow, a faint crisp and crackle as X's boots cut into the newly formed surface. Then the sound stopped and she knew he was close.

She opened her eyes. He was standing in front of her looking down at Silverlawns. From the back he was a long lean figure dressed in leather jacket and Balaclava. He seemed too tall to be Christopher Bellmore. She would know for certain if he turned round but she was almost certain that he was a stranger.

When he looked down he would see two sets of footprints, both his own coming and going from the direction of the main wood and two sets climbing up the hill from Silverlawns. This time, however, only one of them would be his. A momentary check of the surrounding snow would also establish there were no small footprints leading away from the area. The conclusion that the person who had made the smaller set of footprints was still there would be inescapable.

The man looked down at the ground and then turned back the way he had come. Perhaps his brief was strictly to observe and not to contact Jane. Whatever it was she could see him striding back the way he had come. If he was hiding the fact that he knew that she was there he was doing it with consummate style.

After he had gone she eased herself on to the main path. From where she had come there was the track of a man and a dog. In his tracking of her the dog had obliterated her trail, already indistinct because of the fresh falls of snow.

"Good boy," she said approvingly looking round for him.

But the dog was not there. Instead, lying stiffly across the snow was an inert mass of black and grey fur.

Jane went over and lifted the dog's head. This time there was no mistake and there would be no second resurrection.

"Bastard," Jane said. "You bastard."

She should have left it at that. It would have been the only sensible thing to do. If she had been scared of X before, then this should have sealed it. She looked across to Silverlawns, the Peugeot, and safety. Except that some other logic was working in the implacable part of her being. For once, it insisted, retreat was illogical. She knew nothing of her enemies but they seemed to know a great deal about her. This was a moment, just a small moment, when she had an advantage. She knew where one of them was, or at least where he was likely to be.

When she got to the edge of the woods her pulses were racing and her lungs pumping for air. The man's tracks stopped at the tyre marks and he had got into the passenger side. From where she was she could only see the back of the car as it accelerated away.

It was a black BMW like a thousand others in London and unexceptional except for one thing. Its number plate. C -O -B. COB. COB 2 to be exact. So there was probably a COB 1 somewhere. Jane knew who the owner of both cars was, although there was now probably some doubt as to whether he could afford such expensive collecting habits.

She couldn't remember his middle name. It had been something odd Richard had said. Orlando? Orville? Neither sounded right but it didn't matter. She didn't have the same trouble with the first and last names. Christopher and Bellmore.

She didn't believe in coincidence. The car belonged to Christopher Bellmore. One of the two he hadn't admitted owning to his wife. He was probably driving it.

CHAPTER TWENTY-FIVE

She pulled out of the traffic and eased the car off the road. The Peugeot slid to a halt in packed snow and the traffic beside her growled on towards Wimbledon. She looked at her watch. It was barely seven o'clock.

She took the pocket dictating machine out of her briefcase and inserted a tape. She held the comforting black shape in her right hand and placed her thumb on record and her second finger on forward and took a deep breath. She needed to make this sound as matter of fact as possible.

"Richard," she said, "this isn't any sort of joke. It's serious."

She flicked the controls to stop. She didn't know when Richard would be back and he was notoriously bad at picking up his mail. She could send the tape to her mother but Elizabeth Quinn might take weeks if not months to realize that her daughter was dead. Jane started the tape again.

"I need to tell somebody what is happening and what I am about to do. Sorry, Richard, but you get the short straw."

She could add something. She could describe the tape as her last will or testament, something dramatic.

"There's something I'm involved in. I can't back away from it any more, not from where I am. I am going to have to try to sort it out. It's an obligation that I have. I don't have any alternative. I have woken up to a few things in the last day or two."

She clicked the tape off. If Richard could understand these ramblings it would only be through brotherly intuition. She watched the traffic slowly pass the Peugeot, car after car with a single driver, all looking irritated by the delay.

She ran the tape back and erased her feelings. She needed to start again.

"Richard, listen to me, and then act as you think best. This is serious. This is about Mandell.."

Jane summarized everything that had happened as precisely as she could, including everything she knew about Mark Mandell. When she had finished she packed the tape in a Jiffy bag from her briefcase and addressed it to her brother. She wrote 'Please play this as soon as you can!' on a business card and put that in the bag.

She was just about to seal it when she saw a policeman looking at her through the windscreen. He motioned her to lower the driver's window. He looked about twenty, one or two years younger than Ian Hart, but with the same open and honest face.

"Is there a problem Madam?"

"No," Jane said. "No problem."

She didn't sound particularly convincing, even to herself.

"Why have you stopped then?"

"I am sorry officer. I had to dictate a memo. I realise I shouldn't have pulled off the road here but it is something the Chancellor of the Exchequer needs first thing tomorrow." She pointed at the official black leather briefcase on the seat beside her with its authoritative initials - E R - and waved the dictating machine at him to give extra credibility to her story. "Curiously," she added brightly, "it was about police pay. Police pay comparisons that is."

She could see that he didn't really believe her.

"I hope you are going to move off, Madam. You represent a hazard where you are."

"Of course," Jane said meekly. "Sorry to be a problem."

She thought for a moment that the policeman might be having second thoughts but instead he obligingly halted the traffic so that she could move smartly away and then slow as she rejoined the main stream of traffic.

In Wimbledon she decided to park the Peugeot in the road next to Christopher Bellmore's house. There was still some sense in being reasonably discreet.

There were no lights showing in Bellmore's house, or more exactly, his wife's house. Was it only yesterday that she had been here? It seemed incredible. She hadn't imagined she would ever be coming back but it was now clear to her that Bellmore was the key to the whole Mandell business. Bellmore's involvement could mean that the fraud had been carried out from the KM end.

There were criss-crossed tyre tracks on the drive but no cars. There were footprints in the snow but no people. Jane stopped. There were two tracks leading up to the house from where the tyre tracks stopped. She bent down. One set of tracks had been made by the boots with the six pointed stars. But there was another set of tracks beside them, less deeply indented and altogether less precise. They looked curiously familiar. They were much smaller than the first set.

Although the house was dark there was a single lamp shining down on the glistening snow. The Bellmores had invested in an ornamental street lamp to light this end of the drive. It was probably last year's fashion accessory in security lighting. As far as Jane could see it was cast iron, the real thing transplanted from redevelopment in the City to the suburban fringe.

Even by its light Jane could not quite work out why the other footprints seemed so familiar. The two sets led on in front of her past the front door and down the side of the house but, as far as she could see, did not return. She had been almost certain, however, that they had started from where the cars had been parked and she looked behind her to see if there was any indication that they could have got back by a different route.

There were three sets of footprints moving forward to where she stood. The Starman was in the centre and on either side were his two accomplices, identical footprints in the snow. The Starman's other companion could be Jane's identical twin, about five foot six or seven, about eight stone something, and wearing the same sort of sensible walking shoes that the snow conditions demanded.

It had not snowed since the Starman and his friend had got out of the car and now history was recording that Jane had joined them.

She had to go on. There must be more to learn. The Starman and his companion had made no attempt even to approach the front door. There was a clear trail in front of her if she wished to follow it. It would lead somewhere, perhaps only to another entrance to the house, or perhaps they had not been going to the house at all. If the footprints did belong to the occupants of COB 2, and there seemed no doubt that this was the case, they could hardly have got here more than an half an hour before, and whatever they had come to do seemed to have been accomplished because COB 2 had gone.

As she walked to the side of the house the light from the antique street lamp grew dimmer but there were traces of moonlight that were growing brighter all the time as the sky cleared.

Her feet made small crunching sounds in the snow. Now and again she paused and listened. There was no sound.

The footprints led down the side of the house and to a wooden door in a wall. She turned the door handle and pushed gently. The door swung noiselessly open. The footsteps led on past the back of the house and into the garden. Set back from the house was another building from which a dim light shone. The footsteps led on in its direction. She followed.

As she approached she could see that the building was a massive Victorian glasshouse with a curved iron framework arching up into the night. The light was just set back from the main door into the building, a shaded bulb casting the shadows of giant tropical plants onto the white snow outside. The footsteps led up to the door with flat virgin snow on either side. There was no dispute as to where the Starman and his companion had gone.

Jane stood ten yards from the door and looked carefully at the impossible building. Whatever she had been expecting it was not this.

She turned the handle and stepped inside. She was in a little antechamber leading to another door like the one she had come through. That too opened without difficulty and she found herself standing under the light she had seen from outside. It hung suspended over a slightly battered wooden table and an easy chair. The table was bare and looked as though it had been scrubbed hygienically clean. She looked down at her feet. The snow on her boots was beginning to melt and the water run off onto the irregular but tightly packed flagstones. The flagstones ahead of her were unmarked. She knew, however, that the Starman must have gone this way. There was a clicking sound from somewhere in the building followed by a faint hissing. Then she felt a warm spray in her face and moisture on her forehead. It was gentle rain.

She loosened her coat. As the spray of rain fell hot air was seeping up through iron grilles in the floor. The temperature must be 30 degrees centigrade warmer than outside. The spray of rain finished and the moisture began to evaporate. On a supporting cast iron pillar next to the table a control panel had been suspended. She went over to it, took a deep breath, and pressed the button marked lights. The effect was rather more than she had bargained for. In front of her, stretching down the whole length of the now illuminated glasshouse, was a path of flagstones set in gravel. At regular intervals iron grilles were releasing hot air.

At the far end of the glasshouse, perhaps a hundred feet away, was yet another door. Half way along, a path led off to the right. Her finger hovered over the light switch. The illuminated glasshouse would show up for miles in every direction. Planes in difficulties would attempt to land. But at least she could see. She walked down the path.

On either side tropical plants of various sizes, some that must have been at least fifteen feet tall, were growing out of a carpet of close packed green moss. Healthy green fronds showed up against a background of glass and ornate white ironwork. There was no decay that she could see, no traces of weeds or discarded plant matter anywhere. She bent down and looked at the covering of moss. It was like the baize on a billiard table.

She walked to the far door. There were no tracks leading out into the snow on the far side. She turned back and took the turning into the rest of the building.

The path in front of her was probably eighty feet in length and at the far end split to right and left. The glasshouse seemed to be an H shape into which she had entered at the bottom left hand foot. Quite what the whole structure was doing in the Bellmore's garden defeated her.

About half way along the central path on the left the tropical plants ceased to grow directly out of the green moss-like covering. Here they were encased in terracotta pots in neat rows. She was hot but she shivered. There were beads of perspiration running down her skin inside her clothing.

At the end of the central path one way led out. The snow outside was flat and untroubled by human footprint. She walked back down to the other end. Perhaps there was an exit there that she had not been able to see. With a glasshouse this size it would be logical to have an exit at every point of the H.

It started to rain again, a faint spray of water droplets from jets attached to the roof. A straight jet of water droplets clogged her eyelashes making it difficult to see. As she got to the end of the path she slipped on the stones and fell. She put out her hands and arms to break the impact of the fall and felt herself slide on something sticky.

Some of the breath was knocked out of her but she was not hurt. She shook her head and wiped the water out of her eyes with her hands. From where she was, a few inches above the flagstones, she saw that the water was not pure and colourless as it had been elsewhere in the glasshouse but was stained with something faintly pink. She pushed herself to her feet. Her arm was red and bloody; she must have cut herself in falling. She rubbed the blood away to investigate the wound but could not find the cut.

It's ridiculous she thought. But probably no more ridiculous than the overall situation she found herself in. At least it was on a par with that. She found the cut at last, a slight serration on her left index finger. She squeezed the finger hard to see the extent of the damage. A little red blood reluctantly seeped out of the wound and fell onto the flagstone. The red blood landed on top of a little pool of orange pink and started to mix into it. She had come to the end of her journey. The body was lying barely concealed behind a row of palms, arms outstretched, on its face.

Jane moved closer. This was nothing like what had befallen David Mandell or Ian Hart. Any sense of ambiguity had been avoided by the simple fact that a pair of garden sheers was protruding from the man's back. The blades were together, a little above the small of the back, and sticking in at least three or four inches into the body. The handles were bolt upright.

Jane turned the head a little and gave a little scream. Christopher Bellmore, his cherubic features set in sulky repose, lay before her.

Faintly, far away but growing in intensity, she heard the sound of police sirens wailing in the night.

CHAPTER TWENTY-SIX

The sirens left a scar in her mind. She could still hear them when she returned to her apartment. She switched on the television to put some sound on top of the noise and make it go away.

There was blood in her hair, on her body, on her coat. She needed to get rid of it. She scrubbed her hands with the enthusiasm of a surgeon facing the last operation of the week. She rubbed at the stain on her coat till it disappeared. She looked at the spot with suspicion. Had every trace gone? Perhaps it would be better to get rid of the coat. She shook her head. There wasn't time and it wasn't necessarily easy to do.

- You decided to throw your coat away in the middle of winter Miss Quinn?
- Yes.
- It wasn't old was it?
- Not particularly.
- In fact you had only had it three months?
- Yes.
- And you don't have another winter coat?
- No.
- So why were you throwing it away?

Not exactly easy to answer. She needed to behave as normally as possible. She certainly needed time to think. She turned up the sound on the television to finally drown out the sirens. A white UN troop carrier rumbled across the screen. She hardly saw it. Instead there was the face of Ian Hart, freed from his body, and smiling at her.

She blinked. Two of her senses seemed to be slipping out of control. Not that the sight of Ian was threatening in any way. It was almost as if he were encouraging her. She looked at her watch but Ian's face blotted out the dial although she found that if she held her arm out to one side she could just make out the time in the corner of her eye. 9.25. Surely it must be later?

What did she need to do? Perry at the Bank. He was the man to make sense of Ian's numbers. She looked for the cheque stubs in her bag. Where were they? Surely she couldn't have lost them when she fell over in the glasshouse? She must have checked at the time to make sure they were there?

She fumbled around for a few seconds relying on her sense of touch as Ian Hart was still beaming encouragingly at her. Her fingers located the stubs as Ian Hart's smile began to dissolve.

She held the cheque stubs in her hand. The noise of the sirens had vanished from her ears and she could see clearly. She could hear the weatherman on the news programme saying that the exceptionally cold weather was coming to an end. A High was coming in from the Atlantic to sweep away the depression. It would get warmer and the snow would melt away. She looked down. There were two large bloodstained thumbprints on the top cheque stub. Her own. The numbers were unreadable.

She took the rest of the contents of the bag out. She could see no traces of blood anywhere else. Not even the faintest. She looked underneath to see if she could make anything out from the other side. Nothing. The paper was of commendable quality. Perhaps the banks kept cheques for years.

She tore out the stub and walked into the bathroom. She hesitated for a moment and then flushed it away. She could telephone her mother. What page were they hidden? Storeroom? How long would that take her mother to look up?

The telephone answering machine was winking at her. She should have noticed before. Maybe Richard was back. She pressed the play button.

"It's Edward. I'd hoped you would be there. I just wanted to say hello."

Jane could hear Mahler playing in the background and imagined she could hear the fronds of the palm trees flapping in a light breeze. Edward would be in the lounge with the large window looking out on the cove. She wondered when he had telephoned. It had probably been in the afternoon when he had finished his contemplation of the quality of the light changing on the surface of the water in the cove and would be reading a book, an alternate menu of thriller and biography, to occupy the idyll before dinner.

There was a pause at the other end of the line. Perhaps Edward Charles had hoped she would pick up the telephone or perhaps it was just a recognition that life on the West Coast of Ireland did really proceed at a slower pace.

"We were very pleased that you could come at Christmas," Edward said. "I just wanted to say that we hope that you will be able to come back to see us again soon. I know you wanted to talk about Eastwood and please come and do so. But do remember the house is yours to do with as you wish. Simon would have wanted you to do what you thought best. We know that whatever decision you make will be the right one. There," Edward Charles gave a little chuckle, "I've said my few lines. There is another reason for coming back. There is a bottle of the Margaux left after all. It would be a great pleasure to drink it with you. God bless you Jane. Goodbye."

She could flee to Ireland if all else failed. Perhaps Edward Charles's blessings had a special power. She was getting superstitious. She had been impressed by her mother's ability to detect the presence of the Starman.

"Jane? The most extraordinary thing has happened. You seem to have a double!" There was another message on the machine. It was Sally Fry, even more animated than usual. "I've just seen you, I mean of course I haven't, but it was so uncanny, it really did seem it must be you. And wearing your sort of clothes as well. It was really extraordinary. You'll think me crazy so I'd better explain. I don't think I ever pointed it out to you but the end of the garden touches on the edge of the only big estate around her. A mad Victorian who used to like greenhouses built this Kew Gardens imitation. It's used as a commercial nursery now. Well, you'll never guess but I saw this woman running out of the grounds and straight past me. And she simply looked just like you. I know you will find this ridiculous but it's true. Actually I suppose it's going to be one of those occasions where if I ever managed to get another look at this woman I would see that she doesn't look like you at all. That's the normal way of it isn't it? On a second look people find all those differences that they hadn't managed to notice the first time. Actually now I come to think of it I don't think she looked like you at all. Oh well-" Sally Fry seemed to have realised that she was reasoning herself out of the point she wished to make. "I was really ringing you up to say you have remembered the barbecue haven't you? Martin must be mad to do it in this weather but he is determined to go ahead so I hope you and Robert can come. Martin is the only one going to be outside cooking after all. It would be so nice to see you both. And you don't mind looking after George do you? I'm sure he is looking forward to it. Do give us a call. I'd better go. Bye."

A witness, and basically a reliable one, thought Jane as the message clicked off. If Sally thought there was a possibility that she had actually been there Jane had no doubt that she would revert to her initial certainty. There were also two more eye witnesses in Hackney at Ian's Hart's flat and the policeman who had stopped her. Plus fingerprints and blood. And she still had the spare set of keys to the flat that needed to be replaced.

There had been another click on the tape. Somebody had telephoned her but had failed to leave a message. It wouldn't have been Richard. Her brother was incapable of silence on any occasion. It might have been Mark or Robert Stuart. Surely though, Robert would have left a message?

How long had it been since Martin had cooked his first New Year barbecue at the flat she had shared with Sally and Diana? The cooker had failed just as Sally had been about to put the special meal she had planned into the oven and Martin, getting plus points from them all, had managed to change chicken in white wine to a blackened Cajun speciality. She could see him now cooking on the balcony in a slight drizzle with a glass of wine in his hand. The next year Simon had come, invited by Diana.

She wanted to be safe. There was a great attraction in going back to the West Coast of Ireland. She could find some excuse for taking the next day off and fly over. She could be with Edward Charles in the book-lined room overlooking the cove watching the light fade.

She needed to make sure that the last of the blood had been washed off her skin and her hair. She took her clothes off and was about to turn on the shower. Her hand hovered over the control knob. Then it occurred to her that the call could have been the Starman checking whether she was in or not. If he knew about her mother he would know where she lived and her telephone number. All she knew about him was that he had a woman companion and was probably in possession of one of Christopher Bellmore's cars. It wasn't a contest of equals. He might even know that she had been in Wimbledon as well. She had managed not to notice one of her best friends. Why should she have seen the Starman?

She turned on the water and let it cascade over her. At her feet there was a little tinge of something reddish brown that was probably blood. She shut her eyes and felt the water beat over her, a healing stream that momentarily obliterated all her thoughts into a simple physical sensation.

She got out of the shower eventually and poured herself a glass of brandy. It was what Edward Charles would have suggested after the Margaux. She fastened the giant white Egyptian cotton towel tight round her like a dress and sat on the sofa. She remembered her father had done that for when she was a child. Simon had bought the towel, suddenly insistent that nothing else would do. She needed to work a few things out.

Christopher Bellmore clearly had had every reason to feel frightened about something. What had he known? Clearly too much for the Starman's comfort. And the Starman had had a companion, a woman.

Had Bellmore been involved in the whole fraud or had he simply found something out? And why had he warned Jane off?

Jane got up and pulled back the curtains and looked at the river making its calm progress. Maybe there was somebody out there watching her still. But she needed the peace of the river. It was why she had bought the apartment. There was something comforting about the river and its endless daily journey to the sea. Each of the boats travelling back and forth were lives in transit.

She thought about the third set of footprints. There had to be another woman of course. One of Ian Hart's signs of a company in trouble. Paula Black. Roughly Jane's height. About five foot seven, Ian had said. It probably meant that she took the same sized shoe. Paula Black? It was obvious when she thought of it. It was perfectly plausible that she had been the Starman's companion. She had been David Mandell's close friend; and more than an acquaintance of Christopher Bellmore.

There was a gentle knock at the door.

For a moment she thought her senses were playing tricks but she hadn't imagined it.

The knock came again, this time more insistently.

She got to her feet. It was too early for Mark Mandell. In the kitchen area she picked out her favourite small vegetable knife and held it cold against her skin. The knife had a long, thin, extremely sharp blade. She liked it because it always seemed to have the perfect balance for chopping and there was nothing it could not cut through. She thought it would probably be perfect for stabbing into things as well.

Then she walked to the door.

CHAPTER TWENTY-SEVEN

It was Mark Mandell. He was looking away from the door, away from her, over his shoulder. She went back into the bathroom and put the knife down. There was another short buzz from outside. She straightened the bath towel around her and walked back to the door.

There was a cut over Mark's eye and a deepening bruise.

"Jane, I.."

"You'd better come in."

He seemed reluctant for a moment but she took him by the shoulders and pulled him through the door. Colder air swirled in from outside across her bare skin before she pushed the door shut.

"There's something I need to say. I should have said it before."

"Careful."

She had brushed against Mandell and the deep white cotton of the towel she was wearing had become ensnared on a patch of green Velcro on the inside of Mandell's open jacket.

"I'm sorry."

Mark was trying to free himself but his actions only seemed to be tangling them together more closely.

"Leave it to me."

She raised her arms so that both her hands could prize the towel free from his coat but for a moment found them around Mandell's neck. She hadn't noticed before quite how hypnotic his blue eyes

203

were close to, or how tense the events of the day had left her. For a moment she felt she could hardly breathe, and when she could she found that Mandell's closeness had trapped the heady scents of the bath oil on her skin.

She raised herself on tiptoe to kiss Mandell. She could see him on an equal level.

"I do need," Mandell was saying, but his next words were lost as Jane kissed him again.

After a moment he pushed his head away a little. "I do need to.." he started again but this time stopped without any intervention from Jane.

She felt his hands on the small of her back against her bare skin.

"Whatever you need, we need to go to bed," she said.

"I'm not sure that makes sense."

"That's good. I've given up on orderly events. I can't deal with them any more. Give me a crisis."

"I think," Mandell said softly, but he didn't finish the sentence.

"Do you?" Jane asked.

She moved back a little from Mandell releasing the towel from its place between them.

"Do I what?" Mandell said.

"Think? Know what you're thinking?"

She could see Mandell looking at her.

"No," Mandell said. "I don't know. Not at all."

"That's good," she said undoing the buttons on his shirt and feeling the warmth of his skin, her fingertips finding it surprisingly smooth.

"I mean," she found herself continuing, "there's too much going on, so many things to think about, so much to occupy one's time. Better not to have too much of it intrude. The more you need to think about what you are doing, the less you do."

"Probably," Mandell said. "Probably that's right."

For a moment Jane couldn't hear him at all so she only realised what he had said some seconds later. But he had nodded his head.

*

Jane awoke from her dream of warm limbs and comfort and found close to that there was a faint and regular inhalation and exhalation of breath. She looked down and found herself held still. Moonlight had breached the gap in the curtains and silver patches of light flitted across his face; she stretched out her fingers to touch it. He was real. He murmured something soft and caressing in his sleep, an arm inexpertly reaching out for an embrace that subsided away into a turn of his body.

There were ships on the river as she looked out, two boats towing giant barges silently down to the sea; red, green and white lights showing on their mastheads. She watched them passing. What secret purpose they were engaged in the middle of the night it was impossible to tell.

"Jane? Are you alright?"

"I'm fine."

"What time is it?"

"Nearly five."

"Anything the matter?

"No. A dream woke me. That's all."

"You've been staring out of the window for the last five minutes. Is there anything you want to talk about?"

"I talked enough last night. It's your turn. What did happen to you?"

"I borrowed Quentin's car."

"Quentin?"

"He's a friend of mine."

"And?"

"That was mostly it. The car hasn't got an up to date tax disc. The police thought it was stolen."

"And was it?"

"Of course not. That didn't stop them holding me for six hours."

"You should have more law abiding friends."

"It was a mistake. Quentin hadn't remembered to take the old tax disc out and put the new one in."

"Careless. And the bruise?"

"Oh that," Mandell looked as though he couldn't remember.

"Yes, that."

Jane heard an edge in her voice.

"When I got stopped, I thought I should make a break for it. I wasn't successful."

"No wonder they held you for six hours."

"Luckily they were in plain clothes. I managed to convince them I had a nervous disposition."

"Or a guilty one."

"Yes," Mandell agreed. "Look, I haven't any right to be here. I should have told you about the £5 million and my father straightaway. That's what I came round to say last night."

"Ian might still be alive."

"Are you sure he was murdered? There weren't any obvious signs."

Jane sighed.

"I could feel it in the room. Ian was serene because he knew he had hidden the numbers. He was always good at finding the best angle to any situation, however terrible. I can see him picking the bright spot as everything closed down. But it's my fault. I should have told him everything that was going on. He might have detected the danger he was in if he had had the full information to go on. I led him into this situation and all I could give him was a blindfold."

"Come here."

She settled herself back into bed. It was warm and the act of relaxing made her remember how tired she was. She leant back against him and felt his arm around her.

"It's not your fault," Mandell said. "You can telephone your mother in the morning and get the numbers. Then you can see whether Ian was on to anything. There is nothing else you can do."

"There's Paula Black."

"Paula? What's she got to do with this?"

"She knew Bellmore and Bellmore certainly knew something. She was around on Christmas Eve. She is a loose end. I need to talk to her. Somebody was around with the Starman."

"Jane, you are getting into this too deeply. Stick to the numbers. You don't want to involve yourself directly. You don't know this man you saw has anything to do with anything. Perhaps he does but you must be careful. What happens if the police discover these bodies and find out there is a connection to you? At the moment you are safe. There are not likely to be any witnesses, at least not ones that can identify you."

Only Sally Fry, thought Jane, one of my oldest friends and a pillar of the community, who has already left a message on my answer phone tape incriminating me. She hadn't told Mark about Sally's phone message. Then there were the twitching curtain people and, who had it been? Zack? Jazz? People from Mars, but probably reliable witnesses. She shivered. She hadn't done anything wrong - except that the police probably thought it was the duty of a citizen to report any dead bodies that they came across.

"I don't know Mark, I'm too tired to think properly. Where does Paula live?"

"She has a flat in Kensington," Mandell said reluctantly. "Somewhere off Kensington Church Street."

"Where off Kensington Church Street?"

Mandell gave the details.

"It's a good address."

"You shouldn't get too carried away. It is only a small flat."

She thought for a moment of pursuing the question of how precisely Mark knew the flat was small but she was warm under the duvet. There were any number of reasons anyway why Mark might have known about Paula's flat. She might have discussed it at the office. It was not something that had any ranking among the troubles she was actually confronted with. She felt her eyes closing.

"Tell me one thing," Mandell said.

"What?"

"I want to know why you feel so guilty."

Mandell had said it in a matter-of-fact voice as though there could be no argument about the question. She was about to protest that she didn't understand what it was he was talking about, but the words jammed somewhere in her throat. She didn't disagree.

"Is it that obvious?

"I'm a bit obsessed with guilt. I've had a lot of personal experience with it recently. It's not just Ian and the missing money is it? There's something else?"

Jane opened her eyes and looked at him, a shadow in the night.

"I had a child once. Thom. My son. He died. An accident. It was my fault. I was late. I should have been there but I wasn't."

There was a silence. She burrowed deeper into Mandell's shoulder.

"Sometimes when I wake up in the mornings I forget that Thom isn't there any more. Nor is his father. It's silly."

"I'm sorry."

"There is no need Mark, really. I should talk about it, but normally I can't. It only crops up in conversations with my mother. The thing about her is that most of the time she doesn't believe that Thom is dead. I think she wonders why it has been a long time since she has seen him but she doesn't make the obvious connection. She probably thinks I'm involved in a custody battle and don't want to talk about it. I've always wanted to scream at her because of that. I thought if I shouted hard enough I might jerk her back to where I have to live. The strange thing is just at this moment I really don't mind any more. I quite like it that she is convinced Thom is alive. It reminds me he existed and that he lives on in her memory. You see day by day all our memories fade and Thom fades with them. In her memory he is probably as bright as ever."

"I'm sorry. Not about your mother so much, as everything else."

Mandell squeezed her hand.

"It's better said."

She also wanted to say something to Mark about how she wanted him to be with her but she couldn't find the words immediately and she was tired. It was something about the relief she felt in having somebody to trust and talk to. Mandell ran his fingers lightly down the back of her neck and started humming a song. There were only a few notes but very familiar. It was a Lou Reed song that Simon had played a lot, about being someone else, someone good.

CHAPTER TWENTY-EIGHT

Jane paused outside her outer office the next morning. The corridor was deserted. She gave the keys that Ian had given Suzanne one last wipe with the handkerchief held in her gloved hand and took a deep breath.

She had thought of throwing the keys away in the river but calmer counsel had eventually prevailed. Suzanne would not be likely to forget that she had left the keys to Ian's flat in her top desk drawer. If they were found to be missing and Ian was thought to have died in mysterious circumstances, the whereabouts of the keys would be a matter for concern. The number of people who would have knowledge of where they were kept would be strictly limited. As far as Jane could see there would be only one suspect - herself. The keys had to be put back.

The only reason that Jane was hesitating now was that it had occurred to her that there was the possibility that Ian's body would not be found before Monday and that Suzanne, getting no answer, would probably go to the flat to find out what was going on. She must ensure that that did not happen. But Suzanne was not returning to London before Monday and that problem could wait. In the meantime the sensible thing to do was to return the keys as soon as she could. In the unlikely event that she might need them again they could always be retrieved.

She was already later than she had intended. The events of the previous day had left her exhausted and she had not wanted to leave Mark. She had also made several abortive attempts to ring her mother but Elizabeth Quinn was not answering. She had been known to turn the volume control on the telephone down to the faintest of rings that she could not hear unless she was sitting next to it. What had seemed the simplest plan the night before now seemed fraught with difficulties.

She tried to keep her nerves firmly under control. There was no reason anyway why she should not be in her secretary's office. All she needed to do was to retrieve the keys to the desk drawer from the bottom of the box with the computer manuals, deposit Ian's keys, and then return the keys to the desk drawer to their original position. A few seconds would see the task completed. Now or never.

The computer manuals box that was always kept on top of the filing cabinets was missing. An empty space of precisely the right width stared at Jane. On one side was the collection of reference books supported by a red plastic bookend and on the other the first of the green and black box files. She told herself that she had just made a mistake because she had been thinking too much about putting the keys back, that the real cardboard box with the word processing manuals was on the other filing cabinet next to the other box files, that if she just kept her nerve she would find it, the power of the mind.

She knew it wasn't true and that the box and the key to Suzanne's desk were both missing. She had told herself on the way in that she was relaxed and her nerves were unfrayed. Now she knew she wasn't. She took the only logical course of action left open to her and ran blindly forward uttering a subdued shriek.

She cannoned into something soft and felt her feet slip from under her, only controlling her descent by letting the soft object take the brunt of her fall. The soft object emitted a series of sounds that were not far removed from Jane's own initial cry.

Jane's right hand connected with the ground and she managed to absorb some of the shock of her own fall rather than transferring it to the person she had collided with. In another moment she had landed half on the floor and half on the other occupant of Suzanne's office.

Jane scrambled upright, feeling slightly winded, and with her nerves jangling. Her companion was also getting to her feet and picking up the word processing box that held Suzanne's keys. It was Barbara Bell, a gangly young woman with glasses with thick frames, who provided administrative support.

"I'm sorry Miss Quinn."

"No, no, Barbara," Jane said. "It was my fault entirely. I should never have run in to you so carelessly. But what are you doing here?"

Barbara looked as though Jane had accused her of causing the accident rather than having taken responsibility for it.

"I cover for Suzanne when she is off," she said in a nervous tone. "You said that I could."

Jane remembered that she had indeed agreed to the experiment. Brian Lloyd had suggested that it would improve Barbara's confidence to be given a more responsible role and that Jane would also benefit from having someone on hand if Suzanne were away.

To judge by Barbara's dismayed expression the experiment was getting off to a fairly disastrous start. The irritation that Jane had felt at finding someone else in the room when all she wanted to do was cover up her links with a possible murder was obviously being conveyed. Jane permitted herself a minor curse to go with the major curse she had already lodged at this interruption to her plans. She would need to be particularly considerate to Barbara. Brian Lloyd, she knew, had a soft spot for Barbara and taken considerable care to build up her confidence.

When she had more time, Jane told herself, she would sort the matter out. At the moment she simply had to get Barbara out of the room and the keys back in Suzanne's desk.

"There may be a message for me in reception," she said. "Could you go and check please. It could be rather urgent."

It was the best Jane could do under the circumstances and not implausible. For a moment Jane thought that Barbara was going to walk to reception carrying the box with the keys in but just as she was about to go out of the room she thought better of it and left the box on a side table. Jane breathed a sigh of relief.

She dived into the box and pulled out the manuals. Suzanne's desk key was not there. Jane swore. Then she saw that Suzanne's desk drawer actually had a key in it. Barbara must have been about to open it when she arrived. Goodness knows what the girl had been doing kneeling on the floor.

Jane opened the drawer. With Ian's keys returned the first part of what she had to do would be accomplished. There was time to try to track down Perry at the Bank before Norman arrived at ten. She had decided that she must at least alert Norman to the fact that she was concerned that she had not heard from Ian Hart. With the keys back in the drawer there would be no clue to the fact that somebody from the Treasury might have been out to Hackney.

She opened the desk drawer and put her hand in her coat pocket. There was one small snag. Ian Hart's keys were no longer there. She pulled her hand out of her coat pocket and took off her glove. Perhaps she couldn't feel the keys through the leather and fur. She stuck her hand back feverishly into her pocket but felt nothing. The keys were missing.

She pushed the desk drawer shut. If she kept calm she could reconstruct events. She had had the keys in her coat pocket when she collided with Barbara. The force of the impact must have dislodged them. She looked round the floor. Nothing. She dropped to her hands and knees. Nothing. She could hear footsteps from the corridor. It must be Barbara returning. She felt insanity beckon. She would need another ruse to get rid of Barbara for a few minutes.

She stood with her back to the filing cabinets when Barbara entered the room. The girl looked as though she had gained a little of her poise. Perhaps she had not realised that Jane had simply invented a reason to get rid of her.

"You were right," she announced.

"What?"

"There was a message, well not a message exactly, but someone to see you."

"Who?"

"A Mr Norman." Barbara paused. "At least I think it was Mr Norman. I suppose it could have been Mr Norman something. He was a bit hesitant." Barbara's confidence was fading again at her failure to identify Norman properly.

Jane glanced at her watch. Whatever he was called, Norman was ridiculously early.

"So is he waiting in reception?"

"Oh no," Barbara said looking brighter. "One of the messengers is going with him to get a pass. He should be along in a minute or so. He said he had a meeting arranged with you and you were obviously expecting him."

"Oh yes," Jane said. "Now I come to think of it, I was."

*

Jane managed to get her coat off and settle down on the other side of her desk before Norman arrived. She had taken the ninth of the ten deep breaths that she had promised herself when she found him filling the room.

The Inspector had a bodily shape that had no straight, or nearly straight, lines at all. He seemed to have been pumped into his suit. His cheeks had purplish patches in them and his eyes were blood shot. As he sat down on the chair opposite Jane and leant forward against the edge of her desk for support, the top of his jacket fell forward to reveal a pair of red braces against a white shirt. Inspector Norman was a dying breed of policeman. If the Metropolitan Police fitness requirements didn't catch up with him a heart attack would.

"I would like you to explain something," he said. "Why do you lead a double life?"

The Inspector had asked the question in a slightly breathless, hurried way, as though he was eager to press on to other more important matters. For a moment Jane thought that she must have misheard him, although the words had been perfectly clear. A second or two passed. Norman pulled himself more towards the vertical and looked directly at her. Jane couldn't work out quite what it was that he must know. Was it Christopher Bellmore or Ian he was referring to? Maybe it was Mark Mandell. It was bewildering.

"Let me help you," The Inspector seemed to sense she was reluctant to answer. "The facts are fairly incontrovertible. I just want you to explain them."

"What facts?" Jane managed to say in a dry and tight voice.

"Miss Quinn or Mrs Charles?" The Inspector made the question sound a similar proposition to 'Dr Jekyll or Mr Hyde'.

"I don't quite follow-"

"In the workplace Miss Quinn, you are still Miss Quinn. For other purposes, bank accounts, mortgages for example, you are Mrs Charles. It is rather confusing. It seems that you quite enjoy having a dual identity."

Jane didn't think that Norman had been quoting the examples of the bank accounts and the mortgages idly. He had been checking up on her.

"It is very simple, Inspector," she said in a flat tone. "I kept my maiden name for work. That was to avoid confusion among my colleagues. I decided that as far as the Civil Service was concerned it should be once Miss Quinn, always Miss Quinn. It is a fairly common practice."

"If you say so." Norman sounded unconvinced.

Jane's pulse rate had slackened a little but she was still uneasy about what was going on. Why was Norman going round the houses like this? His early arrival suggested that he was in a hurry, not that he intended to spend most of his meeting with Jane engaged in the discussion of a series of propositions about her identity. What did he want from her?

She looked up at the clock above the door. She had intended to give Perry Ian's numbers by now. At the moment she had neither the numbers nor any confirmation that Perry would be available. She hadn't got time for Norman.

Norman might have sensed her frustrations. His next question was more direct.

"You know a Mr Christopher Bellmore?"

That was an easy one. This was what she had expected as well.

"Yes."

The follow up would be more difficult. When she had last seen him? What connection had he with the Mandell business?

"Did you know him well?"

Norman was easing into it gently, waiting for her to trip herself up.

"No. A professional contact. He was instrumental in KM granting the loans to David Mandell."

Norman nodded encouragingly. She felt a little hotter than she had done before. She had an overwhelming desire to fiddle with the paper clips on her desk but held herself back. She had decided not to say anything more unless Norman knew something. She sensed a plausible defence if Norman knew about her first visit to Christopher Bellmore's house. It would be reasonable not to admit to the embarrassing scene with his wife unless pressed.

Barbara came in with two cups of coffees on a tray and managed to spend thirty seconds painfully searching for a suitable surface other than Jane's desk to put the cups on. Eventually she balanced one end of the tray precariously against the end of Jane's desk and managed to scoop the cups off with a display of considerable agility. She managed the sugar bowl with a little more calm and left the room.

Norman stirred a succession of sugar cubes into his drink. Each had to be separately unwrapped which seemed to provide a small problem for him. There might have been a minute steel lock on the package to judge by the concentrated physical effort he put into the task.

Jane felt like shrieking. Norman had not spoken for more than a minute and showed no signs of restarting. Silence always provided a great temptation for her to start speaking and not stop until she had exhausted everything she had to say. She was sure Norman had sensed that. She pinched herself hard.

"I am afraid I have bad news about Mr Bellmore." Norman said as if there had been no interval at all.

Jane said nothing.

"Mr Bellmore is dead."

Jane did her best to produce a surprised exclamation. She didn't know if Norman found it convincing. In any event he went on.

"He was found last night in a glasshouse attached to his home."

Jane felt her legs tense.

"The glasshouse is part of a commercial undertaking owned by Mr Bellmore's wife. Large tropical plants for offices, that sort of thing."

What was Norman up to?

"He had a pair of garden shears stuck in his back."

"Oh that is terrible," Jane said. She didn't have to fake the depth of her feeling. "You mean somebody murdered him?"

"He hardly killed himself."

"No," Jane said. "Of course not. And do you think," she added, "that is has something to do with the Mandell business?"

Norman ignored the question.

"It was a curious thing," he continued introspectively. "I was surprised to see those shears. I was expecting something a little less violent." "Expecting?"

"Oh yes. I was expecting an untouched body. Signs of a heart attack. Something like that. But not marks on the body. Nothing like a bloody great blade through him."

He is playing a game, Jane thought. He knows all about Ian Hart.

"I think I know the man who did it," Norman continued, "but I can't be sure. There is a feel to all of his murders. He has got a thing about it not appearing that a murder has taken place. There's a sort of craftsmanship to it. He glories in being undetected."

"I don't quite see," Jane said. "I thought you said Mr Bellmore was murdered with a pair of shears."

Norman ignored the interruption.

"I've seen his handiwork before. Down in a gym in East Ham. Boxer who apparently had a seizure lifting weights. Peter Jeffries. A lot of people wanted him out of the way."

"I don't understand," Jane said. "Are you saying some sort of professional killer murdered Mr Bellmore?"

"Yes."

It wasn't difficult to know who, Jane thought. The Starman. Somebody had hired the Starman to eliminate people connected with the Mandell case. An X she didn't know, Probably someone with access to a great deal of money to hire anybody they liked.

But there was still something that didn't make sense.

"But if this man operates as you say, I don't see how he can have been responsible for Christopher Bellmore's death?"

"Oh," Norman said. "Oh no. The shears didn't kill Bellmore. He was dead well before that."

CHAPTER TWENTY-NINE

Jane held her head in her hands for a moment when Norman had gone. She felt a sense of release that the ordeal was over, but she also had the feeling that the whole interview had been entirely unsatisfactory. It had been like working hard for an exam only to find that all the questions were easy. Norman hadn't asked her any of the difficult questions she had been dreading. Why?

She looked at the clock by the door. The second hand was moving round with its usual measured hostility. She really needed to think, but she didn't have time for the usual logical and dispassionate analysis that she favoured.

She walked out into the outer office. Barbara was missing. She looked on the floor. There was no sign of the keys to Ian Hart's flat. She undid the desk drawer just in case it was possible that Barbara, in her new super-efficient mood, had actually managed to find the keys and return them.

Inside the drawer in neat sections were yellow labels, biros, pencils, pins, a stapler, scissors, ink, and, at the back, a pile of labels marked RESTRICTED, COMMERCIAL, or SECRET that Suzanne had printed off ready for use. But there were no keys. She eased the metal drawer slightly further outwards. If she eased the sides up a bit the restraining catches would be released and the drawer would come completely free. With Norman on her trail she needed a plausible explanation now on why the keys could not be found.

She pulled the drawer out fully and with a single movement turned it upside down. The contents cascaded to the floor. An ageing bottle of ink bounced twice before coming to rest against the bottom of a filing cabinet. There was something appealing in the act of vandalism. The final resting places of the objects might giver her a clue as to where Ian Hart's keys might have finally ended up. She was sure that she must have dropped them when she was in the office previously. There had been something at the bottom of the drawer that had become the last object falling down. It was a photograph. In trying to see who it was she lost her grip on the drawer itself, which also fell to the ground.

Jane knelt down and picked the drawer up. Below her the smiling face of Ian Hart had been severed. One part of the photograph showed a pair of smiling eyes, a nose and most of a mouth; the other part had the remains of the mouth, most of the lower jaw line, a complete right ear, and a section of curly hair. Jane cursed under her breath. She had already helped end Ian Hart's life. Now she was destroying his memory.

She looked around. There was no sign of Ian Hart's keys near any of the farther flung objects, but she had at least imposed her holding solution to the missing key problem onto the world. She would have risen to her feet but checked the movement. Just visible through an opening at the top of the desk and its front panel was the doorway to the corridor. This space was occupied by a pair of legs. Barbara had returned.

The legs were immobile. Barbara had stopped moving for some reason. There was one straightforward explanation as to why Barbara might be rooted to the ground in shock. She had been coming into the room when Jane had decided to empty the contents of the drawer onto the floor.

Jane stood up.

"I'm sorry," she said. "I thought there was something at the back of the drawer that I was trying to free. I am afraid it slipped out of my hands."

It was clear that Barbara didn't believe her. The girl was not at all accomplished at hiding her feelings. She must have seen Jane tip the contents deliberately onto the floor. She moved forward in a dreamlike way and started to clear up.

"I'm so sorry," repeated Jane. "Do let me help you."

"No," Barbara said. "I'll do it."

She was smoothing out the photograph as best she could and trying to put the two pieces together. Jane took a step backward but could not bring herself to leave. The slowness with which Barbara was moving was profoundly irritating but she was probably fearful that any sudden movement would provoke another violent outburst from Jane.

Barbara had finally managed to put the photograph back together to her satisfaction. Jane saw that the dismay on Barbara's face had turned into a sort of knowingness. Barbara smiled understandingly. Jane might have taken a little time to work out the reason had she not remembered that Brian Lloyd had told her that one of the reasons he was keen for Barbara to broaden her horizons was to try to weed her off her endless diet of romantic novels. Jane backed out into the corridor. Older woman - younger man - even younger woman rival for the man's affections spun together in an office in which they were all working - it was probably one of the seven romantic plots. Jane backed out into the corridor.

"Jane!"

Peter Green was outside her door.

"If we could have a word -"

Peter Green's gangling arms and legs blocked the corridor. Jane retreated back to the area that she was retreating from. She went back into her office and Peter Green followed. She needed desperately to talk to her mother and Perry.

"The corpulent man I've just met," Peter Green said sharply. "Was he seeing you?"

Jane looked at her watch.

"Inspector Norman, Metropolitan Police," Jane said. "He's on the Mandell case."

"I thought the Met were leaving that sort of financial case to the experts."

"I think there are some loose ends to David Mandell's death. Didn't you say a neighbour of yours was involved with the case? He thought David Mandell must have died earlier than had been suggested or something like that? I think that was what it was about although I couldn't be sure."

"So I did. Oh well if Mr Plod is simply covering it from that angle I suppose one shouldn't complain."

Peter Green nodded contentedly.

Jane looked at her watch again.

"Peter, I -"

"I know you're busy. But it will only take a minute or two, I promise. How shall I put it? Ian Hart."

"Ian?"

"Now Jane, don't look so tragic. I think you have guessed what I am going to say."

"But -"

"Please Jane. I know this is difficult but I do assure you I see no alternative."

"Really?"

"None." Peter Green was firm. "The Chancellor's office needs him. The comparative statistics stuff. Completely pointless really but there you are. I thought I had killed it off but the Chancellor does want to go ahead. I know how busy you are and I know how much Ian likes working for you."

"Fine, Peter," Jane said.

"Are you sure Jane?"

"Yes."

Normally she would have argued. She sensed he would have preferred a slightly greater problem, but she hadn't got the time to humour him.

"I'll try and catch a word with Ian now and break the news to him. I'll do it straightaway."

"That's good of you," Peter Green sounded a little unconvinced.

"And it does mean that we do need the extra economists we have been discussing rather more urgently."

Peter Green looked happier. "You're right to remind me. I think there may be a surplus team in the analytical divisions. I'll make sure you get first refusal. We need to bolster our technical effort. Thank you for reminding me Jane. I'll 'phone Colin straight away."

"And I'll speak to Ian."

"Of course. Thank you Jane."

"Thank you Peter."

In Ian's room she treated everything with supreme care. She spent five minutes looking through the papers he had left on the top of his desk. All the official Treasury documents would have been locked away but there were sheets of paper covered with numbers in Ian's sprawling hand. The numbers she had found curled in his hand at the flat had been much more precisely written, as though he had reached some sort of conclusion. On the top of the filing cabinet was the group photograph of the staff at Mandell headquarters. Mark Mandell was standing next to Paula Black.

She looked at the automatic dialling buttons on Ian's telephone. He had favourite numbers. She dialled the first one.

"Jane Quinn's office." Barbara's tone was unduly bright considering Jane's recent behaviour.

Jane put the telephone down without saying anything. If Barbara formed the view that she was being subject to anonymous telephone calls it might jerk her out of her romantic fantasies about Jane. She wondered how long Suzanne had been programmed into pole position on Ian's telephone. She should be able to work out where in the hierarchy Perry was likely to be. The phone rang before she could experiment further.

"Ian Hart's office."

"Sarah Perry."

The voice was young and poised. This was undoubtedly the confidence inspiring Perry of the Bank.

"It's Jane Charles."

"Oh, hello."

Sarah Perry had switched her tone a notch down in efficiency and a notch up in friendliness. Clearly she knew about Jane.

"Ian was working on some numbers -"

"UK bank accounts. Ian reckoned the money had been brought back into the UK. Has he cracked the sequence yet? I was expecting to hear from him by now, although I gather you want to keep all of this fairly discreet."

"We do. He must still be working on it. He decided to go home to concentrate on it. I'll chase him up. Would finding out who owned the account be difficult?"

"It shouldn't be a problem. I just need the numbers."

"I'll see if I can find what Ian has come up with. Can I phone you if we come up with anything?"

Sarah Perry gave Jane contact numbers.

When she put the receiver down Jane looked round the small office. It was strange that she would never speak to Ian again. She realised how much she had come to depend on him over the last year.

"I'm very sorry, Ian," she said. "But I will find out who did this."

She telephoned her mother. There was no reply. Jane dialled again but the telephone at the other end simply rang endlessly. Hadn't Elizabeth Quinn said something about a shopping trip she was taking? Jane remembered that it had been Richard's idea, so his mother had embraced it eagerly. She had a horrible feeling it involved an overnight stay. It couldn't be this week, surely?

If her mother wasn't there to read the numbers out over the telephone she needed another plan than simply telephoning Perry and saying that she had found some numbers in Ian's office that needed to be checked. Her mother's spare keys were at Richard's flat. Richard, despite having expressed the intention on many occasions, had never managed to get a spare set of his own keys to Jane.

Jane closed the door to Ian's office. The corridor outside was deserted. If she hadn't gone away or simply turned the volume on the telephone down there was a chance her mother had simply gone out for some local shopping or was paying one of her rare visits to the common areas at Silverlawns. Jane could telephone again in a few minutes.

"What a mess," she said quietly. "What a mess I've got us into Ian."

She would miss Ian. She didn't really want to have to go back into his office again. She looked at her watch. Norman's early visit had thrown everything out. She didn't want to stay in the Treasury. The corridor she was in seemed to be closing in around her and she had a ridiculous fear that it might decide to turn itself into an endless tunnel from which she would never escape.

She went back to her office. She added the group picture of the Mandell HQ staff to the other pictures she kept in her handbag. She looked at her watch. She cleared some of the paperwork clogging up her desk and then looked at her watch again. She had agreed to meet Mark Mandell later in the day. He was planning to go over to his father's house to see if anything there might give a new clue. She resisted the temptation to look at her watch for a third time. She needed to get out of the building. If she had free time, a walk in St James's Park might give her time to clear her head. She walked back to her office and told Barbara that she had to leave and might not be coming back. She muttered something about her mother being ill that she knew Barbara would pass on if Peter Green or anyone dropped in. Barbara nodded at the appropriate moments to show that she had absorbed the formal excuse. Clearly she still held the view that Jane was a victim of love's passions.

She walked out of the building exchanging greetings with the new security guard, who she realised could testify accurately to almost all of her entrances and exits of the past few days. Something hard in the bottom of her coat knocked against the door.

The snow had brought warmer air and the breeze no longer took the breath away. The snow on the pavement before her was melting with the help of salt and sand and the day was bright and invigorating. The sun shone brightly into her eyes.

She thought of Ian Hart lying in his bedroom. Even though she knew he was dead she had had a picture of him rising from his bed as though he had only been sleeping.

She knew why she had thought of Ian Hart. She knew what the metal in the lining at the bottom of her coat that had banged against the Treasury main door was. She put her hand in her pocket. She could feel the hole that Ian Hart's keys had squeezed through. She thought for a moment she should go back but she knew she wouldn't. Nothing had the power to make her retrace her steps at the moment. She would replace the keys later in the day.

She was aware of a squeal of brakes and someone shouting at her. She looked around. She was two or three feet into the road without noticing and a balding taxi driver was expressing his view that most of his problems were due to careless pedestrians.

CHAPTER THIRTY

Hemingway had once told Scott Fitzgerald that the difference between the two of them and the rich was that the rich had more money than they did. Money was clearly not a commodity that the local inhabitants of this part of Kensington felt to be in short supply. Jane walked slowly down the street. Paula Black's flat was at the end of a short terrace, shielded by the black branches of a screen of trees that showed up sharply against the white painted fronts of the houses.

Most of the four-storey houses were in single occupation. It was only at the end of the street that there was a mild proliferation of doorbells, suggesting the houses that had been turned into flats. Jane looked around. It was discreet, expensive, and orderly; a good area for a man to keep his mistress.

She turned round and walked back up the road. From the bells Paula Black seemed to occupy the top two floors. A yellow and black alarm clung to the front of the building there like a giant wasp. Jane stopped. When she had got into the taxi she had been clear about what she wanted to do. Norman was playing an incomprehensible game and moving with all the speed of a hesitant tortoise. The Starman was still on the rampage and she had no confidence that Norman, despite his background knowledge of the case, would ever catch up with him. If Ian were to be certain of justice it was up to her to follow up on any remaining leads. She was tired anyway of being threatened; of being forced to behave strangely in her own office. Geoffrey Chorley, David Mandell's finance man, and Eve Jackson, his long time personal secretary, had been away on the crucial days. David Mandell and Bellmore were dead. That really only left Paula. Jane needed to make something happen if she was going to feel safe and easy again. Paula Black was the only lead she had unless Mark had managed to get into his father's house, as he had been intending, and found anything that might explain matters. The only thing she hadn't worked out in her plan was quite how she was going to get anything out of Paula. The direct confrontation she had planned when she first got into the taxi no longer seemed sensible.

There was a restaurant across the road that had a full view of the entrance to Paula's flat. She walked across to it and went in and asked if they had a seat by the window. The waiter shook his head but gestured to more distant parts that would only give her a limited view of the road outside.

Jane hesitated. The air outside was no longer the biting cold that it had been but the restaurant was comfortably warm and there were appetising aromas of freshly cooked food. She was hungry and reluctant to leave.

A tall, olive skinned man with a mane of carefully tended black hair and dark-tinted glasses had got to his feet. He had been sitting at a table for two next to the window.

"I wonder," he said, "if you would care to join me. I could not help overhearing your request. I do assure you it would be a great pleasure for me to have a dining companion."

The man spoke with a cultured voice and Jane supposed he might be a Middle Eastern businessman, perhaps Lebanese. The dark-tinted glasses effectively hid his eyes from her so that she had no real clue as to the reaction she was provoking. The rest of his face was quite impassive, the skin remarkably smooth, as though he had just shaved. There was a faint aroma of something intangible and elusive about him, something to make everything new and fresh.

"That's extremely kind," Jane said, "but I really couldn't impose."

"It would be my pleasure."

He sounded as though he meant it.

Jane sat down. She glanced through the window of the restaurant. The entrance to Paula Black's flat was in full view. She turned back to her companion. He had taken off his glasses and was regarding her closely. The eyelids were a little narrowed as though he might be peering into a desert sandstorm but the eyes themselves were a deep grey-green set against pure white.

"I am really very grateful," Jane said. "We know nothing about each other."

The man considered the point for a moment.

"I am not entirely sure that is true."

"No, really, I am sure we have never met."

"Indeed not. But I do know there is something – *someone* - clearly - in the street opposite who interests you. On the right hand side of the road. Really you should be sitting here. It would be easier to watch. You wouldn't have to glance round as you have been doing."

"Is it that obvious?"

"I saw you walking up and down the street. There is something of extreme interest to you about the house at the end of the terrace. You also seemed to be trying to make up your mind about something. You seemed impatient so it was hardly the house itself you had come to observe but something else, obviously someone else."

"I see," Jane said a little nervously.

"Normally it would not have caught my attention but a beautiful woman is always interesting, particularly one grappling with a deep and vexing problem. My other puzzle is that you are not quite the sort of woman one normally meets here. My guess would be that you are a professional woman of some kind - perhaps a lawyer. But there are a number of other things you could be. I am probably hopelessly wrong."

"No, not at all." Jane felt a sense of relief. He was near enough to the general situation for her to be able to talk to him about her predicament, but not to have to explain anything in detail. Perhaps, though, it was a little worrying that he seemed to be possessed of such finely defined powers of observation. Jane was developing a horror of expert witnesses.

The waiter was hovering with a menu for her. In contrast to her companion he was of medium height with no noticeable distinguishing

JOHN NIGHTINGALE

features. He was probably employed by Diana Vere.

They spent a minute or two ordering. The place was filling up. The sound of conversation around them was rising to a sustained background hum, the chatter of the universe. They would not be overheard.

"How can I help you?" the Lebanese said engagingly.

"There is someone who lives in the street I am interested in, as you guessed. But you probably don't know anything about her."

"Perhaps I do. I eat here every weekday. I have a house nearby. But I see by your expression that I should explain. Most evenings, most early mornings, I play Bridge. This is breakfast for me. I wake slowly and even after rising I find there are a couple of hours for contemplation and watching the world go by. The particular world outside this window is the one that I contemplate most weekday lunchtimes. As fortune would have it, it is also the world that you seem to be interested in. So why don't you let me know which part of it that is causing you to look so preoccupied."

"It's a woman," Jane said. She opened her handbag. She took out the group picture of the Mandell headquarters staff and indicated Paula Black.

"She lives across the road on the corner."

The Lebanese smiled.

"I wanted to know," Jane continued, "if a particular man had been visiting her. This man." She produced the bundle of photographs from her handbag - the photograph of Christopher Bellmore that she had taken from the KM staff magazine, the Mandell staff, and then Mark and David Mandell. Robert Stuart's photograph also slipped from her bag onto the table. She needed to sort out the jumble that was the contents of her bag. She pointed at Christopher Bellmore.

"Yes."

There was no hesitation.

"When?"

"Before and after Christmas. I saw him twice, perhaps three times."

Jane wondered if, in reality, it had been Paula Black who had been the last straw for Bellmore's wife.

"Twice together, once leaving, once arriving. I have seen him once alone here and the woman many times alone."

"Did you ever see a young, tallish man with her?"

Jane gave the best description she could of the Starman.

"No. No one that I can remember fits that description."

Jane slid the photograph back across the table. David and Mark Mandell, side by side, stared at her from behind Paula Black.

She had further confirmation that Bellmore had been involved with Paula Black and probably with the Mandell fraud. The link was getting clearer. She inhaled the aroma of the monkfish and scallops that she had ordered. She could relax for a moment. She looked away to gather her thoughts and found herself staring into Toby Jessop's eyes.

He was at a table further into the restaurant, slightly raised from the position by the window. For a moment she didn't think he had recognised her but then she saw the recognition, a slight nod of the head. His companion had her back to Jane, a woman with long reddish hair. She was thinner than Diana Vere, and undoubtedly younger.

Jane looked down at the batons of orange and green vegetables in the shell on her plate and manoeuvred some of them delicately onto the end of her fork.

"You seem to lead an interesting life," her companion said.

"Only sometimes."

Toby Jessop was looking away from her and the olive skinned man was following the direction of her gaze.

"A friend of a friend," Jane explained.

"Of course."

Her companion had adopted a diplomatic tone.

"Is there anything you need to know about him?"

"Who?"

"The MP."

"No," Jane said. "Not at the moment."

The man nodded. "Only he comes here a lot, particularly on a Friday."

"Did you win last night?" Jane was anxious to change the subject. "Or was it this morning? At bridge I mean."

"It is not a game of chance."

"You normally win then?"

"Yes."

"And never lose?"

"It would not be fun always to win. And sometimes I play badly. Once when I was distracted by my partner. A very beautiful woman. I played too rashly."

"Oh -"

"No, please. It was a most interesting experience. I had lost my sense of detachment. I wanted to prove to her that I could beat the odds, that somehow she should trust in me. We went down two hands running, doubled and vulnerable."

"I am sure she appreciated the intent."

"I don't think so. I had been introduced to her as the card player. I think my reputation rested on that fact in her eyes. That was something that should have been safe. An hour later I had destroyed those foundations. It is dangerous to act out of character. The fates are not kind to those that choose the wrong path."

"I believe not," Jane said.

She picked up the pile of photographs and prepared to put them back in her handbag.

"There is another man there who came to the woman's house."

"What?"

Jane felt the hand holding the photographs shake slightly.

"In your photographs. There is another man who came to her house. He was a more frequent visitor than Bellmore."

"Recently? I mean was he here in the last few weeks?"

"Oh yes."

Jane put the pile of photographs back on the table.

"Who?"

Her companion's finger pointed to the middle of the photograph.

"Him."

He was pointing at David Mandell.

"Are you sure?"

"Yes."

"But not this man?" Jane was pointing at Mark.

"No."

Jane breathed a sigh of relief. She was more certain than ever that there was a link between Paula and the Starman. A link with Mark

Mandell, a link into a chain of command that had already killed Ian would be too hard to bear.

"Although, I'm not sure there wasn't another.." the Lebanese was saying.

Jane felt a sudden pounding in her temples. No, she wanted to say. No, I don't want this.

"This man," she said, pointing at Mark again. "Is there any chance that he has been here?"

The Lebanese paused, seemingly puzzled by her question, and then smiled.

"No, no, I don't mean him. Although I would be fascinated to know why you are so concerned. I can assure you this was not the man I meant." He indicated Mark Mandell. "I am sure he has never been here. At least I have never seen him. But this man has, more than once."

He was pointing at Robert Stuart's photograph.

"That's not possible."

"It is always possible to be mistaken and this man was very discreet in his comings and goings. But he has been a visitor here."

Outside the sky had darkened and it was beginning to snow again. Jane put the photograph away. Where Toby Jessop and his companion had been there were two empty seats. She looked round. She hadn't seen them go.

Her companion handed her a business card.

"You should call me if you need anything," he said. "Any time. That number will get a message to me if it is urgent, but perhaps fortune will anyway arrange it. I would expect so."

She looked at the card he had given her. Asil Mutjaba. Outside she saw there was someone walking past amid some sudden flurries of snow, a young woman walking alone. Even though Jane could not see her face the honey blonde hair billowing slightly in the breeze was instantly recognisable. The figure stopped at the edge of the road, no more than twenty yards away, her slim body framed against a passing car.

"It's Paula Black."

"No."

Asil Mutjaba was shaking his head.

"Of course it is her. Surely you can see it is the same woman as in the photograph."

Paula had crossed the road and was going up the steps to the entrance to her flat.

"You misunderstand me. It is the woman in the photograph, but her name isn't Paula Black."

"Are you sure?"

It was hardly a question that needed answering. He had been right on everything so far.

"Oh yes. I knew her father. He was a businessman. Reg White. He made a fortune out of recycling iron, metal -."

"Scrap."

Asil Mutjaba nodded.

"Yes, scrap. He had other business interests, none of them so respectable. He died six or seven months ago. Paula was his daughter. Paula White."

*

They had paid the bill and were finishing coffee when Paula re-appeared.

"I ought to go."

"Not all things are auspicious. You must take care."

"I will," Jane said. "Thank you."

She put her coat on.

"Goodbye."

He took her hand.

"Au revoir."

Paula was climbing into a taxi. There was a second one with its light glowing in the gloom thirty yards behind. Jane hailed it and asked the driver to follow the cab in front at a reasonable distance but not to lose him. The driver nodded as though she was the same as any other fare. They started driving back to central London. Jane looked at her watch. Eventually the taxi in front drove into Trafalgar Square and slid down into Northumberland Avenue. Then Jane saw that it was pulling in just before the Embankment. Her own driver pulled into the kerb.

"Thanks for being so co-operative," Jane said.

"It's your business, love."

Paula was walking towards Embankment Tube. Jane hurried after her. There was a cafe on the right of the station entrance where two jovial Italian men were dispensing hot coffee and cakes. Steam issued from the narrow confines of the building in sudden jets. There was a crowd of three crammed into the inadequate space, but no Paula.

Jane looked across at the ticket machines and beyond. People actually seemed to be queuing up to go through the automatic entrances to purgatory. No Paula.

The she saw her. At the other entrance to the station, the riverside, Paula was talking into her mobile phone. She was silhouetted against the falling snow. From time to time she made a gesture with her hand. Jane watched the private ballet unfold. Paula made one call and started another. Once Paula looked in her direction and made her feel conspicuous. Jane looked round. There was a payphone where she could keep Paula in sight and which would give her more cover.

She telephoned the number Mark Mandell had given her for his father's house. The telephone rang but there was no reply. She telephoned Richard's number. There was the same cheery message as before. This time she left an impassioned appeal for him to telephone her at the earliest possible moment.

Paula had walked back a few paces into the station. Jane put the telephone back on the receiver but saw that Paula was starting another call. She telephoned Diana Vere.

"Jane? Where are you? I called your office but they said you were out. The woman I spoke to sounded rather confused -"

"She is rather confused, but that is entirely my fault. She is standing in for Suzanne."

"Where are you then?"

"A long lunch."

"You don't normally take lunch."

"I do now."

"Well, that is an improvement. Toby was saying what a charming companion you were. You ought to get out and stretch your wings."

"Did he say that?"

"As you ask. Yes."

"That was nice of him. He must be very good for morale."

Diana Vere laughed. "Isn't he? Sadly he is up in the constituency on business. He went up last night."

"Oh."

"Jane, is there anything wrong?"

"There is a little problem I have," Jane said urgently. "One of the people who used to work for David Mandell, a woman named Paula Black. Daughter of an East End operator called Reg White. That's the point. Her real name is Paula White. That's why she is not showing up on your computers. If you have any information I would be grateful. I think she is involved in the Mandell fraud."

Paula was talking with considerable animation. Something was wrong.

"O.K." Diana said. "I will see what we can do."

Jane put the telephone down. She dialled Scotland Yard and asked for Norman. To her surprise she got straight through.

"This Paula Black," she said after she had introduced herself. "I understand her real name is Paula White."

"Yes," Norman said.

"You knew?"

"Yes."

"But you don't think it suspicious?"

"It is not an offence for people to choose what they want to be called.

"You knew?" Jane repeated.

"Yes Miss Quinn, or is it Mrs Charles today?"

"That is entirely different Inspector."

"I am sure it is madam, or is it miss?"

Jane had been proposing to offer some sort of olive branch but Norman was pursuing some fixed agenda of his own. Paula had finished her telephone call and was looking out towards the river. She might move off at any moment.

"Is there anything else I can do for you Miss Quinn?" Norman broke her silence. He had opted for her official name.

"No," Jane said. "I thought you might just like to know about Paula White." She put the telephone down.

Paula was buying a ticket from one of the machines. Jane felt in her pocket for change. She could at least determine on which line Paula was travelling. The machine swallowed her ticket, the barriers opened, and then her ticket was offered up for her to take. She picked it up reluctantly.

Paula was striding forward as though she had a clear purpose in mind and Jane had to hurry to keep her in sight. Jane's hands were sweating and the tube anyway seemed warm after the snow. Paula made an abrupt turn to the left while everyone else who had entered walked straight on. A single short escalator made of gleaming steel churned relentlessly downwards. The last time Jane had been on the Underground as a small child the escalators had had wooden slats on the steps. Then she had been carried out screaming.

Jane told herself that the escalator was so short that she was not travelling far underground. It was no different at this level than travelling in a building in a lift. All that was likely to be above her head was not solid earth but parts of the station itself, storerooms and things like that.

At the bottom of the escalator there was a concourse area with passages leading off right and left and a wide but very low oblong corridor gleaming with white light straight ahead. This time Paula walked straight on. Jane looked round. There was no obvious way back to the surface. She waited for Paula to reach the end and then followed. Down a narrow passage she could see a train opening its doors and a trickle of people getting off. She could feel the sweat building up on the back of her hands, the sense of nausea and panic growing within her. She knew she only had a few minutes before she would need to go back above ground.

She needed to establish where the train and Paula were going and then make her way back to the surface. She waited for the train to leave the station and then edged forward. She would rather not see the entrance to the tunnels but she did need to definitely establish which platform this was. She inched forward to the edge of the little passageway and then stopped. Paula was standing at the far end of the platform. For some reason she had not got on the train.

Jane backed into her own private tunnel. She was finding it curiously difficult to breath in the warm air. She needed to get back to the surface now. She edged backwards into something. The something was really someone, for a man's hand closed over her mouth and a man's arm trapped her arms at her side so that she could not move.

CHAPTER THIRTY-ONE

She was back above ground. The snow was easing a little. The rush hour was beginning early as people decided to give themselves more time to cope with the conditions on the journey home.

"You bruised my leg," Mark Mandell said.

"You are lucky I didn't break it," Jane straightened up. "I meant to. It was a crazy idea grabbing me from behind."

"I had no choice. I went back to your apartment and there he was. I followed him from your apartment to the station and down. I had no idea what was going to happen but it could only be something nasty. I thought we both needed to be out of there as soon as possible."

"What could they do in a crowded Tube station?"

"Nobody stopped me grabbing you."

Jane shivered violently.

"Are you all right?"

"Yes, it's just being in a tunnel. I hate it. I think I might be sick."

Jane moved to one side breathing rapidly. It was too ridiculous a condition to submit to. She blew air out fiercely through her nose and kept her mouth tight shut. She was going to control it this time although a few more seconds underground would have been fatal. She opened her mouth and took a long gulp of air. It was painfully cold.

"Better?"

"Yes, I think so."

"We need to get out of the snow. There is a cafe up there."

Mandell pointed in the direction of the Strand. Jane nodded. The figures before them were like matchstick men. The flurries of snow seemed to eat into the outline of their bodies making them tall and thin against the whiteness.

"I thought you were going over to your father's house?" Jane asked stirring her coffee.

"I was, but I have already looked over the obvious places. I thought I ought to be able to work it out for myself. I should know what my father would have been likely to do. I thought if I could work that out I would know precisely what I should be looking for."

"And did you?"

Mandell looked out into the white blanket of snow.

"I wouldn't say I was making good progress so I went down to the towpath to look at the water. I thought it would help me think. I don't know how long I had been gazing at the surface of the river. I could feel myself beginning to freeze. It was mesmerising. But I caught a movement in the corner of my eye and there he was stamping his feet to keep warm. He must have looked in my direction and just not noticed me because I was so still.

"So what happened?"

"I stayed where I was as I seemed to be invisible. After a bit he seemed to get fed up. Finally he set off back to town."

"Did he have a mobile telephone?"

Mark Mandell looked surprised.

"Why do you ask?"

"Paula spent a lot of time telephoning when she got to the station. She could have been 'phoning him."

"He could have had a mobile. I couldn't keep him in sight all the time. I nearly lost him in the Tube station at Vauxhall. In fact I did for a couple of minutes. Perhaps that explains what he was doing. He might need to stay fairly near the surface to make a call. But he could have been doing something else. Anyway I picked him up again and followed. When he got to Embankment he didn't go out as I expected but went to another platform. That is when I saw you. I just didn't know what to do. So I grabbed you. Sorry."

"And you didn't see Paula? Or the two of them together?"

"No to both questions."

"I didn't see him. What does this man look like?"

Mark Mandell thought.

"Tall, slimmish, but athletic. Difficult to tell. He was wrapped up pretty well against the cold."

It must be the Starman. It was clear enough to Jane except that it wouldn't stand up in the law courts, wouldn't even get to any court. It was more likely that she would be tried for withholding evidence or whatever the crime was for not reporting murders.

"What was he doing when you saw him?"

"Watching your apartment."

"Are you sure?"

"I couldn't swear it was yours. From where he was he could keep a watch over seven or eight."

Jane sighed.

"Let's not kid ourselves. Who else would he be watching?"

"But why are they watching you?"

"I don't know. I have a feeling the flat has been watched ever since I got into this.

"They must think you know something."

"I certainly knew Bellmore. Look what happened to him."

"Jane, this is crazy. You're in danger. You need to get out of this now. Go to the police and tell them everything."

"I'm not sure I can quite go to the police. It would be Norman and for some reason I can't trust him. He's got his own agenda in solving this and I don't know what it is. They would hold me for questioning if I confessed to seeing two bodies. I can't spare the time at the moment. Besides I don't believe Norman is going to be able to solve anything. I owe Ian something, if only to establish how he got killed. It's not a great reward but it is something."

"What about your mother and the numbers?"

"I can't get hold of her on the telephone."

Jane looked round. The only other occupants of the cafe were still examining the guidebooks they had been looking at when they came in. They might have been better advised to opt for a compass and a rope.

The snow was falling with renewed vigour. This did have one advantage. It meant that it would be impossible to be followed. It was difficult enough to see anyone at ten yards, let alone follow them.

"How long is this lasting?" She pointed outside.

"It can't last more than a few hours can it? Why?"

"I could go over to my mother's flat. Talk my way in with the warden. She knows me by sight. I could just say that there was a paper that I needed that couldn't wait. She could come in with me. Ian's numbers are hidden in a book."

"Which book?"

"There's an old family copy of *Roget's Thesaurus*. We've had it since I can remember. If we can find out who has got the money everything is solved."

"I suppose so. But perhaps that was what Bellmore found out."

"We need to know one way or another anyway," Jane said decisively.

Mark Mandell nodded.

"I suppose it can't do any harm. How do we get there? And where is there?"

"It's a place called Silverlawns, and I get there via the South Circular. There is no point in us both going. You were going to check out your father's house. Why don't you do that? It still makes sense. We need all the help we can get - the numbers may mean nothing. I'll see you there. I may be a little bit of time. I have to pick up the car on the way."

"It's too dangerous."

"Not in a blizzard. Nobody is going to follow me in that. Besides you might find something out. We need all the leads we can get. I have this horrible feeling we're rather short of time."

Jane hadn't realised that was how she felt until she said the words. But she suddenly realised that time wasn't standing still but had been accelerating from the time she had first heard of the Mandell loss. For a thousand days time had been static. Now it was hurrying and waiting for no one. Only the obliterating snow was creating a momentary breathing space, confining things temporarily into compartments. She needed to make best use of the intermission. If she was alone it would be easier to think.

"If there is somebody watching your apartment it would be crazy to go back there. Come to my father's house. No one would think of looking for you there."

"How do I get in?"

"When you get to the house gives two rings, count ten and then give three rings. I'll know it's you."

"What happens if the police are there?"

"Stop at the end of the road by the bus stop. I'll get in as though you're offering me a lift."

"Sounds good."

Jane got to her feet.

"Look," Mandell said.

Jane took Mandell's hand and squeezed it gently.

"I have to go."

Jane walked outside. The snowflakes billowed round her thickly, turning everyone not in immediate view into a blur.

The fruit sellers at the top of the street had turned their barrows away from the wind so that the snow encroached only on the edges of their displays. The lanterns hung at the top of their stalls threw yellow light downwards to illuminate the tangerines, dates and apples set between fake green bands of grass. Jane passed the oasis of light and pressed on as fast as she could for Charing Cross Station.

Inside the station, protected from the blizzard, sounds were no longer so blurred. Jane looked back the way she had come. There was no one behind her. There was another thing she had to do as well. She went to one of the telephone booths and looked round. There was no one following her.

"Diana? It's Jane."

"Jane?" Diana didn't sound exactly her relaxed self. "Where are you?"

"That doesn't matter. Have you found out anything about Paula White?"

"When can we meet Jane?"

"There's no time. If you have anything I need to know now."

"I'm not sure that's possible."

"Look Diana, I need your help. What have you found out about Paula White? About her father? He was a scrap merchant wasn't he?"

"Not entirely. His main occupation was local gang boss. Drugs, prostitution, protection. Scrap was just the respectable front. He died last year. He was losing a bit of influence, getting a bit soft compared to the new boys."

"And Paula?"

"Clean."

"The flat in Kensington -"

"She owns it. A cash purchase three years ago."

"Anything else?"

"Jane, we should meet."

"There's no time, Diana. What else have you found out?"

There was something more. Jane could tell from the edge on Diana's voice.

"Paula may not be involved in her father's rackets but she has a brother, Julian, who definitely is. This is dangerous Jane. You need to be safe."

"I will be. It's taken care of," Jane said. She looked around again. No one. "Look, I must be going."

"Jane -"

"Sorry, Diana. Must run."

Jane put the telephone down.

She walked slowly out into the snow. The Strand was clogged with vehicles edging their way slowly forward as the snow fell heavily down. It might be a couple of hours before she had Ian's numbers in her possession again. She was sure she could convince the warden at her mother's flat to let her in. If the numbers did reveal where the Mandell money was or who had stolen it that was all that she could do. Then she could go the police. No one would have any interest in eliminating her once she had done that. She shivered. Even if the numbers didn't reveal anything she would go the police. The situation she was in needed to come to an end. Her experience underground had drained much of her resolve from her. It would be best if it were over that evening one way or another.

She criss-crossed the street to make sure she was not being followed. She felt that it was neurotic and that there was no possibility at all that someone could possibly be keeping track of her given the terrible conditions, certainly not given the fact that she was constantly on the alert to detect the possibility. But she did it nevertheless.

When she had got back to her car and scooped the snow off the windscreen, it occurred to her that somebody might have been watching the car and that all the subterfuge that she had been manufacturing in the last hour could have been totally pointless. She looked about her. She was not alone. The traffic was crawling forward, bumper to bumper, but no one had stopped, nobody was getting into any of the parked cars nearby. The cars were like boulders being pushed forward by a glacier, held fast together and with no possibility of changing one's relative position. One just chooses when to join the stream, nothing else.

Half way to her mother's flat, on a piece of road where the traffic had thinned and the pace was quicker, she was the last car over the traffic lights at an intersection. She slowed. The traffic in front of her faded away and cars from other roads than the one she had been on funnelled in behind. She was sure she was not being followed.

By the time she got to Silverlawns her concern had become focused on the difficulties she might face in gaining entry. She thought the best pretext was the papers that her mother had been signing concerning the winding up of her father's estate. They presented a plausible enough excuse for urgency if she were to mutter on about meeting some Inland Revenue deadlines.

When she got there she didn't need any reasons beyond wanting to pick up some papers from her mother's flat. The warden, a chatty woman in blue smock, detailed some difficulties she herself had been having with the taxman and might have detained Jane longer if there had not been a buzz from another resident indicating that help was required.

"Still," the woman said as she handed Jane the key to her mother's flat, "at least she is taking a holiday so that she can get a few days away from it. That was very nice of your brother. If you would excuse me. Just leave the key here when you have finished."

She pointed at a cardboard box on her desk. Jane nodded, and followed the woman out into the corridor. It had all been refreshingly easy.

She waited till the warden was out of sight and then opened the door. She could remember the word at the top of the page in the

Roget's International Thesaurus. It had been 'Store'. She would look the word up calmly, take the numbers down and take the original scrap of paper away with her. It might be a clue to Ian Hart's death. There could be nothing simpler.

As she opened the door of her mother's sitting room she wondered if it was possible that her mother ever used the book and that the paper might somehow have fallen out. She had a sudden mental picture of herself flicking hopelessly through the pages vainly trying to convince herself that she had been to Ian's flat and had put the numbers in and that they must be somewhere. She need not have been concerned. The neat little collection of books was on the top of the writing bureau as it had always been. It was just that the familiar red book was missing. There was no thesaurus, no 'store' or any of the synonyms listed; no 'stock', no 'fund', nothing at all.

CHAPTER THIRTY-TWO

It had finally stopped snowing. When Jane had gone outside the last flake had landed and the sky over London was clearing. There was now a tranquil backdrop to the questions that were buzzing in her head. The only person who knew about the numbers was Mark Mandell, at least as far as she was aware. Could anybody have seen her putting them into the *Thesaurus* through the window of her mother's flat? It was unlikely. Why, anyway, should anyone, other than Mark Mandell, know that the numbers existed at all?

She had been preparing herself for retrieving the numbers and then finding that no such account existed, or that it belonged to a Mrs Smith in Hull and had never contained more than £1,000 at any one time. She would have preferred that blank wall to this. At least the matter would have been resolved. Why had she taken so long to try to retrieve them?

There were no police outside Mandell's house, no sirens blaring in the night. Instead there were cars gingerly making their way through the deeply packed snow on the side roads and a group of children building a snowman.

She rang the doorbell. Two rings. Count ten. Three rings. A subdued looking Mandell ushered her in and then closed the door quickly behind her. Inside the house was silent.

"There are no numbers."

Her voice echoed round the cold hall of the house, hollow words bouncing off the tiled stone floor.

"You couldn't find them?"

"The book they were in was missing."

"Oh -"

Mandell nodded, seemingly uninterested, as though he knew already.

"Did you hear what I said Mark. Somebody has taken the book."

"Your mother, did you ask her?"

Mandell's tone was still flat. He seemed to be trying to summon up interest in what was going on.

"She is on holiday. A delayed Christmas treat from my brother."

"She might have taken the book with her."

"She might have done. She might have taken her writing cabinet with her. The fact that the book in question has not moved more than an inch ever since she has lived there and only then to be dusted doesn't strike you as suspicious, I suppose?"

"Of course it does. Who else did you tell about it?"

"I didn't. I only told you."

"Somebody has found out about them though."

"Clearly."

"Could someone have seen you hiding the numbers?"

"It's possible, but not really likely."

Mark would have had time to remove the numbers of course. Collecting her car had added the best part of an hour to the journey. Mandell needn't even have done it himself. He could have telephoned somebody. Why hadn't she asked the warden if anyone had been seen around Silverlawns?

"You do trust me don't you?"

"You don't seem upset. You should be mortified."

"I could see it in your face when you came in."

"That doesn't explain it."

"There are some papers upstairs that might explain things a bit more. Why don't you come and look at them. They are in my father's study. First floor."

Mandell turned and walked up the stairs. After a moment Jane followed him into a room at the back of the house.

Mark pulled out a sheaf of plastic wallets and put them down on a small table that David Mandell had positioned by a full-length glass window overlooking Wandsworth Common. Outside the sky had become crystal clear and the snow gleamed brilliant white under the light of the moon. Jane sat down in one of the easy chairs by the table and Mandell switched on a standard lamp. The brilliance of the snow was washed away by the artificial light.

"You had better close the curtains. I am very wary of being watched at present."

Mandell pulled the green heavy curtains shut across the window. Jane looked round the room. The filing cabinet was dark wood and modern. David Mandell's desk was a reproduction of an antique; too unmarked and shiny to be convincingly old. There was also a large television, a few reference books on a shelf and what was probably a cocktail cabinet.

Jane pulled the plastic wallets towards her. There were a series of glossy photographs of houses mostly set against water. The houses were large, white painted, expensive. On the outside of one of the folders someone had written a note on a Mandell Holdings compliments slip -

Mandell,

This could be the one!

P.

The note was ambiguous. It could refer to David Mandell or his son.

The house in question looked out over an extensive stretch of ocean with a myriad of yachts and larger boats gleaming on the blue water.

"So where is this? The States? California?"

"Vancouver"

"You sound as though you know."

"I do. I've been there."

"It seems fairly breathtaking."

"It is."

"A good place to live?"

"Undoubtedly. My father was also a fan, although I hadn't realised his enthusiasm had stretched this far. These are house agent's particulars or whatever the equivalent is in Canada. I think it is fairly conclusive." Mandell's voice was flat. "He was going to buy one of these houses. Maybe he already has. An escape to the New World."

"So he was escaping with Paula White."

"It's her handwriting."

"But why not just go if that was what they wanted to do?"

"A man in his early sixties with £250 million in his pocket could be considered something of a catch. Somebody with access to a few million but with a company to run isn't in the same league."

"You seem to have been busy before I got here. Anyway, why hasn't anyone found all this before?"

"I remembered something that should have occurred to me before. My father was always touchy about letting anyone get access to this room. The door was sometimes locked. There had to be a reason. There is - a safe let into the floor. That is where these papers came from."

"So you think that your father and Paula planned all this?"

"I think it is more than a fair bet, don't you?"

Mark Mandell put a blue British passport down in front of Jane in the name of Mr S Watkinson. She opened it and found herself looking at a photograph of David Mandell.

The passport had apparently been issued two years previously but looked surprisingly new. She flicked through the pages. There were no visa stamps, no marks of any kind.

"One might suppose that Mr Watkinson had never been anywhere, and I don't suppose he has. He would have made his first trip after Christmas, possibly with a glamorous younger companion. I imagine Bellmore was involved as well, presumably to take care of the KM end. He panicked and so Paula and her brother got rid of him. It is an explanation that fits what we know."

"If your father were planning to leave the country - "

"What other option did he have? There would only be one person to ask where the money had gone and that would be him. He was bound to leave."

"Paula is still here."

"I imagine a sudden disappearance might not have been desirable. It would indicate that it was likely that she had been involved."

"Could anyone else have been involved? Are we sure Geoffrey Chorley couldn't have had anything to do with it?"

Mandell laughed, a sudden humourless sound that echoed through the empty house.

"Chorley? He'd have no appetite for this. Geoffrey was always whiter than white."

Whiter than white.

The words circled their way through a million connections in a million different cells in Jane's brain.

"Your father's safe. How did you get into it?"

"The tumblers hadn't been engaged. It just opened."

"Curious that your father would just leave the safe open?"

"Isn't it?"

She could feel a cold draft from somewhere in the house, but perhaps it had been there before. She saw the curtain over the long window looking out over the Common move as the current of air insinuated its way into the space between the fabric and the glass.

"This open safe," Jane continued, "I suppose it would have been a complicated combination?"

Mandell looked up from the pile of papers. "Very, knowing my father."

Very lucky then that David Mandell had not bothered to set the combination, although he had bothered to put back the floorboard and replace the covering rug.

Almost absurdly unlucky that someone had stolen the *Thesaurus* from her mother's house. Perhaps the extremes of fortune cancelled each other out. Or perhaps she could not see what was obvious.

The draught behind the curtain was creating little waves of undulating fabric. It was hypnotic and dreamy. She felt it dulling her intuition.

"I think I could do with a breath of fresh air, Mark. I need to get my brain into gear. I can't do it here."

Mark Mandell gathered the papers into an untidy bundle.

"There doesn't seem to be anything else that is startling."

"Nothing on the KM transactions?"

"No."

She hadn't been expecting that there would.

"We could go out onto the Common," Mandell continued. "There is a gate leading directly out from the end of the garden."

"You don't need to come Mark."

But Mandell was on his feet.

"I insist."

He touched her cheek with his hand.

"You're very cold."

"Just a little numb."

*

Outside the moon was high in a clear sky.

The snow was glittering and unmarked. The air was still, but the fumes that had hung over London since the New Year had been carried away by the snowstorm. Jane looked behind her. Two straight virgin footprint tracks were marked on the snow in two straight lines leading back to David Mandell's house.

Mark Mandell walked beside her. For the last five minutes he had said nothing, seemingly as preoccupied in his own thoughts as she had been.

They were walking towards the bridge that crossed the railway line that ran through the Common. Jane could see the headlights of cars moving in the distance on the outskirts of the Common through a thin curtain of trees that stretched in front of them.

"It seems warmer."

Jane looked up. She was far enough from sources of light to make out faint stars. In Ireland the stars in the night sky had been a carpet of bright lights that had seemed to fill the whole sky.

"What is it?"

"I was wondering. Paula and her brother - if they have got the money why are they still here?"

"Why should they go away? They can stay and let my father take the rap."

Jane looked at the snow. Perhaps that was what Paula and her brother were planning to do. Sit it out and end up - whiter than white. Then it struck her that there was an alternative explanation, one that was far more plausible in the light of events. Paula and her brother were still here because they didn't have the money. They were still trying to find it. Perhaps that was because somebody else now had it.

"Jane? What is it?"

She had stopped.

"Oh nothing, I was trying to work something out."

She felt his hand on the back of her arm.

"You were swaying; I thought you might be feeling faint, or something -"

She put both her hands on Mark's arm and unlocked his hand from her body.

"No, I'm fine. I'm tired, that's all. Let's go back to the house."

He was in front of her, the white face of the moon behind him, his own face in shadow.

"Jane, I'm in love with you. I thought I ought to tell you."

Mandell's arms were around her shoulders. The moon had disappeared from view leaving his face in shadow.

"I'd like to get away from this, start somewhere new."

Jane took a step backward.

"There's nowhere we can go until this is sorted out."

"I know you need to escape. We could go together."

The moon reappeared.

"Look at me, tell me you will. Tell me at least you will think about it."

What was Mark saying? Did they have £250 million to start a new life together? Or maybe the £5 million hadn't been diverted to supporting Mandell Entertainment.

Jane's head was bowed, looking at the ground. Then she looked up but not at Mark Mandell. There were the tracks they had made coming from the house here and there overlaid with their footprints returning to it.

She looked round behind her. There was no one to be seen on the Common, but there was another set of tracks running at an angle to their own. They were crossing. Had they been there when they had first walked out?

It was one of the footprints of this track she had seen when she looked down.

"It would be wonderful, a new life." Mandell said. "We could go now, this very minute."

"No," Jane said. "I don't think we can."

There was no mistake however hard she looked. The tracks were perfectly clear in the virgin snow. It was very easy to make out the star design.

CHAPTER THIRTY-THREE

"What is it Jane?"

"The man you were following from the apartment. There might have been something distinctive about him. I wondered if you looked at the footprints he left."

"No, why -"

Mandell was bending down. Jane pointed to the star prints.

"You're not saying that those are his footprints?"

"They can't belong to anyone else. I have given up believing in coincidence."

"But it can't be. Surely we would have seen him? He can't be invisible, can he?"

"Of course not. It's probably just that we can't see him."

Mandell looked round. There was nothing, animal or human, moving or still. The moon was now bright and the white snow left no hiding place.

"Where can he be?"

"Trees, bushes, the railway line. He must be somewhere but we are not going to find him."

Mandell pointed at the Starman's footprints stretching away on a track at right angles to their own.

"We could follow his tracks."

"There's no point. They would just end somewhere. Probably

abruptly."

"He's not a superman, Jane. I followed him. He didn't know that was happening."

Jane had a mental picture of the dog lying dead in the snow. Only a puppy.

"We're out of out depth, Mark. According to Norman this man is a professional killer and extremely dangerous. I am sure he killed Bellmore. I think he killed Ian. I'm not sure that Norman isn't involved in all this in some way. He seems to have some sort of private vendetta going on where he is prepared to take some casualties - us - to get his man, or whatever he wants. We need to get the normal police involved. And we need to get off this common."

"Back to the house?"

"Yes. As quickly as possible."

They stumbled back as fast as they could, through the gate at the end of the garden and then through the garden itself and back into the house. There were only their own tracks leading towards them.

Mandell pushed the kitchen door shut and stood with his back to it.

"Are you sure it is locked?"

Mandell tried the door and pushed the bolts at top and bottom home.

"Solid."

Jane was checking through her clothing looking for her mobile but couldn't find it. She couldn't even remember losing it.

"Where is the nearest telephone?"

"On the dresser. I'll put the light on."

"No," Jane said. "No need. I can see it."

There was a shaft of moonlight coming through the window, which had panels of coloured Victorian glass down its sides. It bathed the end of the kitchen in icy unreal white with patches of distorted blue and green.

She walked across the room, her heart pounding from the exertion of running and picked the receiver up. She looked behind her. Mandell was still standing by the outside door, a comforting shape in the gloom. She started breathing slowly and deeply. She needed to keep her nerve. The telephone almost dropped from her hands as she picked it up. The receiver clattered against the edge of the dresser, the sound absurdly loud in the silence. She started pushing the buttons. She saw a shadow move in the light in front of her. She turned round. Mark was still there, unmoving. She had an overwhelming desire to check that it was still him, that he hadn't somehow changed, but she fought it down. She knew she was being ridiculous. She needed to concentrate on the telephone call.

She put the receiver to her ear. The number was not ringing. She must have got it wrong. She pressed to get the dialling tone again. Nothing.

"It's dead, Mark."

"What?"

"The line is dead."

"It can't be. The jack plug has probably been pulled out of the socket. My father's cleaner is always doing it. There have been times when I have had to come round because she has disconnected anything within range of my father's hearing. Look, I'll turn the light on. You can't see what you are doing."

"No!" Jane hissed. "If you do that he will know for certain where we are. I can check."

Jane bent down and traced the telephone wire to a socket in the wall. It was firmly in place but the line was dead. She took it out and put it back in again. The line was still dead.

"It's no good," she whispered over her shoulder.

"There is another telephone in the hall. It may just be this one that is dead."

Jane knew that that wasn't the case, that what they had to do was get out of the house fast and get to a place of safety. Every minute they spent in abortive actions was a minute lost which would count against them.

She saw the shadow grow in front of her. Something had cut off the light. Death comes as a shadow, as the fairy tales say.

Looking out of the kitchen window she saw that the moonlight in the garden was undimmed and that it was only a local shadow that was affecting them, and that was hardly possible. That was when she heard the noise, somebody outside.

She had risen to her feet and turned round. The warning to Mark was just about to be uttered. But it was too late. He would not have heard. Her words would have been drowned out in the noise of the stained glass panes in the garden door shattering and the million splinters of glass exploding into the room.

Mandell grabbed at the spade as it was being withdrawn but only succeeded in being pulled into the broken glass edge of the window. A flashlight from outside shone into the room and the light spun everywhere off its new crystal flooring. Then the spade came shattering through the other pane and the door itself buckled under a tremendous blow. A long arm in leather appeared, reaching inside for the door handle.

She would have screamed but she needed her energy to survive. Mandell, clutching his shoulder, was close behind her as she opened the door into the hallway.

Mandell switched the light in the hallway on.

"No -"

"He knows where we are."

Mandell was pushing internal door locks into place. This door was plain wood so they could not be seen by whoever was in the kitchen, nor see into it. Neither could they see what was happening. They could hear a splintering sound. The garden door was giving way.

They had a few seconds. Jane ran across the tiled hall to the main front door and pulled at it. Nothing happened. It was deadlocked. She remembered that Mark had locked it after she had come in.

She turned to him.

"The key!"

He was bleeding. Flying glass had cut into his cheek and the blood had run down his face and on to his coat. There were drops on the floor.

"It's in the kitchen."

The door behind him shook under the force of a heavy blow.

"The basement," Mandell said. "There is another way out from there."

Stairs ran down underground from the side of the hall, a wide circular staircase that coiled its way downward.

"Stop Mark!"

She pulled Mandell back.

"There is nowhere else to go!"

"Look."

Jane pointed at the dozen stone steps which they had come down. There was a clear trail of drops of blood.

"Back to the top!"

"That's crazy."

"No." She could hear that the blows on the kitchen door were more regular, the initial frenzied speed having given way to measured force. With each blow there was a further splintering of the wood round the locks. There was not too much time, but there might be a little, probably enough.

At the top of the stairs she managed to staunch the flow of blood by tying her scarf round Mandell's head. The trail of blood led down and then back up.

"Now," Jane said. "We go down, but carefully."

She led the way, avoiding the drops of blood that would smear if she trod on them. At the bottom of the stairs they were face to face with David Mandell's swimming pool. The flat surface of the water reflected what little light there was back at them. Round the edge of the pool were the dim shapes of columns. In front of them wide steps led grandly into the water. Above them they heard the door give way.

"This way."

Mandell pulled her to one side to what seemed like a solid wall but in which there was a concealed door. Mandell opened it. There was a narrow passageway and steps leading upwards. Upstairs the locks on the door to the hallway had finally given way and silence had replaced the hammering.

"The pump and filtration room," Mandell whispered. "This leads out to the garden again."

They were moving upwards when somebody turned the lights in the basement on. There was a ventilation slit that Jane could see through. It began with light in the water, at first faint but growing in intensity, bubbling up from the ever-brighter blue depths. An orange light on a control panel on the wall beside her was suddenly lit and the silence was filled with the hum of machinery coming back to life. As Jane watched recessed lights in the walls shone their own light upwards revealing an orange pink marbled ceiling and columns round the edge of the water. David Mandell had obviously had some admiration for the classical.

Then Jane saw him. He had neat dark hair, a stylish short leather jacket worn over a thick dark green ribbed sweater, waterproofed trousers and designer commando boots. He was dressed more for a survival course than a stay in central London. He showed no signs of the violent exertions he had been engaged in. He was moving competently and lightly round the edge of the pool with his arms slightly outstretched to ward off any threat or danger. This was Paula White's brother. This was the Starman.

Now he was close to her, no more that ten feet away. He was hardly more than twenty and had a handsome and intelligent face in which adolescence seemed to have been forgotten long ago. She had to force herself to remember that he had killed Bellmore, almost certainly Ian Hart, and Norman's victim in the East End. There was nothing overtly threatening in his presence and he held no weapon. For a moment he was motionless and she wondered what he was doing. Then she realised he was listening for any sound they might make. He should, of course, have been searching the upper floors of the house if her ruse had paid off but he didn't seem to have spent even a second considering that option. There was only one hopeful sign. He was now moving away from them along the side of the pool.

She felt a touch on her arm. Mark Mandell was pointing upwards towards the ground.

"C'mon," Mandell hissed. "This is our chance."

"Are you sure?"

"Of course, follow me."

Jane took one last look behind her as Mandell eased himself forward. The Starman was on the far side of the pool. Mark was drawing back some bolts at the top of the steps. It seemed they would soon be out in the air and free. Mandell threw back a trapdoor. Jane could see there was another roof above and the moon shining through a glass window.

"Quickly!" Mandell said. "It's the workshop my father had built on. You can't get to it directly from the house. We should be safe."

Jane followed him up and Mandell lowered the trapdoor carefully back into place.

Jane was just congratulating herself on the effectiveness of the escape when there was a faint clicking sound and she and Mandell found themselves caught in a pool of light. It was the light from a powerful torch blazing into their eyes. Jane was dazzled.

"At last," a woman's voice said. "I have some questions you need to answer."

CHAPTER THIRTY-FOUR

It was rather a welcoming voice, like that of a hotel receptionist. It was also perfectly calm; rather calmer than Jane was feeling. The overhead lights in the workshop clicked on. A young blonde woman was facing them. Close to she had the rounded, flawless face of a model, vacant of emotion. Her purpose was, however, clear. In one hand she had a torch with a large head and a long slender stem that looked suitable for a club. In the other she had a more immediately effective weapon, a small revolver, equipped with a silencer.

"How?"

Jane stopped. She knew the answer to her question. Paula and her brother had always had the situation worked out and every angle covered. If Paula had had an intimate relationship with David Mandell she would probably know the layout of the house as well as Mark did.

Paula was examining her. Her eyes were scanning backwards and forwards across Jane's face. Jane tried to look as though she could think of any number of plausible reasons to explain the situation that she and Mark found themselves in. She could see it wasn't working. Paula's expression was as unmoving as the gun in her hand.

"Where's the money?"

"I -" Jane said.

"Let him answer. Where's the money Mark? Make it easy. Tell me now."

"I don't know Paula."

"It's me Mark. I know when you're lying. I thought your loving father had given up on you but clearly not. You were the fall-back if anything went wrong. You have to be."

"I don't know where the money is."

Paula shrugged.

"We'll see. Just lift up the trapdoor and go back the way you came. You first Miss Quinn, and then you, Mark. Just take it slowly and easily."

Paula motioned them backwards with the revolver.

With the light from above shining down, the steps downwards and the area they led into were less mysterious than before. Next to the array of pipe work and the pump there were shelves with tubs of blue pool paint, and chemicals to keep the water clear of algae. Jane got to the bottom of the steps.

"I'm caught," Mandell said.

Jane looked up. Mandell's jacket was hooked to the edge of the trapdoor so that he could no longer move downwards. Rays of light from above shone past his head and shoulders, illuminating swirls of gold coloured-dust so that Mandell resembled nothing so much as an angel in disguise.

Mandell turned to look below and his eyes switched pointedly to one side; Jane saw that a number of tools had been hung onto the brick wall by nails. One of them was an axe. It was small, the sort of axe used for chopping firewood, but still an effective weapon.

Jane had never hit anyone or anything since childhood. Attacking the Starman with an axe did not seem the most opportune way of resuming the practice. If only she had been more efficient they could have had the account number that Ian Hart had produced. Clearly they hadn't got it at the moment and it wasn't the Starman who had taken it from Silverlawns. Not that any further information would mean that Paula and her brother would then go away and leave them. Eternal silence would be a better option if £250 million was at risk. It seemed to have been the method they had favoured for Christopher Bellmore and Ian Hart. From the angle she was at she could only see a small part of the pool through the slits in the wall. There was no sign of the Starman. She put out her hand for the axe, took it gently from the wall, and stood to one side.

Mark Mandell acted at the same moment. He had been releasing his coat. To pull it away he had had to brace himself against the edge of the trapdoor. Now he simply jumped, pulling the trapdoor closed in the same movement. There were two bolts on the underside. Mandell pushed them home.

"Mark!"

"Out!" Mandell said.

Jane had the axe in her hand and was running to the concealed door.

There was a faint popping sound like a cork being pulled abruptly from the neck of a bottle, not once but twice. Something passed through the wooden trapdoor and ricocheted in the confined space before exploding into a paint tin.

Mandell swore. "She wants to kill us. Out of the door!"

Mandell was right behind her. They could hear Paula shouting behind trying to warn her brother. Her cries were muffled and with the trapdoor bolted shut there was no way that she could get to them from above. They had a momentary advantage, albeit more academic than real. Luckily there was not time for consideration of the true hopelessness of their position. Mandell was already ahead of Jane pushing open the concealed door back into the swimming pool area proper. As the door opened Jane could see that the Starman was twenty feet away and turning towards them.

Mandell's charge took him clattering into the Starman who teetered on the edge of the pool. For a moment Jane was convinced that nothing would stop the Starman toppling backwards into the water but somehow he twisted to one side, immune from gravity also, and kept his footing. He disentangled himself from Mandell and took a step back. One of the mock Roman pillars supporting the roof was immediately behind him. The surround to the swimming pool on this side of the room was very narrow and there was no way Jane could help unless the positions were reversed and the Starman had his back to her.

For the moment Mandell didn't seem to need help. He had his hands pressing tightly around the Starman's throat, the knuckles white with the pressure he was exerting.

Jane looked at the steps connecting the swimming pool to the rest of the house. Perhaps they could get out of this after all. The Starman was hardly moving and that part of the war, surprisingly, seemed to be being won. The trouble was Paula. Even if she didn't have a key to the front door she could get in through the kitchen. Surely that couldn't take her very long? Jane needed to do something. If she could get nearer to the bottom of the steps she might jump Paula if she came down from the floor above, or perhaps they could retreat back to the trapdoor.

Then she noticed that the Starman's hands were moving slowly along the line of Mandell's shoulders. At first Jane thought the movement was some automatic reflex that was no longer under the Starman's control, so small and precise were the movements. The Starman's thumbs pressed inwards into the top of Mandell's spinal column and Mandell suddenly went limp and his hands dropped away from the Starman's throat. With exaggerated care the Starman lowered Mandell's head and body onto the marble tiles and pulled himself fully upright. His eyes met Jane's. They were calm, graceful eyes. Jane took a step backwards. There would be no marks on Mandell's body. She wondered what they would conclude he had died of. Probably the same thing that was going to kill her.

The Starman was moving forward. She waited for him to produce a weapon. No weapon. He killed with his gentle hands. She took another step backwards and he moved after her. His eyes were following the axe she had in her hand.

"What do you want?"

The Starman seemed not to notice Jane's shrill question. He moved forward a little more quickly. The gap between them was narrowing. She found herself at the end of the pool. She could run or she could attack. She wanted to weigh the odds and give herself an edge. She told herself she was good at taking decisions under pressure, weighing all the odds. Everybody was vulnerable to something, even the Starman must be. If she could only work it out. She tried to make herself as calm as he must be. That was the paralysis that he preyed on - the knowledge everyone had that he was invulnerable. She didn't have to accept that.

Into the calm that she had tried to create came an irrational anger. Someone, probably his wife, had stuck the shears into Bellmore.

Otherwise he would have been like Ian Hart, another body, another sudden and inexplicable accidental death, another execution. She sprang forward wildly and hit out at the Starman with the axe. She could see the little smile in his eyes as he waited for her.

She slipped. She had pushed off with too much force for any hope of reasonable support from the gleaming poolside tiles and stumbled as a sprinting athlete would whose starting blocks were not secured firmly to the ground. She came forward head down in a wild and unpredictable movement, arms flailing to help keep her balance. The back of the axe blade hit the side of the Starman's head, a solid and direct contact, and he collided with one of the stone pillars and fell onto the tiles. As she stared, mesmerised, a thin trickle of blood appeared from under his head and meandered unhurriedly to the poolside before spilling over the edge into the water. Jane found that she still had the axe in her hand. She had managed to cling on to it despite the force of the blow she had delivered. She felt a mixture of numbness and an unholy exhilaration.

"Don't move!"

Paula was at the bottom of the steps at the other end of the pool. At thirty yards she wouldn't miss.

"Put it down!"

Jane's energy was subsiding. She tossed the axe into the pool.

She looked where Mandell had fallen. Paula was walking towards him, arm and gun outstretched. It was either the way one did it or she had seen too many police movies. She looked at Jane and then kicked Mandell viciously in the back before she stepped over him. Mandell did not move. Paula came forward. She nodded her head towards the Starman.

"Feel his pulse."

Jane bent down. The face was still calm and peaceful. So convinced had the Starman been of his immortality that death had not been recognised by him.

"I can't."

"You incompetent."

Paula raised the gun towards her. Jane had the Starman's wrist held in her hand.

"No, I don't mean that. He doesn't have one."

"You're lying. He is faking it."

"No," Jane said with finality. "No he isn't. Why should he?"

"Back up," Paula said gesturing with her revolver. Jane retreated back towards the wall until she could go no further. Keeping the gun pointed firmly in Jane's direction Paula bent over her brother. Her hand felt along his outstretched arm towards his head and into the little river of blood flowing to the pool.

She withdrew her hand slowly and looked at her fingers. There was incomprehension on her face.

"You've killed my brother."

"It was an accident."

It was almost a true statement, certainly more true than false. The Starman had insulated himself against anything but an accidental blow from an amateur.

Paula was looking at her with incomprehension. Jane stared back unblinking.

"It's not possible."

Behind Paula, Mark Mandell was getting slowly and carefully to his feet.

"So where is the money?"

Jane was silent. Mandell was creeping forward.

Paula gestured with the automatic.

"I'm not losing my brother for nothing."

"I don't know."

"That is not an option. You have to know."

Paula thought she was lying; that, at least, was clear to Jane. It might keep her alive for a few more seconds if she said something. She only needed ten more. Mandell was nearly upon her.

"I am going to kill you."

"No," Jane said, "I'll tell you where the money that you and Mandell stole is. It's in a bank account. I have got the number but not here - "

Jane's eyes must have betrayed something about Mark because Paula whirled round as Mandell launched himself forward. The gun was fired as they collided, a faint pffft, and then Paula fell down on her back, the scorch marks of the bullet on her coat.

Jane moved forward as if in a trance. Mandell's face was grey with shock.

"What have we done, Mark?"

"I don't know."

Mandell was bent over the body.

"We should call an ambulance, the police -"

"It's no good. They are both dead. No pulse, no signs of life."

"We need to get out of here Mark."

"I know."

"We ought to do something. We could telephone -"

"It might get us both into gaol."

Mandell held her.

"I'm tired Mark."

"We have to leave here."

"There's nowhere to go."

"The apartment. They were the people watching it. They must have been. It is safe now."

"When they find the bodies -"

"They might come for us, but not for certain, and not just yet."

"No, I suppose not. There's tonight I suppose."

"Nights are long in winter."

"Or short if they end too early."

They had got to the ground floor.

"Out through the back."

- So you left the scene of the murder Miss Quinn?

- Yes.

- Without a second thought?

- No. I was deeply upset, Inspector. I had seen a horrible series of events that had left me quite numb.

- But you were able to proceed to your apartment in the company of Mr Mandell?

- We walked and then we took my car. I was able to drive. We had to have somewhere to go so we went to my apartment. We were tired.

- Too tired to telephone the police, Miss Quinn?

- Yes.

- I am not sure I understand that Miss Quinn, or is it Mrs Charles?

There were cars on the road as there always were in London at any hour of the day or night. The snow on the road was turning to a black slush. By morning only the common would be pristine white. They came to a red light and stopped.

"I can't remember how many days it was since we met at the Pompadour," Mark said.

"A long time. Too long to remember if you're tired. If you don't concentrate too hard it seems to stretch back infinitely into the past."

Placing things, regularising them, so that your life slips away into an infinite series of routines, constructions that enable you never to have to think at all. Or that was the way it had been.

- Miss Quinn?
- I'm sorry, Inspector.
- You went back to the apartment with Mr Mandell, your lover.
- No.
- You deny that you went to the apartment?
- No.
- That Mark Mandell was your lover?
- No, no, you don't understand. Of course he was, but not then.
- You had every reason to want to protect him?
- No, it wasn't like that.
- What was it like?
- You don't understand, Inspector. It was a great shock.
- You had every reason to shield him from the police. You knew he had fraudulently removed £5million from his father's companies. You had no intention of going to the police then or at any other time. Did you Miss Quinn? You went back to your apartment with your lover without any thought of contacting the police. What were you planning to do? Flee the country with the £5 million? Or was it £255 million?

"We need to talk about what we are going to do Mark."

"I know. We must talk in the morning. Now I'm tired. Very tired."

She came into the bedroom with two glasses of water.

"My father always used to drink a glass before he went to bed.

Cleans impurities out of the system."

"These boots are extraordinarily tight."

"My father advised me never to go bed with a man with boots on. You had better take them off."

"We have to do something in the morning."

Mark Mandell struggled out of the boots and crossed to the window and looked out.

"Can you see anyone?"

"There is no one to see anymore. He's dead."

"It's difficult to believe."

But then everything was difficult to believe, not just what had happened immediately beforehand, but Bellmore, and Ian Hart. Easier to believe there was some other universe where all that had happened had not occurred after all, how very reassuring that would be. She looked at Mandell. His head was bowed.

"I think my father was planning to run away with Paula and the money."

"You don't know that. It clearly wasn't Paula's plan."

"There is no need to be kind, there is no doubt really is there? Nothing makes sense unless he was planning to abscond with the money. If he was just involved in a deal there would have been no need to hide the money as he did. It is just that he didn't trust them, so he took precautions to make sure they couldn't get the money unless he was around. Anyway that's not the point. He was a thief. Like father, like son, I suppose as it turns out."

"The money might still come back. My mother might have had a reason for taking the book with her."

Jane didn't really believe her mother had suddenly developed an overwhelming interest in words.

"Let's hope," Mandell said without conviction. "That light seems very bright."

"Illuminating our sins," Jane said. She turned the overhead light off.

- It that your explanation Miss Quinn, or is it Mrs Charles? You believed Mark Mandell was guilty only of foolish behaviour?

- I told you Inspector, I keep my maiden name for business purposes.

- How convenient to be two people. But you really think embezzling £5 million is just one of those things?

- I was confused Inspector. I couldn't make sense of what was going on. I thought I needed to do everything I could to find the missing money. I don't know what I thought about Mark, or even, I suppose, if he might have stolen it.

"I would like to do something good," Mandell said. "I would like to be someone good."

"You're getting quite Victorian, Mark. All this concern for your soul."

Mandell lay back on the bed.

- Extraordinary.

- I'm not sure I understand Inspector.

- Extraordinary you should be on the premises when Paula White died.

- I explained.

- And Christopher Bellmore.

- There are reasons.

- And Ian Hart.

- Coincidence.

- Are you sure?

- They were all involved in this Mandell business

- And there are other matters.

- No.

- Your husband.

- It was a long time ago.

- Your son.

- I don't want to talk about Thom.

"You're shivering Jane."

"I'm just tired. Take your clothes off and get into bed. We need to sleep."

"You're in the centre of a pool of light," Mandell said.

He was in the shadows she noticed. He was looking at her but she couldn't make out the expression on his face.

"I feel as though I'm floating."

"This is a very large bed, you could get lost in it."

Mandell lay down next to her, his body warming hers. She felt his hand move up across her to her shoulders and neck and rest there. She felt the vein in her neck pump warnings to her brain and then Mandell's hand wasn't there; and he had turned away to the other side of the bed and she wouldn't have known as she drifted slowly into the borderlands of sleep that he was there at all if it had not been for the sound of breathing, their breathing, together.

She saw a long line of screens showing her dreams. The office, her mother and father, Richard chasing a blonde in Paris. She saw that you could step through the screen and be part of the events taking place the other side.

She heard a voice calling, faintly at first and then with a growing insistence. She turned away from watching the screens in front of her with a sense of reluctance. Richard had caught up, at least temporarily, with his chosen conquest. On the next scene she thought she saw her father look in her direction and smile. She wanted to stop but there was something insistent about the voice. It was coming from the screen right at the end. It was faint but she could make out the word. It was her name. It came to her softly on an eddy of sound, repeated again and again. She began running.

It was an English country road. There was a figure in the foreground walking forward. He was trying to wipe the blood from the wounds on his head off his jumper.

"I can't make it stop," the little boy said.

"I can help," Jane said as she walked forward.

Thom smiled at her.

"No, Mummy, you know you can't."

CHAPTER THIRTY-FIVE

They would come sooner or later. Jane had always known that. She heard the hammering on the apartment door and knew she could delay the moment no longer. She slid reluctantly away from the warm body beside her.

"Mark! It's the police."

She shook him by the shoulder but he was still deeply asleep. The hammering had started again. If she didn't open the door they might break it down.

She got out of bed, put her dressing gown on, and closed the bedroom door behind her carefully. She adjusted the dressing gown, took a deep breath, and swung the apartment door open with as much confidence as she could muster.

"Jane, you *are* in!"

Sally Fry stood in the doorway.

"Sally?"

"You do remember don't you? You're looking after George."

Jane was aware of movement against her knee. She looked down. The small face of George Fry looked hopefully up at her.

Jane remembered. "What's the time? I must have overslept."

"Ten o'clock. One of your neighbours let me in at the front door, the man with the ginger hair, so I came up. I hope this is still alright -"

Jane thought she could hear movement behind her in the bedroom. She had a premonition of Sally uncomfortable in the witness box, hesitantly confirming that Mark had been there with her in the flat.

"Of course," Jane picked George Fry up. "There is no problem. I know you're on a tight timetable."

"If you're sure."

"Don't be silly. I'm sorry to have be so disorganised, but I have been looking forward to it, haven't I George?" She yawned theatrically. "I've just been working too hard. I must have overslept."

"I really shouldn't take up your weekends."

"No, no, George is great fun. Just what I need to unwind."

Sally nodded, not entirely convinced. "Spare clothes and juice in this bag, favourite toys in that one. Look after him well won't you?"

"Of course, Sally."

She could sense that Sally had worked out there was a man involved somewhere. Jane took a step forward. There was further sound from the bedroom, slightly louder than before. It was time for Sally to go.

"Have a good trip. I'll keep him safe and sound."

Jane picked George up.

"Bye then."

"Bye."

Jane closed the apartment door with the same flourish with which she had opened it as Mark Mandell appeared from the bedroom clad in a white hand towel. He looked at George who returned his glance without apparent interest.

"Jane?"

"I'm sorry. I'm looking after him for a few hours. I just forgot about the arrangement and I didn't think it was a good idea to let his mother see you before we had sorted out what we are going to do. It seemed easiest to agree."

"So what are you planning to do?"

"Go out for a walk, get some food. There's absolutely nothing in the apartment."

Jane lowered George to the floor and he ambled off contentedly enough on a tour of the flat.

"What about going to the police? I thought you had decided that."

"That was last night. I'm not so sure there is anything I want to say to them. I've been thinking about the deal with KM. I'm not sure your father isn't entirely innocent."

"It's a nice try Jane. But the fake passport is pretty conclusive isn't it?"

"In an open safe? Somebody was meant to find out. Probably Norman, if he had ever got his act together. Just think about it. All KM had been waiting for was the final yes. Your father was known to hang on to the last minute on deals. Di Rocca probably wanted to get back to the States for Christmas. All the key Mandell Holdings staff like Geoffrey Chorley and Eve Jackson were also away. Bellmore had been left in charge, probably with orders to play hardball if your father wanted any last minute changes. It didn't matter. Your father was already dead. It was always the intention to murder him and make the death look like an accident. The money would disappear and there would be evidence that he was planning to disappear with it. When the money couldn't be found the conclusion would be that he had salted it away somewhere. It should have been foolproof, but things didn't go entirely to plan. The swimming trunks, your evidence on when you had seen your father which made the death look suspicious, and your father himself. He liked puzzles and codes; he may have been suspicious of Paula who must have been involved closely in all this somehow. Maybe he had a sense she might be after the money. So he ensured that when the money was transferred only he would know where it had gone. Perhaps he really was planning a takeover or building up a share stake."

Mandell shrugged.

"You could be right. I suspect my criminal tendencies aren't inherited. But I'm not sure where that gets us."

"There might be a way of putting everything right."

"I doubt that Jane."

"No, listen, neither Paula nor her brother had access to the money. That's clear from last night. They suspect you of having it but really either someone else has got it or it is lying around somewhere in an account. Ian saw a pattern in the account numbers in the first transactions. He detected a pattern that was going somewhere. If nobody has the money and the only people we know who were dealing with these transactions - Paula and Bellmore - are dead, it's becoming a better bet that the money is actually safe somewhere. Don't you see? You said your father was secretive. Perhaps he was involved with Paula and her brother but decided that he needed an insurance policy. If he managed to arrange matters so that only he knew where the money had gone, Paula and her brother would have nothing to gain by getting rid of him, provided, of course, that they understood that was the position. Perhaps it was only after the event that they found they could not trace the money. Anyway, don't you see, if we can find the money your father is in the clear. He may not be whiter than white, but nobody can prove it one way or another."

"That's fine for my father," Mandell smiled wryly, "but not so good for me. Establishing my father is innocent only ensures that I am guilty."

"Not if we find the money. Nobody is going to be too concerned if the £250 million comes back."

George had somehow managed to prise the sky blue parcel out of the cupboard. He was feeling the arms and head of the bear under the paper and pulling idly at the assorted string Elizabeth Quinn had, for some reason, enveloped the parcel in.

"So what are you going to do?" Mandell said as George wandered away with the parcel clasped closely to his chest.

"Telephone my mother. She has got to be in sooner or later."

"I'm not entirely convinced that is the whole story."

Neither, Jane thought as she dialled her mother's number, was she. But there was another connection that she had thought about and that she didn't want to mention to Mark. She had talked to Robert Stuart about George Mandell and Ian. Robert had known Paula. She waited for the receiver not to be picked up.

This time, however, there were a couple of rings and then her mother, as usual, clearly annunciating the number.

"Mother? You're back."

The silence at the other end of the line indicated that Elizabeth Quinn took the statement to be a self-evident truth.

"I'm looking for some numbers," Jane said. "I left them in the *Roget*."

She expected her mother's usual bewilderment. She was

disappointed.

"It's a double roll-over." Her mother's voice was perfectly decisive.

"What?"

"Tonight, the lottery, it's a double roll-over," Elizabeth Quinn said slowly to cope with her daughter's mental incapacities.

"I don't understand."

"I saw the *Roget* had been moved. It wasn't quite in line with the other books and I do so dislike that. The woman who cleans the room is always moving it. As I was putting it back straight I saw the numbers you had left. Your father always said you were lucky so I thought I might do them as well and as Richard had arrived I took the book with me because I thought you might have done another entry. I didn't think your first numbers were very good, you see you only have a choice of six, not seven, even if there is a bonus ball, so one of them would not have counted anyway."

"I understand," Jane said quickly as her heart fluttered wildly. "I just wondered. You still have got the *Roget* haven't you?"

"Of course, dear. It really is a family heirloom you know. You should-"

"And the numbers?" Jane interrupted.

"The numbers?" Her mother sounded confused.

"The piece of paper with my numbers on. The piece of paper with the numbers that I put in the *Roget*. Have you still got that?"

"Oh no dear. It blew out to sea when I was coming out of the shop."

"Blew away?"

"Oh yes. It was really quite windy. But very bracing. A very good choice of Richard's."

Her mother added the last words approvingly. For once, however, Jane felt no inclination to react to the usual one-sided praise. She was already feeling quite numb enough.

"You've lost them?"

"Yes dear."

There was no note of regret in her mother's voice, but then even if Jane were to explain the full enormity of the position there would be no note of regret either.

277

"I must go, Mother."

"Goodbye dear."

Jane put the receiver back in place.

"It doesn't matter." Mark Mandell didn't sound particularly convinced, but he had put his arm comfortingly round her shoulder.

"No," Jane said. "I don't suppose it does."

"You should sit down."

"No, I'm fine. Sorry Mark, crazy mother."

"Something may crop up," Mark said encouragingly. "Look, I need to think what I'm going to do. The police are going to catch up with me again sooner or later and I need to think what I am going to say. We're going to have to do something about the bodies in my father's house as well. I need to go back there."

"You don't have to say anything about the £5 million Mark. You never know, your father might have agreed if he had still been alive."

"It's a big if, Jane."

"Promise me you won't do anything hasty. Please."

"OK, but I need to go to the house."

"How long is that going to take?"

"Two hours, maybe two and a half. I'm not going to linger. I could see you back here or out somewhere by one."

"The Embankment. One o'clock."

"I didn't think the Embankment was your favourite place."

"I'm not going underground. The gardens are fine. I need to get out and clear my head anyway."

She kissed Mark and held him close.

She felt a little shaky the moment he had gone. The events of the previous evening and the past few days were beginning to take their toll. She looked out of the window. Mark Mandell was on his way to his father's house to look at two bodies. It did seem that it was possible that such a statement could be true. There were little drops of water falling from the edge of the roof. She sat in the chair. There was something that she felt she should have worked out. But she couldn't place it. There was something else she needed to do anyway. She dialled Robert Stuart's mobile.

"Stuart."

"Robert, it's Jane."

"Jane? There was a pause and for a moment Jane thought the connection might have failed. Then Robert started speaking again, this time in much more animated tones. "It's great to hear from you. I did call a couple of times but it's been so hectic here. How are you? How's London? Are you making any progress on Mandell? Are you coming over?"

"I don't think so."

"That's a shame. Are you sure you can't find the time?"

"It is not exactly time that is the problem."

"I don't understand."

"I have been thinking Robert. There are one or two things that have happened that don't make a great deal of sense. I thought you might be able to provide an explanation or a missing link."

"Look Jane, I am not sure what this about but I am not sure this is the best time to discuss. It's three in the morning here and I was just about to turn in. It's been one hell of a day and I'm dog tired. I'll phone you later – evening your time – if that's convenient."

"I don't think it is."

"Sorry?"

"Just answer me one question. Do you know somebody called Paula Black, or perhaps Paula White?"

"Yes," Robert Stuart said a little reluctantly, "I do."

Jane hadn't expected him to admit it, had almost hoped that he wouldn't, but he had. She felt numb as he continued speaking.

"I've broken it off with Paula, Jane. It was just a mad fling. I was tempted, I suppose, but she doesn't mean anything to me. That's why I wanted to give you the earrings. I've been stupid but really it is you I care about. Please forgive me."

"Did you tell Paula about me?"

"I may have mentioned it. I said it was all over and she asked why. I said I was in love with somebody else. You, Jane. Please believe me."

"Did you mention my name? And Mandell?"

"I could have done, I don't know. Please Jane, it didn't mean anything."

"I'm sorry Robert, but it means something to me," Jane said putting the phone down.

279

It rang a few seconds later but Jane left the receiver where it was and disconnected the answering machine. It rang again and for a third time but Jane stared into the distance. She knew why she had a warning message and why her car had been tampered with. Robert Stuart had told Paula that Jane was on the track of the money and they had needed to slow Ian and her down to give themselves time to find it first. She sighed.

Then she realised there was something else wrong - George. He might not speak but he did make a sound moving about, and there had been no sound for some time. He was no longer by the window or in any part of the main room that she could see. She hadn't left the apartment door open had she? More than anything else she couldn't lose George.

With her heart beating violently she walked as calmly as she could into the hallway. No George. Not in the bathroom or bedroom. She felt desperate. Then she noticed an edge of sky blue behind the open cupboard door,

"George, you shouldn't go in there!"

She took George with her into the bedroom and started getting ready to go out. She found herself remembering the Lou Reed song that Mark had been humming the first time he had stayed. Someone else, someone good.

She put George into his anorak and then into the collapsible pushchair that Sally Fry had brought with her. She remembered the look on Sally Fry's face at the prospects of riches when it had been discussed in the restaurant. She smiled. Even her mother had seemed peculiarly coherent about the lottery numbers. £250 million was anyway on a completely different scale even from the lottery jackpot prize.

They got to the Embankment Gardens early, George hanging on determinedly to the side of the pushchair with one hand and to the sky blue parcel with the other. The biting chill of the previous days had blown away. Flags were flying on the newly cleaned white stone of the Adelphi building and the paths were cleared of snow and drying in the sun. She stopped and looked around. Elizabeth Quinn's advice on the lottery numbers came back to her. *I didn't think your numbers were very good, you see you only have a choice of six, not seven, even if there is a bonus ball, but one of them would not have counted anyway.* She stopped and repeated the words to herself. For the lottery at least her mother was prepared to live in the present, although why she should have assumed that Jane's numbers were for the lottery was probably just an indication of a new fixation.

Then it hit her, a bolt of enlightenment from the blue sky, the niggling problem that had been troubling her, the fact that she should have worked out. There was no reason why her mother should not have assumed that the numbers on the piece of paper were lottery numbers. There had been fourteen numbers, but each with another - seven groups of two. The six lottery number and the bonus ball number. And if one of them hadn't counted that must mean it was higher than the top lottery number of forty-nine.

She propelled a slightly protesting George into the pushchair with the sky blue parcel and pulled out her mobile.

"Mother? You did enter my numbers didn't you?"

"Yes dear."

"Have you got them there? I'd like to check how I did."

"Just a minute, I'll get the ticket, but remember that last number you had, sixty-six, is too high. I didn't do that."

She looked around in the seconds before Elizabeth Quinn returned to the telephone. The world seemed indifferent to this possible change in fortune.

"I have got them here, dear."

Jane made her mother repeat them twice so there could be no mistake. When she put the telephone down she made a separate copy of the numbers.

She looked round for Mark. The gardens were virtually deserted. Perhaps he had been optimistic in thinking that he could complete his search of his father's house in the time, or perhaps the police had found the bodies and been keeping the house under observation in case somebody returned.

Where was George? A little edge of the alarm that had been washing over her in waves in the previous few days returned. She must keep as calm as possible and not do anything silly. Everything dangerous was over and perhaps the situation could be sorted. If they had found the money there would be little purpose in opening questions like the time of Mandell's death. Norman probably had no evidence. Mark would be in the clear.

She looked round. George had crawled into the bushes in pursuit of something.

"George! Come here."

The small figure stopped and then turned. George was clearly on his best behaviour but he didn't move back to her. His feet were moving but the hood of the anorak was now caught in the bush behind him. A look of dismay began to grow on his face as he was unable to make any progress.

"It's alright George you need to be unhooked."

Jane scrambled into the bushes. It would be best, if possible, not to deliver George back with his clothes wrecked. It would be sensible to strap him back in the pushchair once she had got him free.

She moved behind him and untangled his hood. She looked out into the gardens. There was still no sign of Mark. George was now contentedly holding the sky blue parcel close to his chest with both arms.

"Time for a ride George!"

She was about to pick him up when she heard a rustle in the bushes behind her. She was in the act of turning to find out the cause when she found she couldn't move. A man's gloved hand was clasped firmly across her mouth. The grip was so tight and so violently applied that she was having difficulty in getting any breath at all.

The man behind her had his other hand clasped tightly round her waist pulling her, off-balance, further back into the evergreen bushes.

One part of her brain, immune to the general panic buttons that were firing, was trying to work it out. There must be somebody else, somebody who had been close to David Mandell and had managed to spirit the money away and had every reason to want to tidy up loose ends.

She kicked out with her legs and sent the pushchair rolling back towards the path. She knew she could work out who it was if she had time, but her vision was becoming distinctly hazy round the edges and now the blood was pounding crazily in her head. As consciousness began to ebb away she felt her right leg become heavy. She knew George must be clinging to her, trying to save her.

CHAPTER THIRTY-SIX

She could see Mark Mandell's face. It was strained, almost distorted.

She hadn't blacked out, as she had feared. The grip round her throat had been eased and she could even breathe a little.

She was being dragged backwards. Mark was in the middle of the round open space that the bushes bordered on, but was disappearing from her sight. Surely he could see the pushchair? But would he even remember that she had a pushchair with her? It had been folded up when he left the apartment.

"Where is the money?"

The man's voice was a whisper but the words were precise.

"I - can't - breathe."

Jane forced the words out one by one in little breaths of their own. The grip the man had on her mouth was relaxed again. She looked down. They had left a blurred track but, here and there, star marks were clear in the snow.

"Talk."

"It's in - an account. I have - the number."

Jane tried to look around. There was no weight clinging to her leg. Was George still with them?

"Well?"

"I can't - remember it. I've got it - written down in my handbag."

The handbag had fallen to the ground.

Why had she lied? Neither bit of paper on which she had written the numbers was in her handbag.

The grip on Jane was released and she stood upright again. There were people twenty feet away beyond the bushes and the railings walking to the station, but she could hear them rather than see them. Surely somebody must have noticed something? Mark must at least know that the Starman's body was not in the house. She should cry out, but that wasn't an option. She had found George. The Starman's hand was hooked round the hood of his anorak. George for the moment was more concerned with hanging on to his parcel than anything else.

"You did kill David Mandell didn't you?"

The Starman nodded gently as though he had been complimented on his professional expertise. Delicately he tightened his grip on George's collar. George was beginning to look uncertain, no longer convinced that what he was engaged in was entirely safe.

"The account number?"

It was more a command than a question. She knew that if she didn't do anything he would tighten his grip on George's neck again. She bent down to pick up the handbag. There was a long discoloured area down the side of the Starman's face that she knew she had caused.

They couldn't both still be alive could they? She didn't believe that. It was the Starman who was immortal. Anyway, that didn't matter. She needed to concentrate. Perhaps Paula had been the brains of their side of the operation, but the Starman could work it out for himself. If he had the account number there was still nothing to stop her preventing him getting the money. He was going to kill her.

She opened the handbag and offered it to him.

How would he know if she was lying? He would check to see if there was a number there. If it looked like an account number that would be something, but not final proof, not a guarantee.

"Give it to me!"

He wasn't going to go burrowing in her handbag, diverting his gaze, even momentarily, from her. But then she hadn't thought he would, although how he was going to solve his problem of whether the number was genuine or not was another question.

Then it clicked. He would take George away with him as a guarantee that she was telling the truth.

She opened her purse and took a cash receipt from the bag with exaggerated care. Then she dropped it.

The Starman's eyes flicked away from her and at that same moment she lunged forward for George. For a vital moment the Starman's attention switched to the scrap of paper floating down to the snow. When he did look back he was off balance. They collided over George and the Starman fell. Jane, whose adrenalin surge had started in the seconds before she dropped the paper, somehow scooped George up and scrambled away.

She was running with George clasped more to her waist than in her arms. She managed to adjust George upward. There was a chance that the Starman would not follow. No, there wasn't any chance. She knew that as she completed every heart rending stride. She looked behind. The Starman was behind her as she ran towards the tube station.

There were people in the station entrance. She was already panting. She would have no breath left to explain anything quickly. And how could she keep the Starman away from her? If he was close he would have some method of disabling her instantly, such skills were part of his stock in trade. Why didn't anybody notice what was happening to her? Why didn't anybody want to help her?

She couldn't run through the station out on to the Embankment, the Starman would catch her. She could joint the people, but that wouldn't stop him doing what he wanted. As she approached she saw the gate on the left was being opened to let the woman with the stick through.

Jane dived forward into the gap, pointed behind her at the Starman, mouthed the word "tickets" at the station guard and was through.

There was a passageway to her right or a dulled silver escalator in front of her descending endlessly downwards. George was wriggling in her arms. She wanted to stop but she knew she wouldn't. She ran down the descending steps. At the bottom was another passageway.

She heard a commotion behind, an eruption of irregular noise in a normal quiet Saturday. She knew she had to get out of the passageway before the Starman got to the bottom of the steps. She scrambled down the long round tunnel that seemed to stretch on for ever and which was barely wide enough for two people to pass. She turned the corner at the end and stopped.

She told herself she was in a building, albeit one that extended far below ground level, but nevertheless a building and not a tunnel burrowing through the earth. Jane listened. She could hear nothing. A normal person would give up at some point, but that rather ruled the Starman out.

She wondered what the Starman was doing. Had she lost him? She adjusted her grip on George and hurried to the end of the new passage, a wall with signs pointing to the northbound and southbound platforms. This passage was smaller still and nearly round, more claustrophobic with hardly room for two people together and internal pipes hanging from the roof.

There were people on the southbound platform. An elderly woman in bright colours, a young man and woman obsessed in themselves. She walked forward. Rats were scuttling across the blackness that lay under the rails. At either end of the platform she could see the dark circles of the tunnels that led down under the river. There was the noise of a train approaching.

She forced herself backwards and felt the platform wall, comforting and solid, behind her. She noticed she was sweating, drops of moisture on her face and on the backs of her hands.

The tube train stopped and the doors in the carriage in front of her swung open. She looked along the platform. She was at one end. The elderly woman had already boarded the train. The young man and woman were sliding on as a single entity. No one had got off. She could see the guard looking at her. She just had to step forward and board the train. Then she and George would be safe. The train was about to start its journey through the lower depths in endless tunnels in the earth below London.

"Isn't this fun George? We're having an adventure."

She would do it. Get on the train and off at the next station, wherever that was.

She stepped out and took a deep breath. The Starman appeared at the other end of the platform and looked at her. Time seemed suspended. The empty carriage looked less enticing. In slow motion the doors slid together.

THE SKY BLUE PARCEL

She stared straight ahead watching the Starman out of the corner of her eye. She edged slowly backwards to the tunnel behind her. The public address system crackled as though it were about to burst into life but then went dead. The Starman was starting a leisurely movement in her direction. Jane quickened her step backwards. When she was out of sight she turned and ran down the passage nearest to her.

She turned the corner. What had once been a single escalator led upwards. It was boarded off. A sign announced that the escalator was being replaced and the work would take thirty-two weeks to complete. Arrows pointed back the way she had come or to alternative routes that could be taken.

The escalator to be replaced had been shielded behind plywood boards tacked over a wooden frame. A makeshift door gave entrance. She tried the door and it pushed open. In front of her the metal plates at the end of the escalator had been taken away and, bending down, she could look up into a square metal shaft that led upwards at a steep angle, but in which there were metal struts. It would hide her and George.

She buttoned George up as best she could within her coat and supported him with one arm. He was still clinging tightly to the sky blue parcel. She used her other arm to hoist herself onto the first of the metal struts that would normally have provided the support for the casing to the escalator machinery.

George grew heavier as she climbed upwards. Thirty feet up she knew she needed to rest. Her arm was numb under George's weight and all the muscles in her back were creaking in protest. She braced herself against the metal framework and looked down. There was first a shadow and then the lower half of a man's body was in view. He was wearing boots and green trousers as the Starman had been. She shook her head. There was no point in fooling herself. There was no suggestion that it could be anybody but him.

He was not moving. She tensed her body, held her breath, and willed him to go away. Then she started counting. It was a mildly helpful technique for controlling panic. On the count of ten he disappeared from view.

Jane breathed out and George began to cry. He started with a faint little moaning sound that was hardly audible but which to Jane sounded so loud that the Starman was bound to hear. She leaned towards George and started singing as softly as she could, a lullaby that she used to sing to Thom. She edged closer so that really she only had to mouth the words to quiet him down. Then she lost her balance and had to grab wildly at a metal strut to steady herself, gashing her hand. George's little cries that had temporarily subsided started again and she realised he must be hungry. She looked down. She was sure that the Starman must hear.

There was the flicker of a match below. The Starman was lighting a cigarette. An eddy of smoke was drawn upwards past her in an air current seeking the surface and she thought they had escaped detection, at least for a moment. Then the top half of the Starman's body appeared below and he looked upwards. He saw Jane and smiled. He beckoned to her to come down, as one might beckon a naughty child. Jane shook her head and clenched her teeth together to stop herself from screaming. She levered herself up to the next struts with a renewed energy which, even as it was acquired, began to ebb away. Her heart started beating violently and she looked down. The Starman beckoned to her to come down again. She shook her head violently.

The Starman shrugged more in pity than in anger and felt for something in one of the pockets in his trousers. When he next looked up Jane could see he had a knife in his hand. It was a short, stubby knife that had a concave indentation on each side to let the blood run more freely. The Starman threw the cigarette to one side, put the knife in his teeth like a pirate and started climbing easily up the metal framework after her.

Jane reached for the next metal support and started climbing again. George's cries were getting louder.

"I'm sorry George. But you shouldn't worry. This isn't real."

She said the words in short bursts as she climbed upwards. In climbing it was impossible to look down. Only when she stopped and re-positioned herself would she able to tell what the true position was.

She was gasping for breath, her last burst of adrenalin exhausted, and she knew she must finally stop. The struts were getting more difficult to cope with and when she looked up it was clear that there was no way out at the top. She leant back, and looked down.

The Starman was three supports below and could probably grab her foot if he stretched, but his head was down locating his footholds. She watched as he prepared to lever himself up onto the next metal strut. She felt the muscles in her face become distorted and her leg tense. As he hoisted himself upwards she stamped down with her foot and felt the jarring impact of the sole of her shoe against his head. She nearly fell and thought triumphantly for a moment that she had dislodged him. But then she saw that he was levering himself upwards to the next support, and still had the knife clasped between his teeth.

She lashed out again but this time her foot caught his upper chest. He was levering himself up and would soon be beside her. There seemed nothing that she could do to stop him. He seemed still to be enjoying himself. She hadn't even managed to kick the smile off his face.

She lashed out again and started screaming.

"Mark!"

The Starman was moving up beside her.

"Mark!"

She could feel George wriggling against her.

"Jane!"

It was Mark Mandell's voice, not very far away.

But too late of course. He might just have well have been on the moon. She twisted to move George away from what was about to happen.

The Starman calmly removed the knife from his mouth, transferred it to his right hand, and plunged it into her.

CHAPTER THIRTY-SEVEN

She felt the tip of the knife penetrate her skin but nothing else. It was the shock she knew. In a moment she would feel the pain.

"Jane!"

She could see Mark Mandell below, a figure in a dream.

The Starman looked down to make an estimate of the risk being offered by the newcomer. Then he turned back to Jane. She could see from his face that he had concluded that Mark Mandell was too far away to have any influence on the outcome of the immediate matter in hand – her execution.

The smile was reforming on the Starman's clinically handsome features, nothing gratuitous - just a positive technical assessment of the situation. Jane hit him between the eyes with all the strength she could muster. The force of the blow swung her off balance so she and George started sliding forward into the Starman as well. She was surprised she still had the strength and that the pain was not more pronounced. She could see that there was now a dazed expression on the Starman's face, as though what was happening was a professional affront. As she watched she saw his eyes glaze over and his supporting arm loosen its grip on the metal until it became detached.

Her own hand fastened over the support that the Starman had just let go of and her slide was halted. A rough edge of metal ripped through the arm of her coat and scraped down her skin, but she stopped.

The Starman was falling, first slowly, and then with increasing speed. His limbs were splayed out but the air would not break his fall. He bounced off one support after another, each impact reducing his subsequent capability to stop his descent. Mark Mandell, who had been climbing upwards, fended off an outstretched limb as the Starman fell past him. Then the Starman hit the ground. First his body, and a split second after, with a cracking sound, his head.

"Jane, are you alright?"

She felt violently sick. The Starman was unmoving.

"Yes."

"Hold on, I'm coming."

"Be quick."

George was going quiet again, his wriggling about under Jane's coat more subdued. She fought off the sudden tiredness and nausea until Mandell was in front of her in much the same position that the Starman had been. He looked at her as though he was seeing a ghost.

"Mark, what's wrong?"

"This."

He pointed to the hilt of the knife sticking out of her coat.

"Oh," she said. I hadn't noticed that."

She felt perhaps that she should laugh. Being dead seemed no great difference from being alive.

Mandell was carefully pealing the coat back. The blade had passed through the coat and embedded itself in the sky blue parcel. Only the point had nicked Jane's skin.

"That's lucky."

"Yes," Jane said, "it is. I suppose I have to thank George and my mother. I'm glad I didn't give it away. But I don't understand. What is going on Mark? What happened at the house?"

"There were no bodies, no sign that anything much had happened at all unless you were looking for it as far as I could see. Even the broken glass in the door had been boarded over. I thought for a moment the police must have come, but they would have treated it as a crime scene. Everything would have been left as it was. I couldn't believe it. Somebody had moved the bodies and cleared up."

"If there were any bodies."

"One of them may have been immortal, but not both. He clearly wasn't dead. He must have moved her body. I could have telephoned the police but I couldn't think of any explanation I could get through in under a day. And then I thought that one of them, or one of their associates was still active so I came back here. And then I saw him, running into the station. I couldn't think of anyone he was likely to be following except you."

Jane nodded.

"At least it's over now," Mandell added.

"You'd better take George."

She untangled the little boy from her coat and handed him to Mark. George grabbed the sky blue parcel.

Jane felt her limbs aching from the unnatural exertions that she had experienced over what could only have been a few minutes since she had been underground. Climbing slowly down she felt her claustrophobia coming back in a wave. She needed to return to the surface.

There was another problem, though, when they got to the ground.

The Starman had gone. There was a thick red trail on the ground that was darkening as they watched.

"He couldn't get up from that."

"He has."

"He can't have got far."

"Paula thought he was immortal."

"Not when it mattered. He can't do any harm now, not losing that much blood." Mandell sounded confident.

"He must be somewhere."

"We can follow the trail. Look after George."

Mandell handed George and the parcel back to her and moved cautiously forward. Then he started coughing.

It was cloying, acrid smoke that was seeping around them.

"It's nothing," Mandell said unconvincingly.

Jane hugged George.

"Still, we had better get out of here. C'mon"

Mandell was moving forward when there was the sound of a shot, deafening in the confined tunnel. The Starman was not using his sister's silencer.

"Look." Mandell said.

Jane moved forward to the corner. She could see the other way along the curved platform to the driver's mirror at the entrance to the tunnel.

The Starman was dragging himself along the platform with one arm. In the other, pointed in their direction, he held the gun. In his mouth was a lit cigarette. Behind him something that had been stored on the platform under a green tarpaulin was giving off a trail of thick black smoke. As Jane watched a little flame appeared, died, and was then replaced by another and then two more. In a few more seconds the whole of the tarpaulin was ablaze and the Starman's figure was silhouetted black again the red smoky flame.

Mark Mandell was pulling her by the arm. The smoke seemed to take the oxygen in the air away, denying life.

Somewhere close at hand there was a little explosion as something else on the platform caught fire.

"We'll have to go back," Mandell said.

Jane nodded but she knew that it was hopeless. She had been here before.

*

Sometimes time fragments. It doesn't run in its normal order but breaks up so that some moments keep repeating themselves.

Jane had smelt smoke the other time. The scent of fireworks in the damp November air, burnt manganese and exploded gunpowder. It was what she had remembered vividly, night after night, after it had happened. She had been driving home late, much later than she should have been. She found herself in the house at Eastwood knowing that they should have been there. Even now she could hear her feet crossing the floor and her voice shouting up into the empty house. Only the echoes of her own voice had replied. There had been a heavy rattle of rain against the window and she had stopped midway across the hall. That had been the last moment she remembered on the right side of the divide. Her husband and her son should have been back hours before, even though they might have set off late because she had promised Thom that this year she would take him to the fireworks in the village.

Despite the flames of a thousand bonfires and the star rockets bursting in the sky their deaths had been simple. A tree collapsing into the road, weakened by the previous week's storms, the day's rain softening the ground and fatally weakening the grip of its roots in the soil. The tree falling as the Mini had rounded the bend. No one else involved. It was a local road and not much used. The bodies were being put into an ambulance when she arrived.

A breeze had been blowing up. Autumn had come late that year as the villagers had noted with faint disapproval over their pints of warming winter ale in the *North Star*. The main outlying branch of the tree, two feet thick, had crashed into the car between the driver's and the rear seat. Both occupants, or so they said, must have been killed instantly. When she arrived a rocket had burst overhead spilling white and gold stars downwards and illuminating the loading of the bodies into an ambulance.

She had gone to the hospital and the coroner's court, identified the bodies and filled in the relevant forms, wound up her husband's affairs and gone to their graves in the churchyard in the village at least once a month.

She had looked in the car, ignored the stains although she knew what they were, and picked up her son's book that he had taken with him for company that evening. A lot of bears go on an outing, one disappearing per page until there were none, and then, on the last page, all appearing again. Fiction.

*

"Jane!"

Mandell was shaking her.

"We've got to back up there. It's the best way out."

She was holding George, she noticed. She didn't remember picking him up. The smoke was thicker too and some of the lights on the platform had failed but there was now an orange glow of flames licking along the platform.

"Now!" Mandell said. "You go first. I'll take George."

"There's no way out Mark."

"There's a side passage just below where you got to. We can't stay here!"

There was the noise of a train running somewhere and a rush of air into the station and the crackle of newly invigorated flame.

"Time to go," Mandell said.

He picked George up and started climbing.

Jane didn't know how long it took to climb back up again. In the gathering smoke she would never have made it had she not climbed that way before and, every time she looked upwards to locate the next support, seen George's face looking down at her.

Mandell pulled her into the passage he had seen. Wire mesh was being cemented into the wall.

"It leads to another passageway, the next level up."

He was sweating, probably not so much from his exertions as the increasing heat. The air was becoming hot to the touch. They edged forward across rough concrete and through another door. They were in another tunnel with signs pointing to the Northern Line. Along the top part of the tunnel a thick ribbon of smoke was floating.

"We may need to crawl," Mandell said. "Better air."

At the end of the tunnel they saw an escalator leading upwards.

At the top of the escalator, through the smoke, there was a faint flare of orange. Up above them, on the way back out to the surface, another part of the station was on fire.

"Back the other way."

As Jane ran she saw that the tunnel was getting smaller all the time and closing in around them. The ribbon of smoke was getting thicker so that the visible tunnel was contracting all the time.

They got to the end. The air became more acrid. Somewhere rubber was burning. Jane could feel it sliding ever lower into her throat. It was becoming difficult to breathe. They had two choices of which way to go. It was not difficult. One way there was an orange glow.

"Fire that way."

Jane found her voice calm. It was a simple statement, just recognising a fact. There was fire behind them everywhere they had been and facing them in one of their two possible exits.

"There is nothing much here to burn." Mandell sounded as if he thought the logic of the position were enough to quell the flames.

They ran on, the other way.

Jane thought it would not be the flames and the heat that would kill them but the lack of air.

The lighting on the left hand side of the tunnel faded and died. The air became grey and their shadows dimmer. They were gradually fading away, losing substance. The pattern of tunnels and their path through them also became a blur.

They came to a dead end. More work was in progress. More wire mesh had been attached to the tunnel walls and the floor was uneven.

"Where now?"

"There must be somewhere," Mandell said.

Mandell gave George to her and then he was pulling away at the wire mesh.

Jane looked at George. For a terrible moment she thought he might be dead but then she saw that miraculously he was sleeping, oblivious of anything that was happening.

Mandell was on his knees.

"It will be all right George," Jane said softly. "Don't worry."

"Jane!"

Mandell was pulling her to the ground.

"Don't you see!"

"What?"

"The air."

It was clean, breathable. Ian Hart would have approved.

"It's coming from somewhere."

Mandell was pulling a wooden cable drum aside. There was a hole in the wall from which there was a stream of fresh air. The only problem was that at its maximum it was no more than a foot high and not much more wide. Jane bent down. Light was also showing from the other side, fifteen or twenty feet away.

Mandell was taking his coat off.

"You can get through there."

"You're crazy. Even if I could, you couldn't. And what about George?"

"That's easy." Mandell was ripping the shoulder of his coat and threading the belt through it.

"Tie this to your ankle and you can crawl through with George tied into the coat. I can guide it from this side."

"There's no time. We should get back to the passage. Then we all have a chance to get out. I'm bound to get stuck. That would be hopeless. The tunnel is the best bet."

"I don't think so." Mandell was fastening George into the coat. "You'd better take your own coat off. If you do you can get through there. I might even be able to make it myself."

"But if you can't -"

"Nothing lost but a few seconds." Mandell smiled. "Besides I always wanted to be a hero, or at least someone good. Not much chance of that I realise, but it's not too late to start."

Mandell kissed her and Jane found herself crawling though the constricted space depending on her arms to drag herself forward. In her nightmares the space always got progressively narrower and narrower. Here it was too small to begin with. Halfway through she was stuck.

In her dreams she awoke before dying. Here she could feel the concrete pressing down on her stomach and hips. She had stopped.

It was then George started crying. It reminded her of Thom. She closed her eyes. She could see her son beckoning her forward. She hadn't thought that she would be seeing him again so soon. She made a movement to reach out to him and found there was space above her head if she could just move her shoulder. She pushed with controlled pressure and felt the concrete grate against her skin, but she was moving; at first imperceptibly, then an inch, and then two.

She managed to get her arm and hand free and pass it over her face. There was an eternity of room if she could move, all the room she needed. She found an edge in the concrete above her to pull herself along. She could feel George's weight pulling at her leg as he was dragged forward. He had stopped crying and was coughing. She pulled harder. Her shoulder scraped against something that felt like a nail but she was moving faster than before, more than a foot in the last completed movement. She was now also able to use her legs braced against the side walls to propel her more quickly.

She stopped. There was something solid against the back of her head. She couldn't understand. When she had looked into the opening before she started to crawl she was sure she had seen an opening out. She should be free but instead her path was barred at the last moment.

She worked her arms and hands to her face. Whatever was blocking her path was smooth. She felt along it to see if there might be some way round and tried to push herself forward. The smooth object was suddenly removed from her fingers and fell away from here with a crash.

A billow of grey dust appeared in front of her and sought out her eyes, nose and mouth. She started coughing as the dust seeped into her lungs, but her hands and arms were free. She had reached the other side.

She emerged into a pile of equipment. She was shaking. All her limbs seemed to have been stretched and contorted by the physical effort. She pulled on the belt attached to her leg. George appeared, his crying subsiding.

"Mark!"

She shouted but there was no reply.

Smoke was beginning to seep out of the opening she had managed to slide herself through. She picked George up and headed for the surface. He was still holding the sky blue parcel in a limpet like grip.

Above ground, at the entrance to the station, a fire engine was blocking the road. Its twin blue lights were flashing but the siren had been turned off. Hoses were stretched over the ground and beyond them a crowd of people looked on.

CHAPTER THIRTY-EIGHT

The thaw was well established and there was the drip everywhere of melting ice.

The £250 million, after completing its journeys, had ended up in the account that Ian Hart had identified.

Jane turned away from the window. For a moment she was sure she had seen a figure behind her, but she knew that was not possible. She low newspaper and read the story again. "Two bodies found in Tube Fire". Next to the paper the bear that had arrived in the sky blue parcel was laying face up, some of its stuffing protruding through the puncture in its chest caused by the Starman's knife. She needed to sew up the wound.

She walked out of the flat and went down in the lift. She thought that she might go to Eastwood. It was a decision she could make later in the day.

In the flowerbed by the river she saw that green shoots were already pushing through the remains of the snow. The pale disk of the sun was visible through the thin cloud and growing brighter by the moment.

She remembered the last words Mark Mandell had said to her.

"Au revoir, Jane, not goodbye."

He had been quite insistent upon it.

If you enjoyed "*The Sky Blue Parcel*" you may like to read this extract from "*In A Secret State*", the Second Jane Charles Thriller – to be published in 2007.

From *"In A Secret State"*

SHE was close, so close, to plunging the knife between the shoulder blades in front of her. Ergonomic grip it had said on the packaging, easy and comfortable to use. She felt her hand tighten on the handle. It was simple. One restraining hand on the shoulder and the other to plunge the knife into her victim's back and twist it as hard as she could. She closed her eyes.

She always had the same image of Jane Charles in her mind. The black hair ruffled eternally in the breeze, an enquiring look across whatever London street it had been. Jane hadn't seen the camera, couldn't have seen it. And the picture looked like something from a fashion shoot, except the model was relaxed, not self-conscious in any way.

She looked at herself in the shop window. She could see clouds of her own breath in the cold damp air, but her face was drawn and bleached of colour. She slipped on the greasy pavement and nearly stumbled to the ground, but she didn't fall.

Jane Charles was twenty yards in front of her and had turned into the high street. The pavements were suddenly busy; women with prams, children, a pensioner on a motorised chair driving all before him.

She would have liked to have told Jane what she was going to do and make her suffer as she had suffered for the last six weeks but she knew that wasn't possible. Death would have to be as quick as she could make it.

They had turned off the high street. There were no shops here, no people, just rows of little houses. She didn't know why but she had always imagined there would be people around her when she did it. Suddenly that didn't seem sensible. It would be so much easier to kill her in a deserted pace. There would be no one to help Jane and no one to stop her getting away. That was smart, what Paula would have wanted. Paula was always telling her "TTT Sharon" – Think Things Through.

The knife had tangled in the lining of the pocket and she needed a second or two to free it. And Jane had quickened her pace. She found herself panting as she tried to catch up. Jane was out of sight in a moment. And she had taken a wrong corner, she wasn't thinking, and Jane was getting away. She started retching as a wave of nausea swept over her, she couldn't lose Jane now, not now. And if she hadn't gone round this corner she must have gone round the other one. TTT Sharon. There wasn't anywhere else she could have gone. That was where Jane must be.

She ran forward and almost collided with a sleek Asian man in an expensive dark blue business suit. Jane was smiling at him and he was looking admiringly at her. There was a vintage white Mercedes sports car with the driver's door open beside them. She brushed against him and then she was past.

She slowed her steps and looked back. They were still there wrapped up in each other, unaware of her. Behind them the white lighthouse loomed up above the neat little houses and in the distance the grey sea merged into a greyer sky.

She felt like laughing. Jane Charles didn't know about her, didn't know that she existed. She had been so afraid that she did. It was simple now. The body had to be found, the knife wounds had to be counted so that they would know how hated Jane had been. But it didn't have to be here. She didn't have to be caught.

She had found Jane Charles. She had found her house by the sea. She knew where she lived in London. There was no rush, no particular urgency. Killing Jane was only a matter of finding the right time and place. Only it would still have to be quick. Jane couldn't be allowed to die in a state of grace. She needed to be surprised by death so there would be no time for prayers and preparation, no hope of Heaven…